I0637803

A Whisper *of* Demons

KATE CHAMBERS

Copyright © 2023 by Kate Chambers

All rights reserved. No part of this publication may be reproduced, distributed or transmitted in any form or by any means, including photocopying, recording, or other electronic or mechanical methods, without the prior written permission of the publisher, except in the case of brief quotations embodied in critical reviews and certain other noncommercial uses permitted by copyright law.

For permission requests, write to the author at: katechambersaz@gmail.com

Kate Chambers

A Whisper of Demons / Kate Chambers. —1st ed.

Paperback: ISBN: 978-1-956989-35-9
Ebook ISBN: ISBN: 978-1-956989-33-5

For Mom.
She never got to finish her novel; she would be so proud.

I will not wish thee riches nor the glow of greatness,
but that wherever thou go some weary heart shall
gladden at thy smile,
or shadowed life know sunshine for a while.
And so thy path shall be a track of light,
like angels' footsteps passing through the night.

~ AUTHOR UNKNOWN

WORDS FOUND ON A CHURCH WALL IN UPWALTHAM, ENGLAND

Contents

Prologue

There is a library, filled with books of souls and lives; an eternal library filled with names, one name lettered on each spine. Very few can enter—even fewer can read these books.

But he can. He is the Guardian. A fighter in his former life: fighter and philosopher, an educated man. He served with his blood, his sweat, his tears, and his soul. He is one of the Faith. As his reward for patience and perseverance, he is allowed to sit and read in peace for eternity, until called upon. When needed, he is expected to give the utmost. It is never questioned by him, or any who knows of him, what the outcome will be. So, he sits, and he reads. He reads about people he's loved and lost, about people who intrigue him, and, most of all, about those he fears. 357 years march by, but he knows that years mean nothing in this place of eternity.

It is time to read again. He scans and patiently waits; it is always this way. One of the books will talk to him. It is his job to listen. He listens hard, he listens well, and very softly he hears it, *Seraphine*. Behind the neat rows of books there is one that has been pushed back. *Pushed?* he ponders. It is old, sad, and forgotten. *This one,* he reaches in and grabs the book. Her name, her soul, shimmering on the spine: **Seraphine Macguire.**

His brain whispers, a familiar warmth like a dear friend from long ago, and, also, another Chosen One. Curious, he handles the book carefully. A delicate inscription of three ancient symbols from three ancient empires covers the front of the pebbled leather. Singly, they hold power. All three together—they create magic.

He is intrigued. His gaze rests for a moment on his only companion: Garm, sleeping and silent (for the moment) at his feet. He is a Dog who Knows; a guardian, a protector, the original warrior beast. Garm feels his stare and stirs. His blue eyes open slowly to stare back. He is ready, always ready, to fight, to protect, to guard.

This man—half Viking warrior, half educated priest—smiles at his confident companion, then settles in and starts to read.

I am descended from warriors; a destroyer of demons. Curled up in my bed under covers, cozily trapped between a snoring dog and a sleeping cat. I could stay here; nothing bad happens here. Here, life doesn't run over me, doesn't ask questions I can't answer, and it doesn't demand strength that seems in such short supply; strength from a well dangerously close to dry.

◇✳◇✳◇✳◇

PART ONE

Seraphine: A Woman Who Fights Demons

◇✳◇✳◇✳◇

Chapter 1

Present Day

Seraphine Macguire liked to run at night. It was 8.6 miles round trip, out to the small airport and home again. She would stop at that halfway point to watch the private planes take off and land; there weren't many, some nights none at all.

Follow the chain-link fence, Serah thought as she ran. *Left turn on Sky Parkway into the lot, push up a small rise, then jump to the view atop a low cinderblock wall.* She sighed a heavy breath, *no planes tonight.* The winter night was quiet, and the air felt soft on her sweaty skin.

A thought of sweet Sam tumbled in, and she felt her gut twist. She wished for the thousandth time, "Ahhh, normal. To just be Normal."

"Remember what you used to wish?" Serah asked herself out loud. She huffed a laugh, remembering a time when all she wanted was a reprieve from her boring life.

She could hear the electrical hum of the radio tower announcing its presence to an ocean of purple sky. Serah scanned the soft darkness. The airfield was as empty as she felt.

"Some Demon Hunter, eh, Mom?" Serah asked the wind. She snorted a laugh and tried not to cry. She felt as if dust flowed through her veins. The fights made her weary. She was so tired of not understanding her adversary, tired of not winning—whatever that even meant—when it came to those encounters. The white feral cat, whose home was the nearby hanger, trotted over and hopped up onto the wall nearby. Serah could see the reflection of his eyes shine.

Hey, bud. How's the hunt tonight?" Serah asked quietly. "I wish you could tell me what *you* see…what you *know.*" Serah smiled and chuckled, as the large, white tomcat leisurely yawned and licked his paw.

A tiny beep barely pierced the dark as Serah restarted her watch and turned for home. She smelled the demon before she saw it. The salty air.

She cursed, "Not tonight. NOT tonight." But the Rage Demon did not care.

"Always avoid the fights, if you can, Serah. Pick your battles. The time will come." Benjamin's wise advice sounded clearly in her head, and her ponytail nodded sharply. She agreed with her trusted confidant and dearest friend. Serah turned and ran.

I am not afraid. I am brave. I am not afraid. I am brave: a mantra against the demon who chased her in the dark, a macabre race to any eyes that watched. Serah ran, leaving behind the hiss and yowls of the tomcat, as he witnessed but dared not interfere. Legs pumping, arms moving, forcing exhalations like she was taught. Rage Demon had caught her unaware. Her foot stumbled in the shadowed street, and Rage was on her in an instant.

Eyes wide, her pain masked by the diamond-hard clench of her teeth. At the demon's touch, rage consumed her. She managed to stay on her feet, but not at the same pace.

"Keep running. Run *more.* Do. Not. Stop." A prayer against what she knew would happen if she did. Her hands became curved claws of fury. Mentally, she pushed against it. Rage pushed back. Images were vivid in her mind: kicking a head, kicking a face until teeth break off and fly through the air, the jaw shoved back into the throat, skull dents, then crushes. It is Rage. Seductive in its power, it would be so much easier just to let it in—let it win. She starts to believe she cannot prevent it.

"No! I am strong. I am the destroyer of demons," her voice ending on a whimper. "Please." She could not run anymore. Her eyes closed, as she recognized her mistake: never say please to a Rage Demon. *Rookie.*

"Sugar, just have fun." Her mother's face floated in her mind, and Serah remembered. The loving face faded into the desiccated skull that was her mother, laying on a hospital bed with a Betty Boop shirt on. Her last breath, unwitnessed, except by the pink Betty Boop.

Serah howled. The sound ripped out of her and with it, despair, that was a different demon pushed hardest. Rage took its claws and fled. Serah dropped to a crouch on the ground, dry heaving and shaking, hands balled up against her head. Time passed silently on little feet tiptoeing past the remains of the fight. It was a draw.

"My words are powerful, as is my will. You will not destroy me," Serah whispered in the direction Rage had scattered while hobbling home.

"Ouch." Serah sat up in bed, smushed between a dog and a cat. Diego spread out on his side, his back pressed up against the length of her leg. Both offered a feeling of security to the other. Rubi the cat, always thwarted from her favorite spot on Serah's belly or chest, had given in and curled up right next door. Serah laid back down and took stock. Encounters with the Rage Demon always left the worst hangover.

Serah absentmindedly patted Diego's sleeping belly. She liked the noise it made against her hand, a hollow sound, but a solid warmth of soft fur between her fingers. She clicked her cell phone screen on: 5:47 a.m. *Ugh. Early. Too early.* She remembered it being midnight when she fell into bed.

Achy, Serah knew the bruises would already be in bloom. Calm for now, the residual anger would bubble up intermittently for the next few days, as well as the craving for Jack…or gin. She hoped she could keep the shots to a minimum. In this mood, she craved her liquor straight. She liked to feel it burn, as it traced a path down her throat. Before, when she didn't know what these encounters would leave behind, she would find herself in the middle of a bar fight or two. Her friend Sam was often called to scoop her up off the bar room floor—battered and bloody, but oddly smiling.

"The others look worse," she would tell him. Her rescuer chalked it up to booze and boredom but grew suspicious after the third time, in as many weeks. Each time, on the drive home in his pickup truck, she would start to calm.

"The Rage made me do it," she whispered not looking at him; her arms clutched across her chest, as if an attempt to keep her soul safe. A giggle escaped—death and dismemberment passing across her field of vision—then choked back with a look of horror.

If Sam was her rescuer, Benjamin was her priest. One for the body; one for the soul. I am lucky, Serah thought.

Hot under the heavy blankets, she could feel the sweat drip from between her shoulder blades and down her tank. Serah groaned and threw back the comforter. The clamminess chilled her, and the cool air of her bedroom made her shiver. She hated that feeling.

"Ugggghhh." Laying back down and tossing a layer of covers over her, she saw that her bedmates were snuggled in tight. It almost made her laugh that she actually slept like this for her pets. *It was comfortable,* came her retort to herself, and they were worth it. An empty bed is not always a safe place to be.

The need for coffee finally drove her from the nest. Serah constantly fought the urge to stay in bed until late in the day; a lingering "gift" from her demon encounters. She wondered when things had changed—her past—before her first encounter was always hazy. She found memories written in her journals, accounts she knew she wouldn't have remembered without reading their words on the page. Her memories felt sanded off at the edges.

Benjamin, her best-friend-turned-demon-hunter-trainer, could recall conversations, often word for word, and, most often, they were conversations he had with her. Serah snorted a little laugh at the thought of what he would say in answer to that title. It irked her, at times that he had that ability. But when he used it to prove how valuable she was—how unique, how strong—she could only thank God that he was her friend and confidant.

Serah threw on leggings and UGGs and put her hair up in one quick, efficient motion, then jogged over to the heater.

"Brrr, shit, it's cold." She looked and stabbed her finger at the little red up arrow. She tried to be frugal, but every chilly morning she told herself, "Just until I warm up." Outside it was bright and clear.

"What a pretty day," she whispered, and she started to recall one of the memories she wished she could forget. A shake of the head cleared the thoughts she didn't care to pursue.

As the coffee maker burbled happily, Serah fed the pets, gave medicines, tossed dishes into the dishwasher, and then turned to grab a cup just as the coffee was finishing up. A lover of all flavors of coffee, she had beans delivered once a month from exotic, expensive locations; a recent favorite, all the way from Istanbul, was her only nod to snobbery.

"My vices are coffee and cursing," she would say with a grin to those whom she had just met.

A little bit of cream and the hot concoction was ready. Serah was always disappointed that it didn't taste quite as good as it smelled, that it wasn't some magical elixir for the apathy that plagued her, that its juice didn't course through her veins with sudden energy for the day. No, it was more of a simple comfort than a panacea.

"I need all the help I can get," Serah said softly to her coffee mug. Diego wagged his tail, the only one that heard.

Her yellow kitchen was sunny and warm. Sitting on a stool at her small two-person table, she sipped and contemplated. It was quiet. She always hated the quiet of the morning in her tiny little house; Serah thought she could feel its heart break. It occurred to her that maybe it was *her* heart that broke in the lonely quiet.

She remembered her first demon encounter.

It was such a pretty day. They were lying in bed.

Heaven, she thought, this is what heaven might be like.

Serah stretched, "What a pretty day!" She laughed with delight.

"What a pretty day," he mimicked, exasperated, "You always say that." Surprised, Serah turned her head on the pillow to look his way. His blue eyes were sleepy, and the hatred burned. She could feel it. It took her breath away.

"What's up, baby? You seem...mad," she hesitated, "at me?" Grimacing, she hated when she got this way, panicked at his anger. Directed at her or not, it didn't matter. If she couldn't fix it, it meant she wasn't loved enough.

Rubi the cat was out of the room on her tower perch. Diego and their second dog, Max, were sleeping on the floor in the next room—unperturbed—leaving the bedroom to their two sleeping people.

There had been no one there to protect her or to understand. She knew that now. Shaking a little, back in her sunny kitchen, she closed her eyes against the relentless quiet that pressed in. Another sip of coffee out of her favorite mug; an attempt to keep it all at bay. Keep it away. The memory came anyway, and she remembered what happened next.

His eyes started to bleed. The blood slowly dripped onto the pretty blue-flowered pillow, and then it didn't drip, it poured.

Horrified, Serah screamed, "Jeremy! What's happening? Are you okay?!" His lips curled, jaw clenched. No words to spit out at her. Dogs barking now, then growling and howling. The cacophony of noise competed with another sound. She scrambled up to grab a towel, but his seizure stopped her. Changing directions, she turned and ran for the phone. Sliding around the corner, she grabbed her cell phone in the kitchen and sprinted back to him. Trying to hold him down with one arm and dial with the other. The dogs were frantic.

Serah remembered calling 911. She dropped the phone once, twice. "Shit, boys! Stop it! STOP IT. SHUT UP! SHUT UP! SHUT UP!" she screamed.

A frantic search for clothes to wear, dogs to control, people yelling to control the dogs. Questions—so many questions. A short ride to the hospital a few miles north on the freeway. Sitting in the front passenger seat twisted around, contorted, turning to see. She had to see. Blood down her shirt. Blood on her hands. Blood on her face. Dried blood is difficult to get off skin. And even harder to get out of dog fur.

Shaking off the memory was hard. It pulled her in and constricted around her. That was Demon Horror. She hadn't known it at the time. She would meet Horror again, but that time was the first.

Time to walk Diego. He was patient, as if a saint sent from somewhere demons cannot go. His wise eyes watched, and his tail thumped twice on the floor saving her from remembering more.

"It does no good to dwell on the past," she heard Benjamin's voice again; his teaching embedded in her mind from their many training sessions. "We all wish, but no one gets a mulligan. There are no do-overs, Seraphine. Not in this world."

Oh, Ben, you have to be wrong. With a sigh, she turned and smiled as she took in Diego's expectant face. Setting down her coffee cup, she went for the leash. It was time to go enjoy this pretty day.

Chapter 2

Four Years Earlier
Year One of the Demons

The answers are in the quiet,
Listen hard, listen well.
The answers are in the quiet,
And the quiet waits to tell.

~ FROM THE BOOK SEEKERS OF THE TRUTH

It may have been that summer, slowly going crazy with the quiet. Serah often rose early to do chores but found herself wandering around the house, drinking coffee, whiling the morning hours away. Then, finally forcing herself outside in the broiling heat of the afternoon to start work in the yard. It felt like a penance of some sort—sweating through her shirt, trimming roses in the sweltering afternoon sun.

As she hacked into an overgrown section of the plant to reduce it to the size needed for the trash, she was struck by its shape. It almost looked like a weapon. A handle could be made at the bottom—removing thorns and affixing some sort of padding—and the rest could be swung quite effectively. A deterrent.

She did not know where this thought came from or why. She was not a particularly violent person. She lived a quiet life, and she was only trimming the roses. But she saved that piece, placing it aside for later.

Living in a suburb of Sacramento, Serah was grateful to buy her little house near the American River Parkway. Her 900-square-foot single-car-garage house, with its teeny tiny kitchen only a two-seater table would fit in, was a dream realized, because it came with a big yard for Diego and a beautiful place to walk for them both.

Serah looked up from her chores and noticed the sun starting to dip down in the sky. The cool evening breeze off the river came through the yard like clockwork every night, with hints of the faraway ocean carried in. She whistled to Diego, who was smart enough to have grabbed his favorite spot of shade in the corner of the yard while he watched her work the afternoon away in the broiling sun.

"Time for some dinner, my boy." Together they crossed the yard—roses and thorns and violence forgotten.

She sighed, "Another Friday night in, and I'm knitting. At least I will be well prepared when spinsterhood finally hits," she said out loud. She locked the doors against the dark and curled up in her favorite spot on the couch.

He stood over her shoulder. He was big. A Viking in one of his former lives, a lawyer and monk in others, he favored his time with the Norse—wild, long beard matched by greying tousled hair—Poseidon crossed with a mountain man. He was the Guardian of the Chosen Ones.

He stood behind Serah with a pensive look on his face. Not that Serah could see it. The cat stopped her bathing and stared back at him. Green eyes met brown. He smiled at the cat, and Rubi turned her back to him in a huff.

"Cats," he whispered matching Rubi's disdain.

What stood behind Serah was nothing she could see. But there was something there. The cat knew it. The house knew it, creaking and groaning with the wind. Serah did not know it. The dog huffed and squeaked through a dream, oblivious. Her cat sniffed lazily, continuing to clean herself as if nothing of importance was occurring.

The Guardian remembered his education: Cats are half-in, half-out. They are comfortable with the night and the shadows that pass through it, treading around on silent feet—watching. Always watching. They are the keepers of the records, recording the comings and goings of those from the other side, as well as the humans who encounter them. Cats have been witnesses to these events since the time of the First Choice. Their memory is long and unwavering. Unfortunately, few still living have the skill to access this information. In time, the knowledge will pass into oblivion as the line between this world and the other grows more pronounced, more of a barrier than a gate. Soon, no one will remember what it means to see a ghost—to encounter a demon.

Dogs are in our world. They are the protectors of humans. They are here to bring peace, protecting their humans from most often unsavory contact with the other side. Many are now scared themselves, causing encounters to go awry. Unexplained, the numbers of Dogs Who Know are dwindling out of existence.

Rubi turned, leapt nimbly over to Serah, and gave her a loving lick on the hand, as if to say, "Mine." The man chuckled and silently agreed. At his chuckle, Serah's head came up suddenly—her knitting forgotten. She stared first at Rubi, who froze at her sudden movement, ready to jump away. Serah turned, placing one hand on the back of the couch for support, as she twisted to see behind her. The man froze, too, even though he knew that she could not see him unless it was dusk or dawn; it was a natural response. A human response.

Serah stared but only saw her kitchen doorway, the darkened room beyond, and the dog sleeping peacefully. The man watched and slowly let out his held breath. He was close enough that Serah's bangs stirred. She let out a yip of nerves and looked around for the source of the breeze. Up at the vent—not blowing. Then to the windows—not open. Then to the front door—both locks turned.

As she went through this mental checklist in rapid succession, the logical part of her mind took over and pushed away the irrational belief that something strange had stirred; it pushed away the thought that her bangs were ruffled for no apparent reason. She could feel the anxiety creep on slow feet into her stomach—up into her throat—where she knew it would tighten and soon become difficult to breathe. With a tense hand on her chest, she leaned forward to grab her new medication that always stayed close. Biting half a pill, she tossed the bottle back onto the coffee table and took the pill with a swig of her wine.

Serah closed her eyes and waited; it never took long. Slowly she forgot what had actually caused her to check her surroundings so carefully. Soon she couldn't remember anything but a vague uneasiness, as she paused from her knitting to take another sip of her wine.

The man sighed, "So, this is the one, eh? She's a newborn babe, not even marked yet." Shaking his head, he looked around the room for anything to tell him she was the warrior—could *become* the warrior—he was led to believe. *At least she has the dog and the cat,* he thought, turning disappointed and walked through the doorway to the kitchen. For one brief second, he saw his reflection in the shiny, silver horseshoe nailed up to the doorframe. He had an instant to register surprise, and then he was gone.

Chapter 3

Serah yawned and pushed her bangs back from her face.

"Late night?" Ben asked. They'd met for lunch near the downtown library where Serah worked.

"Oh, yes, you know me and my hectic social life. Ha," Serah snorted. Ben smiled, knowing his friend's habit of staying in.

"No, I've been having some weird dreams lately, and I feel like I'm not getting restful sleep," Serah explained.

Ben lifted an eyebrow at her words, "Are you dreaming about the day Jeremy died again?"

A year and one month since that day, Ben will never forget answering his phone to a screaming Seraphine. It made his gut twist to think of that sound again, and he tried not to. For six months, she barely left the house—only to go to work and buy food for Diego. Ben helped find Jeremy's dog Max a new home with one of his law professors who was looking for a reason to walk the beautiful campus paths. After that, he left Serah alone, believing she needed the space to grieve. One night, he decided he had had enough of waiting, waiting for her to come around and join the living. Ben found a sad looking kitten outside the law library, crying like it had lost someone it cared about too. He watched for a cat mom, or anyone to claim it, but after two days he couldn't stand it anymore. With ease, he grabbed the friendly red-black kitten, named her Rubi, and immediately drove her over to Serah's. Banging on her door until she answered with wild hair, wearing the same robe (they burned that robe later in a bonfire of Jeremy's things), and a look of "what the hell!" he remembered thrusting the kitten into her arms. *I saved it, and now she will save you. Her name is Rubi. I'll be over tomorrow to take you to lunch. You better be ready. You are getting out of this house.*

Ben shook his head to clear out of the memory. At the same time, Serah shook her head, "No. Some weird things about rose thorns and a book...," she trailed off, knowing she gave the impression that she had dreamt this.

"Rubi has been acting odd lately too. I feel like she's watching something. I probably just have a case of the *heebie-jeebies*." Serah used that term to explain when living alone just creeped her out for no specific reason.

"I found this new book—tome rather—in the ancient historical section. I'm sure it's a copy, but it sure does look like the original. Though how could that be, right? I mean that would make it thousands of years old, so it can't be. But, of course, I had to open it," Serah chattered as Ben listened. With his quiet, focused way, he was always able to get her to reveal more than she wanted.

"You need a special pass to even enter that area, due to the age of the documents. And you know I was just promoted, so my pass can unlock that door now. The other day I was sent to 'clean those old dusty things,'" Serah mimicked her boss's thin, high-pitched voice. "And so, of course, I pretended like I was being punished, but you and I both know that I LOVE historical documents. Anyway, when I started to clean it, I swear Ben, it...rustled!"

Ben, clearly expecting something more significant, asked in a bemused voice, "Rustled? Rustled how?"

"Well, rustled! You know, the pages kinda ruffled like there was a breeze. Only there wasn't, of course. Historical documents are protected from normal air conditioning, from anything that would increase their decay. There shouldn't be any breeze at all...," Serah trailed off again, no longer confident that she had seen anything of significance.

"I mean I don't even know why we have it. Seems to me, it should be in a museum," Serah continued. "But, of course, nobody asks me, so there it sits."

"The front of it has a few—three—symbols inscribed in the material that looks like leather. One that looks like a snake; two hands, sort of a double high five and some odd stick drawing. I don't know; I don't know ancient Egyptian,

Greek, whatever it is."

"Take a picture next time. Maybe we can figure out the markings," Ben waited quietly now for Serah to say more.

"When I told you about the rose bush, did you think it was my dream?" Serah asked hesitantly. Ben looked at her and nodded.

"The other day, I was pruning the bushes. You know, in the back of my yard on the fence line. I trimmed this one branch, and it occurred to me that it looked like a weapon. Umm. I didn't throw it away. That's weird, isn't it? I mean, why did I think of that?" Serah trailed off once more.

"Nothing is *weird* in life, my dear Seraphina," Ben liked to use her full name, with a bit of a twist, when he was making a point. "All life is connected. Everything we see is a symbol of what's to come—what has passed. Some of us are just more able to understand the language."

Serah poked at her salad, took a bite, and chewed as she thought about what to say. "I saw one of the first pages. Thorny rose bush was there—in the book. And a drawing of Diego sitting next to Rubi. It looked so much like them!" Serah paused, then shook her head. "I know. I know what it sounds like. I'm probably just bored. I think my mom went a little nutty, you know, maybe it's genetic," Serah sighed and put her head in her hands. Ben watched her in silence, as if made of the Earth.

"You're doing that thing again," Serah opened one eye and peeked between her fingers at him.

"What thing?" Ben laughed.

"That thing where you go really still as if listening to the radio channel of the universe or something," Serah smiled. "You are like my own secret decoder ring for life. But you hardly ever tell me what to do! Ben!"

"Because it's not for me to say, Seraphina."

"The answers are in the quiet...," Serah's voice echoed Ben's, because she knew what he was going to say. It is what he always said.

"Jinx!" laughing together, the two friends turned their attention back to their lunch, law school drama, and the latest amazing thing Diego and Rubi did.

Walking quickly, Serah arrived at the library and ran up the steps. Breathless, she pushed through the heavy double doors, past the metal detector. She quietly made her way to the employee locker area on the first floor.

She took the staff elevator; a silent ride down to the underground basement level. Serah stepped off cautiously and looked around. The area was deserted. Not much traffic in the historical documents area during lunchtime. She scurried over to the glass door, waved her pass over the electronic pad, and pushed it open after hearing the lock disengage.

The door slowly shut behind her, and she could feel the cold air greet her as she entered.

Shivering, Serah remembered her training class, "Old documents are required to be kept at fifty-five degrees in order to slow their decay."

Serah could feel the silence press in on her, and then thousands of tiny unintelligible whispers filled her ears. When she tried to focus on them, they were gone under the whirring of the air conditioning. She looked around nervously. There, again under the *schiirrring* sound of the forced air—whispers.

I am off my rocker. I definitely need more sleep, Serah thought. She walked over to a table where a clear plastic box sat containing the tome. She lifted up the lid, stared down at the book, and looked at the symbols inscribed.

She stared—as if willing the book to give her answers—and saw the pages ruffle. Serah jumped back, a squeal on her lips.

Turning to look at no one, eyes wide, "SEE, I told you," she said in a breathless whisper to the empty room, closing her eyes and sighing to herself. Each symbol was stacked, one on top of the other, as if in a specific order. She leaned over the book and snapped a quick picture with her phone.

Serah's pocket vibrated and made her jump. "Thirty minutes WORK." She clicked off the reminder alarm on her cell phone. Licking her lips nervously, she stood in front of the book and reached out to trace the designs on the cover. Her finger left a glow, like a tracer, that quickly faded.

She tugged on nearby white gloves to prevent oils from her hands from further decaying the old material. Without waiting to think of all the reasons not to, Serah grabbed the book and sat cross-legged on the floor, her back up against the far wall, so she could watch the doors.

"Breathe," she whispered. Taking a deep breath, she opened the cover gently, slowly. *Please, pleeease, don't fall apart.*

The first page was what she knew: images of Diego and Rubi. It was striking how much the drawing looked like her two. The markings—Diego's light eyebrows, the varied coloring of his scruff, the light patch on his chest, and his multicolored tongue, all the way down to one black paw. Rubi was a little less clear, but it was uncanny. Her left whiskers were only an inch long, leftover from a dramatic, but luckily not too painful, candle accident. Rubi's right side was normal, with a spiderweb of mottled red-black coloring all over her head. Serah grabbed her phone and snapped another picture.

"Hello, page two," Serah whispered turning the thin pages clumsily and awkwardly with the gloves. Odd stick lettering was written across the top in big bold print. It looked intense and "scary." Serah breathed the word out.

ᛏᛁᚤᛉᛏᚾ

ᚷᛃᚱᚱᛃᛘ

ᚱᚼᚤᛁ

ᛦᚠᛒᛃ�htᛁ

ᚠᛏᛘ

ᚴᚼᛁᚴᚼᛁᛉ
ᛏᛁᛉᛒᚼᛊ
ᛁᚼᚢᛁ
ᚠᚼᛁᚴᚢᚱᛁ
ᛒᚼᚢᛁᛊ
ᛏᛒᛒᛏᛊ
ᛁᚼᚠᛁᛏ
ᛁᚤᛒᚼᛏᛁ
ᚠᛁᛏ

Click! Picture taken. Anxiety started to fill Serah's gut, as she took in the page. "Maybe page three is better," she said to herself, careful to keep an eye on the time.

ᚢᛏᛒᚼᛉ

Again, pictures of a cat and a dog—this time more generic looking—and a large rose bush with one branch shaped like a weapon, just like the one she now had in her garage.

A large shrub labeled:

ᚱᚼᛉᛁᚤᛏᚱᛁ

An image of a compass with the words

ᚠᚨᛚᛚᛁᚾ ᚷ ᛞᛁ ᚷ ᚠᚢᛏᚱᛏᛁᚱᛏ

Click! Without even trying to decipher what was on the page, Serah took the picture.

Page Four:

ᚠᚨᚱᚣ

Serah's eyes widened even more, as she scanned the page. A large, ferocious dog that looked very similar to her Diego, filled the page. His snarling face looking as if he was ready to commit violence, something Serah had never seen in Diego. She felt mesmerized by the grip of fear and could see her hands shake a little as she snapped the picture.

A chime pierced the silence and made Serah jump—her phone alarm again. Time to start her shift. Getting up, she carefully placed the book back in its case and shoved the gloves into her pocket, not wanting to leave any evidence. *And to have for tomorrow when I come back,* Serah smiled into the dim room.

Six hours later, she walked back into her house and, at once, felt better. Diego ran scrambling from the bedroom to greet her as if reuniting with a centuries-gone long-lost love. It never failed to make her smile.

"Careful, buddy. Easy, easy," Serah softly admonished, worried as always about his structural health. He grabbed her tennis shoe, the first within easy reach by the door, and ran in circles, tail thumping wildly, holding the shoe in his mouth as if to say, "I would give you the world if I could."

"Come on, bud." Both headed to the back door and into the yard.

It was dusk, her favorite time of day. Actually, early morning and dusk—just as the sun came up and just as the sun was going down—were times she wished she saw more. There was something magical about the change. From day to night and back again into day. It felt like, for those brief moments, neither dark nor light held the power to sway those beings under its control. Those who lived by the dark could venture out or venture home; their power gained was lost to them as was those who lived by the day. It was nature's equilibrium.

Leaving Diego outside to roll in the grass and attend to outdoor business, Serah went back into the kitchen; it was dinner time. Rubi sat purring on the counter. Dog food mixed, fresh water poured, Serah looked up at her sliding glass door to the backyard—no Diego waiting patiently to be brought back in.

"What is keeping him?" She walked over, turned on the back porch light and stopped—turned to stone. A man. He stood on the other side of the glass. He stood like no one stood anymore, Serah thought, like someone in the military— ramrod straight. But he also looked a little wild with a long beard and Poseidon hair. Serah could see her reflection superimposed over him on the glass from the light above her and the darker night beyond. Her hand was poised on the door latch, her foot up ready to take another step that she hesitated to take now.

Beyond, Diego was happily rolling in the grass. He did one more shimmy and then caught the scene. Popping up with the grace only dogs can show, he padded over to the man.

"Diego! Diego, no!! Come here!!" Serah, almost frantic, clapped her hands, shouted, and moved toward the door. Diego stopped next to the man and sat. The man looked down and placed his big hand on top of Diego's head in a gentle gesture. Diego only stared at Serah.

That got Serah to move. She leapt forward, "Don't you DARE hurt my dog!! WHO are YOU?!" She raged at the perceived threat.

"Get away from him NOW! I swear to God, I will KILL you if you touch one hair on his head!" Serah, at the door, fumbled with the screen that never opened smoothly. As she ripped the screen door off the track, she looked up to see both the man and Diego watching her. Diego sat stock still.

She rushed up to him and knelt down running her hands over his body assuring herself that he was okay and unharmed. Then she pivoted on her heel, coming face-to-face with the man. *Viking.* That word popped into her mind as she took him in. *Monk?* Serah stared, and he stared back. He was tall—she had to crane her neck back to look up at his face.

"Betri til fit ok fall þan live without vætta." His voice was soft; his face was not. (*Better to fight and fall than live without hope.*)

"Wha—?" Serah stopped as the man grabbed her hand and forearm in a tight grip.

"Protect þessi einn." (*Protect this one.*)

The man dropped her arm, and Serah dropped to her knees on the grass, almost sick with panic and pain.

"Protect þessi einn," he repeated softer, almost kind. He touched her head, and then Diego's, in a gesture of respect, turned, and strode toward the gate. Serah coughed, staggered to her feet, fear for Diego making her brave, and raced toward where she last saw the stranger. When she rounded the corner, he was gone.

"CREEP!! Stay away! I'll call the cops!" Serah shouted into the night air. Diego huffed softly, which got her attention. She uneasily ushered him back inside. Racing to the kitchen cupboard, she grabbed her inhaler and pills, then paused to look down at her companion. He ducked his head and wagged his tail softly. She wished at that moment, more than any other, that he could speak something she could understand. Serah realized she was breathing normally, excited and fast, but she could *breathe* full, deep breaths. The medicine fell to the table. On her wrist, a scar had formed and healed with no pain. Diego sniffed her intently.

"Holy cow," Serah scrubbed her face with her hands. "Well, that was…different," Serah turned to look at Diego who was now at her feet. Diego thumped the floor with his tail. Rubi hopped up onto the table between them with a quick purr of inquiry.

Why am I not freaking out more? Serah wondered. *Because it is time.* She almost looked around to see who said that but realized those words had popped into her head in answer to her question. Serah turned and with the scarred wrist opened her fridge, grabbed a beer, sat down at the kitchen table, with a quiet sigh and shake of her head. This time she was glad she was alone.

Serah returned to the book two more times during her week. She would arrive thirty minutes before every shift, descend the stairs or use the freight elevator if it wasn't occupied, and try to learn more. She felt drawn to the book, compelled to hold it, sit and stare at its pages, often forgetting she only had a few precious minutes, sitting in almost a trance, watching her fingerprints leave a glow on the pages at every touch. Serah felt significant for the first time in her life.

With each page she turned and took a picture of, her interest grew. Page five was filled with signs and symbols that looked Greek or Egyptian; Serah was not sure.

"Holy shit," Serah gasped. There on the page, the third symbol in a long row of equally odd symbols, was the same as the scar that now marked her wrist, "What the heck?"

Click! Her phone camera pierced the silence. Much too loud for the quiet of the room and the quiet of her heart, Serah flipped the button to silent mode.

Page Six:

Just two symbols adorned the next page. Tracing her finger over the symbols in a reverent gesture, she felt these were more important somehow. These symbols were somehow stamped into the page, making their edges raised like braille. Serah closed her eyes as she traced over one then the other. One felt cold, and one felt warmer, one made her want to cry. Her free hand came to rest gently on her throat, the other turned the same hand into a fist of...*victory*. The word materialized in her mind like a wall of fog or maybe smoke. She didn't feel foggy at all, she felt clear and fully alive.

ᚠᛁᚱᛁ

"Fire," she whispered and her eyes flew open. Looking down at the book and over at her fist in the air, giggling a little she turned the page with a quick shake of her head. Page Seven: Another page of mysterious stick writing, and an odd drawing with an eye in the middle of what looked like six wings. *Creepy looking creature,* she thought as she took the photo of the page.

Page 7:

ᚼᛁᚼᛁ

ᚼᚼᚠᛁᛢᛢ

ᛏᛁᚱᛏᛒᛈᛁᛈ

Serah shrugged into the jacket she finally remembered to bring with her against the chill of the room. Glancing through the pages she already saw, Serah let the book fall open on her lap to whatever page it wanted:

Inscription til seekeranórr truthrinn

Picking up her phone, she quickly used Google images to help her identify the language:

"*Norse*," she whispered to herself. She didn't understand the words, yet her eyes soaked it up. Power. She felt power in those words. Circling the words was a thorny rose bush branch, the compass, and the creature with six wings.

Serah felt the book grow warmer and warmer under her touch. Then, suddenly, it burst into flames.

Serah shrieked, and the fire-retardant system activated on cue. Under the deluge of the powdery mixture, she grabbed the door handle and ran. Racing to the elevator, she neared the doors and heard a "ding!" Panicked, she looked up to see the up arrow light up. Skidding to a stop on the slick floors, her mind shouted, "Stairs!" She turned to the right and slammed through the doors into the stairwell. Flinging herself up three flights under the torrent of the sprinkler system that poured down in areas where there were no books, she paused on the last landing to catch her breath, intending to walk calmly toward the lockers. Taking a deep breath, Serah pulled open the stairwell door to chaos. People running, employees trying to shout instructions, a few children crying, and one elderly woman had fallen next to a stack of periodicals. Serah flattened herself against the wall for a few seconds as she took in the scene. Chest tight with breath starting to shorten, she could feel a panic attack coming on. Eyes closed, Serah gripped her chest with her hand as if willing her heart and lungs to respond.

"Can you help me, dear?" A sweet voice broke through, Serah's eyes popped open, and she briskly walked over to the woman on the ground, as the sprinkler system slowed and sputtered to a stop.

"Thank goodness they stopped. That was quite a shock, wasn't it?" Serah helped her into a kid-sized plastic chair.

"Oh, yes, honey," the lady replied. "I was due for a visit to the salon for my weekly hairdo, so it was good timing." They both chuckled.

"Are you hurt? In pain anywhere?" Serah asked.

"Oh, no. I'm a tough lady, I don't break easy. Just a little unsteady." Serah looked at her new friend who nodded, "I'm fine. Go. Go, young lady."

Serah could see the front parking lot of the library from where she stood.

"The fire department is pulling up now. They will take good care of you." Pushing her wet hair back from her face, Serah stood and wound her way quickly through the stacks, rummaging in her pockets for the extra hair tie she always kept in various places. Pulling her long hair back into a quick, loose ponytail, she strode toward the staff offices to find her boss and see what she could do to help.

A handful of long hours later, a tired Serah made it home. Shaking her head she thought of the long list of cleanup chores that still needed to be done and would most likely be her tasks for the coming week, if not month. Though still in the afternoon hour, Serah marched to the fridge and popped open a beer, took a swallow and a seat at the kitchen table.

The house was quiet. Serah sat, conflicted between wishing this had been a normal day: Easy morning shift at the library then back home to do some chores, enjoy the backyard with Diego, cook a nice dinner, the house filling with comforting smells, maybe curling up with a good book or watching a show.

Yet another part of her was excited. She was bored, she realized, bored deep down to her core. Bored with her life, with her day-to-day existence. Nothing she could complain about she knew, yet each day stretched out ahead of her with a sameness that, if she bothered to admit the truth to herself, made her want to scream.

"What the heck," Serah scrubbed her face with her hands, taking a swig of her beer, and turned to look at Diego who took his place at her feet.

"I need to do some research. We need more information. There's got to be an explanation for what happened…," Serah trailed off. Diego thumped the floor with his tail. Rubi hopped up onto the table between them with a quick purr of inquiry.

"What's up, my girl?" Serah asked as Rubi chattered while rubbing her irresistible coat against a mason jar of dried flowers at the center of the table. As if catching a scent, she turned and stalked straight across the table to Serah, intently sniffing her hands, twisting under Serah's wrist to remain attached by the nose to her palm.

"Hey, girl," Serah said rubbing her cat's soft face and head for a moment. She was hot, she needed fresh air. Taking the last sip of her beer, she stood and stepped out the side door where the breeze hit Serah with relief. She felt almost as if she had a fever. Though she wasn't chilled or clammy on her skin, her insides felt burning hot. Slowly, she opened her fist. There, plain as day, seared onto her palm where the pointer finger joined her hand, right under her knuckle, was scar number two. She recognized the symbol from the book. Pulling her phone out of her back pocket, she quickly flipped through the photos she had taken of the pages. "Bingo," she said, finding the one that showed five symbols all in a row. Taking another screenshot of the photo, Serah edited and narrowed in on the one that was now on her palm. She clipped the photo down to just that one symbol and uploaded it into Google image search. "I'll be damned," Serah sighed those words into the afternoon air. "Hecate's wheel, the sign of the witch." She looked down at her new scar. It didn't hurt, though it looked like it should. She just felt…warm. Shrugging a little, she turned back inside, ready to make dinner and settle in to a quiet evening at home, Serah couldn't shake her nagging feeling. A feeling that maybe these quiet evenings she had come to despair, these evenings that filled her heart and mind with a desperation, a certainty that life ahead was a long boring line of quiet evening after quiet evening, that this was in fact not the truth. She began to believe these evenings would be like diamonds in the future—luxurious and rare. Turning back to her patient companions, she reveled in the quiet, her mind wondering and wandering, looking for answers and intuitions about the adventure ahead.

Something was definitely happening; Serah felt it. And instead of being scared, she was excited—excited for what was to come. *What's next?* she wondered. A slow smile spread across her pretty face.

Chapter 4

Serah dreamt.

She stood in front of a beautiful woven basket. She was being watched. The white cobra rose up from the basket to almost shoulder height and flared its hood. Serah could feel her eyes widen, and her blood shoot adrenaline to every part of her body in a rush. Panic. The white fangs looked as if made of pearls. As she turned and ran, she felt the cobra strike. She was prey. Her head turned to see its fangs caught in the fabric of her white sleeve, an inch from her unprotected hand. In an instant, she reached out with her other hand and grabbed ahold of the cobra's silken body. It wasn't a good grab; it was too far behind its head. She felt terror fill her, and she pulled and pulled with everything she had.

"Noooo bite, no bite. No, no, no, no." The snake's body started to separate, started to tear apart. Serah gagged her revulsion at the sight of it, but she was stuck. She didn't know what to do. The panic filled her. She lifted her eyes and there was Ben, her best friend, standing nearby. He was watching.

"Help me," she begged. He was silent.

Serah woke as if shot through a gun in the dark. Breathing fast, her hand went to her chest as the image of her nightmare slowly faded from her mind. She turned her hand over and looked at her new scars, hoping for insight. The same hand reached out to rustle the fur of her sleeping cat. Rubi opened her eyes and contorted herself to gain more pets with a short trill of a purr that Serah loved; she always wondered what she was "saying" when she did that. Serah absentmindedly obliged the request, thinking about the snake from her dream. Was it an omen of some kind?

The air grew still. Rubi reacted and sat up instantly, sitting in that pretty curved-back cat posture. Serah watched as her cat's head seemed to be molded into place, all her muscles tight. Nothing could force her to look in a different direction.

Startled, Serah asked, "Rubi, what's up?"

The cat continued to stare at the foot of the bed. The room grew so still it seemed as if the actual molecules stopped moving. Serah felt her chest tighten in that familiar way and attempted to take deep breaths.

"I can breathe. I am okay. I can breathe. Everything is okay," she repeated to herself, worried it was another panic attack—self-taught calming that seemed to work only when she was desperate. Rubi leapt up as if tased, turned, and landed back in Serah's lap. She quickly licked Serah's arm. Once. Twice. The pressure and stillness remained. Three licks, then a fourth. Finally, Serah's ears popped, and her breathing eased.

The demon sat, perched on the foot of her bed. Its world was a hazy one, as if looking through stained glass. Movement and emotion were the easiest for its eyes to see in the wavy distorted view. Emotion *moved*; it could gather speed like a train, or it could sit like a smoke signal wafting, and it *stunk*. Oh, how the demon loved it so. The sweetest scent was its own particular brand of emotion. The kind it was made for. When that came, it was devoured. Devoured like an orgasm of rage or fear or despair, whatever the case may be. There were many kinds, eight to be exact—some more rare than others.

The demon sat and stared. It could see Serah's arm glow from being marked by her cat. It was patient, not eager to test what protection might have been given. Its name was Apathy. Apathy had made a home here for quite some time, feeding off of Serah's slowly dying energy. The days she couldn't make it out of bed early enough. The nights she felt like watching *Alias* reruns imagining what her life could be…what it *should* be. Yet, doing nothing. Doing nothing but sitting on her couch as her life crept by. Its name was Apathy, and it was content.

Apathy smiled at the cat's gesture; a smile that a sociopath would love to emulate. It didn't understand much of the human world, but it knew power.

Emotions were energy, and the words that came with them more powerful still. Names were the most powerful of all. Rumpelstiltskin was no fool. Only a fool at the end.

Apathy sat and stared at Serah's marks. Rubi was vigilant, waiting. Purrs grew into growls, and growls escaped her louder and louder as her anxiety increased.

"I can seeeee you," the cat tried to say. "Stay away. I know you are here now," she purred.

Apathy blinked and moved forward. Rubi let out a yowl like nothing Serah had ever heard. Diego roused and quickly stood to find himself nose to nose with IT. He pranced backward in fear and trampled over Serah, a German Shepherd on a queen-sized bed does not make for room to prance.

"Diego! Down! Down, Diego! God you are walking all over me. Stop it! What is going on here?" Serah hollered and held out her hand against the onslaught of her German Shepherd's feet.

The marks seared on her palm and wrist, turned outward. Apathy's blue eyes narrowed, and it hissed out its attempt to reject the symbol and its power. Much more power if wielded by an owner who knew how to use it, but power nonetheless. It was enough. Rubi matched it hiss for hiss. Diego whined, a nails-on-the-chalkboard whine.

Serah yelled, "Jeez, what the hell is with you two?" Apathy had no use for this chaos. It vanished.

"Guys, guys! Calm down...please," Serah tried to use her soft calm voice, looking around for any cause to the mayhem. Diego stopped, turned, and joyously started licking his person's face. Serah couldn't help but laugh as she ducked and dodged to avoid that wet tongue. Rubi the cat sat quietly. Serah managed to settle Diego into a pile half on half off her lap rubbing his ear in that perfect way and took stock of Rubi sitting still, tense, staring at what the demon had left behind. Serah followed her stare to the edge of the bed.

"Wha—?!" Serah leaned closer to examine what she saw. "Mouse droppings? Ugh! Dammit!" she said and groaned.

"How did they get there? Is that what all the fuss was about? Mice?!" She asked her furred companions. Throwing back the covers with a grimace, her feet hit the cold hardwood floor. She stomped out of bed to clean up the mess and paused as the quiet thought passed, *Freakin' brave mice…Huh.*

An extra energy inhabited her, and she shooed everyone off the bed. Serah cleaned vigorously. The thought of sleeping in a bed with mice droppings was more than she could handle. She stripped the sheets and hauled them off to the washing machine. Nothing less than a full cleaning to be done: new sheets, new duvet, new blanket to handle paws. Before the washer even started its rinse cycle, Serah began to pace. It was only 4 a.m. Maybe she was getting too much sleep, she thought.

Serah clicked through her emails on her phone and paced more. She saw one from her mom, *Happy Birthday, my daughter.* The subject line made her almost laugh.

"My birthday was two weeks ago, Mom," she whispered to the darkened kitchen.

Serah, I hope this finds you well. I am out of the country again, but wanted you to know I was thinking of you, as I always do. I want you to fly like you did in your dreams as a little girl. Please use this present; it would mean the world to me. And it will help you in ways you don't see yet. I have only ever wanted to keep you safe.

Love from Austria,

Mom

"Now that is actually interesting," Serah muttered. A gift of thirty flight lessons at a nearby flight school. The small local airport was only a few miles away; she passed it often on her way to her favorite Mexican restaurant.

"Thanks, Mom," Serah set her phone back on the counter, her uneasiness felt slightly calmed.

She started to pace again and decided it was time for coffee and an episode of *Alias*—the perfect solution. As she settled in front of the TV, the restlessness enveloped her. Leaning forward she set the mug on the coffee table and stayed in that posture, resting her head in her hands. She rocked back and forth, not paying attention to the TV. Diego looked up. *Okay, okay, okay,* she thought, a bit frantic as the pent-up energy welled. It warped into an anxiety she could feel in her chest. It was familiar. But, this time, Serah couldn't. Sit. Any. More. Up from the couch, into the bedroom to throw on workout pants, top, jacket, and running shoes, the pavement was going to feel it too.

"Going on a run!" she said to no one in particular; her voice grim because up until now Serah knew she hated running. She grabbed her key, tied it to her shoe. No headphones, no music, just her thoughts and her breath. That was enough.

Thoughts tumbled. Serah picked up the pace. By mile two she was panting hard. She had never run this fast or this far. The thoughts started to smooth out, and she recognized it. She could feel a certainty—not peaceful—just a quiet feeling where she was certain of who she was and what she did. She ran on. By mile three, she could think again. She turned for home.

The sweat rolled off her in rivulets. It was as if rivers of toxins were oozing right out of her body. It always felt that way after a good workout. She wondered why it had been so long since her last good slog at the gym. Once home she showered and got ready for work.

A few minutes to spare, she logged in to print the email from her mom. There it was, the coupon for a set of thirty flight lessons. She snagged it from the printer and headed out the door.

It's going to be a good year, she thought. And for the second time in twenty-four hours, a smile grew to cross her pretty face.

Chapter 5

Serah walked into her favorite local spot, A Cuppa Joe coffee shop.

Over in the right-hand corner sat Ben, law student studying for his most recent exam. Studying was a loose interpretation of what he did when he was there. He was friendly and warm and gained energy from being around others, mostly his friends. Thinking of their friendship made Serah smile as she waited for her coffee.

Ben slouched with earplugs in, not seeing her approach. She tossed her keys down on the table and threw her bags down with a sigh.

Ben looked up at Serah with affection as he pulled out his earplugs and set them aside knowing studying was done for a little while, as she launched into her story.

"Bennnnnn. It's official. I'm crazy. Off. The. Deep. End. What's it like having a crazy friend, by the way?"

Patient, Ben chuckled, "You are one of the sanest people I know, so what's up?" he asked. At Serah's pause, Ben waited for a minute.

"Talk to me, Goose." He didn't like to push, but he knew sometimes she needed one. Serah stared for a minute at the gorgeous tattoo of a glossy feline curled around his forearm. She held out her hand, the one with the new burn scars and waited for a response.

"Holy crap. Ouch!" Ben's eye narrowed as he focused in on the scar. "Those look like...something. What does it look like?"

Serah nodded as she responded, "It's Greek, the sign of the witch and some other Norse symbol of protection, I think," Serah spoke quietly and sipped her coffee as she told him the story of the book in the library and the man in the yard. Waiting for him to reply to her wild story, she looked around the coffee shop at the other patrons. One woman with impossibly-long nails was talking quietly on her cell phone. A mother with two boys was attempting to order an apparent lifesaving dose of caffeine, in between their play. A silver-haired gentleman—*yes,* she thought, *definitely a gentleman*—relaxed with legs crossed in a comfy leather chair reading the paper.

Why are they here and not at home? What do they expect or want out of life? Do they search like her? Serah wondered.

"So, the book actually burned up? We couldn't go look at it?" Ben's first question brought Serah back to their table.

"Yep. Actually burned up. Wish we could. Might explain a few things. I did manage to get pictures of some of the pages." Serah pulled out her phone and together they scrolled through the photos: picture of the dog and cat, the strange lettering, the long list of unknown words.

"It's Norse, from what I can gather. But I'm not really sure how to translate it. Look, it's them!"

Ben nodded. He agreed that did look exactly like Diego and Rubi. "Text me those photos when you get a chance, would you?"

"Sure, but is this just a wild goose chase? I mean why would this happen to boring old me? What's going on here? I feel strangely calm about it all Ben. Have you ever seen or heard of anything like this?"

Ben ignored her question, "Let me see your hand. Does it hurt?"

"No, not at all actually. Looks almost healed, no?" She uncurled her hand and held it out to him. He grabbed it and felt the scars, both a bit raised but more shiny-white than an angry-red of a recent injury.

"This one happened yesterday?"

"Yep."

"Huh, well, kiddo, I don't know what to say," came Ben's quiet answer. Serah swallowed back her frustration. She knew it wasn't fair, but she relied on him a lot. *Too much,* she thought and took a breath. She didn't know what to do.

"Well, that's an answer. It's not sexy, but it's an answer," Serah said, and they both laughed at one of their favorite lines.

"I think that this might be just the beginning," Ben added.

Serah's eyes went wide when he said that. She was always talking of her boring life, but now that it was heading toward decidedly unboring, she wished she had never had such dangerous thoughts.

"Damn. Okaaaay. I guess. At least it's not boring," she said and tried to laugh off her nerves. Ben's eyes were a bit unfocused. He was thinking hard.

"I think for now, just be more aware of what is going on around you. Might be some answers there that you aren't seeing yet."

"Okay. I'll try, but what am I looking for?"

"I don't know. I just don't know. Look for anything. Anything at all," Ben turned back to studying for the bar exam, and Serah opened her computer to research flight training, a mutual decision to leave it at that. For now.

A few hours later they decided to pack it in and head for home. Each of them felt better after having been in the presence of a good friend since they both were overwhelmed by all they had going on in life. Serah and Ben walked out into the beautiful September day.

"See ya, Ben. Thanks," Serah said after a quiet stroll to their cars.

"Any time, my friend. You give me strength. Keep moving forward. We will talk again soon, 'kay?" He said and smiled at her. Those small shoulders of hers seemed to carry a great burden. At times he thought he knew and then sometimes, including today, he found himself wondering again what that burden was. Maybe now was the time they were going to find out. He wasn't sure why he thought that, but he did. Ben always listened well to his quiet thoughts.

"There are answers in the quiet, Seraphine. Just make sure to listen," he called to her as she got into her truck. Serah nodded, smiled, and waved. He turned on a sigh, time for class. *Good luck, Seraphine.* He sent that thought out to her and hoped it helped. It was all he could do, for now.

Ben looked down at his watch and decided all he could do wasn't good enough; class was almost over and studying could wait. Shrugging his backpack on amid the rustle of goodbyes from classmates, Ben walked out and instead of heading to his car, he turned toward the main library on the other side of campus. Maybe more answers could be found today.

Ben walked the beautiful treelined paths of campus, but lost in thought, he didn't see any of the beauty today. Memories came calling especially painful ones of his friend Ethan—tortured by the things he saw, eventually not able to sleep hardly at all, using booze and beer to medicate, the bar fights, so much rage and despair. Ethan seemed to envision himself a superhero of sorts, talking about the spirits he vanquished, the emotions he conquered, how he seemed to see bad events coming and was able to stop them. Ben always wondered—did Ethan create this world to explain what he didn't want to admit—a mental illness of some kind? Ethan was brilliant, really too brilliant for school. Bored quickly, he dropped out of college after two years saying he couldn't concentrate and had better things to focus his time on than learning calculus and geometry. Ben laughed as he remembered, at the time, how envious he was of Ethan's decisive attitude. Ben hated math and chemistry too; it was words that held his attention and what ultimately drew him to the law. The law was filled with powerful words that made an impact, words that changed the course of history.

But the law couldn't teach me the right words to change the course of that night, Ben sighed. His mind settled on a memory he would most like to forget.

As he walked, he heard the ding ding ding of his phone, as multiple texts came through back-to-back, pulling him back to the present moment. Knowing he had the pictures from Serah to help his research confirmed his choice as the right one today, though he had an uncomfortable feeling he wasn't going to like what he found out.

Chapter 6

The house was quiet. Serah heard the click of Diego's nails on the hardwood floor, as he padded down the hall to say hello. When he saw her at the table where she was studying for her upcoming flight lesson, his ears tucked back, ducking his head, giving a small wag.

"Time for a walk, buddy?" His ears perked slightly, so she knew he understood, but it seemed he wasn't willing to hope too much in case he was wrong. She had been known to fool him before. When she went to the hall closet and grabbed the leash, Diego leapt into the air turning 360s to land back down on his large paws. His excitement never failed to make her laugh.

"You'd think you were a prisoner, and I never took you out!" Serah shook her head with a smile. Once outside she turned her face up to the sun and closed her eyes. Glad for her hoodie and vest, they started down the sidewalk to a small neighborhood park. She scanned the area and didn't see any people around at this hour, so Serah clipped off Diego's leash once they entered the park property. Together they played ball and chased wind-swept leaves and watched the sun start to set behind the tall pine trees that edged the quiet block.

Diego saw it first. It sat in the half-light between dusk and dark, lit slightly by the pool of soft light from the streetlamp that had just turned on announcing the pending night. It hugged the border where light stopped and approaching gloom began.

"What is it, buddy?" Serah asked. She watched his nose flare as he tested the wind, his neck stretched forward unwilling to move closer before he knew. He was patient. Serah squinted to try to see ahead to the next block and decided best to clip Diego's leash back on for the walk home.

"Come on, bud, let's go home. It's time for dinner, and I want to get ready for my flight lesson tomorrow," Serah said as she tugged on Diego's leash.

"Forward motion, let's go."

Diego growled; he could smell it. The shape in the dark snapped its eyes around at that noise and fixated on the pair in the street. It was Demon Fear, and it could smell them too.

"What the hell? Diego!" Serah couldn't remember the last time she had heard him growl. The sound curved through the air and landed in her gut. She looked up the street but saw nothing.

Nothing.

Diego looked up at her, wagged one short wag with his tail and then continued to watch ahead. Serah strained to see.

Blue eyes. *Did she see blue eyes?* Confused she shook her head and blinked. When she looked up, the blue eyes were bigger. It was closer now. Diego's growls intensified in equal measure as the space between them decreased.

"Diego. Diego. DIEGO!" Serah shook his leash hoping to get his attention. "Diego let's go. NOW."

She could feel it, the nausea forming. Fear. She could taste it, saliva filling her mouth. Fear invaded. Serah's heart sprinted. She could see it, a formless shape with those eyes. Its eyes were big and blue; they did not blink.

"No, no, no, no, no, no," Serah pressed her palms against her face. She turned and spit, and tasted salt.

Fear wafted over to that spot and lingered there. It circled the spit and sniffed. Like an addict to a line of coke. It circled, and it sniffed. It sniffed, and it hissed. It hissed at Diego as he growled. His growl grew as wild as his fear. He growled and yipped loud enough to echo down the quiet street. Yet, every blind stayed down. Every curtain was shut tight.

Fear danced. It twirled around like a dancer on a stick, reaching out tendrils of smokey fear to touch the terrified girl. It played with his prey eating up the waves of emotion as they snuck by. Such a delightful snack—an appetizer before the main course. It waited for full dark. It was in no hurry.

Alone. She was dying, alone. Like Jeremy did. Like we all do. There is nothing there. Nothing out there at all. We are all alone. Me, fly a plane? That is stupid. I am too clumsy. I will just kill us all. Stupid girl. Stupid, ugly lonely clumsy girl. No one will EVER love you.

Serah stood stock still as the words and images reverberated in her head like a mantra, a spell, with soul crushing power. Her eyes popped open and swept back and forth. She knew someone followed her. She knew they intended her harm.

"Hey, pretty girl. Heyyy." Her head snapped up to see a figure crossing the street. Grey hoodie and jeans, he looked normal. She wanted to run. She felt crazy. Why was she acting this way? The large blue eyes of the demon swirled at her feet. It blinked in anticipation and let out a slow, almost silent "hisssssssssss." It knew what was coming, and it was ready to feast.

Diego looked from one opponent to the other, confusion turning his growl into a whine. He looked up at his human for guidance. She watched the man so he did too.

"Hi, ummm. Just walking my dog. Thanks," Serah stuttered, encased in fear.

"What a nice night for that. I've seen you around here before. I always remember the pretty ones," he said. But he didn't smile. He just watched as he moved closer. His words spoken by others would have made her flush and flirt back, but his sounded dirty and almost...evil. *Evil?* She didn't understand. The stare from his blue eyes she couldn't counter.

"Yeah...it is...for sure, thanks. I, uhh, gotta keep going. Dinner time, you know?" *So scared so scared. RUN!* "So, ummm, see you later," she edged away, as he reached out a hand.

"So pretty," his fingers touched her dark brown hair and caressed down from the crown of her head to the flyaway ends. "Shiny like," he whispered.

"Noooo. No, no, no, please," Serah begged, her teeth started to chatter. She closed her eyes and leaned away from the dirty hand. Frozen, she could not step away. His hand closed on the end of her hair and tugged. Hard. He pulled her head back with a sharp snap. Serah flinched, and she sucked in air in surprise.

Demon Fear sipped, then drank the air in gulps. This was what It waited for.

Diego lunged. A cacophony of barking peeled down the street as he jumped at the man. He could reach the man's chest with his paws as he forced him away from his girl. The man hissed and stumbled off the curb.

Serah tripped backwards onto the green lawn behind her and passed out. Fear blinked. It swirled around the girl's head, but there was nothing left to eat. With one last hiss at the annoying canine, Fear danced down the now darkened street, sated.

"Seraphine. Seraphine, wake up. Wake up, NOW."

Serah cracked one eye open to see Ben's face swimming above her. His hands on her shoulders, he tried to pull her up. She resisted.

"OhmyGod, did I pass out?! I never pass out," she said, throwing one arm over her face. "Aaaagggh."

"Seraphine, seriously. Sit up, please. Let's make sure you won't do it again," Ben cajoled and tugged. She let him tug her into a sitting position. He watched her face to make sure it stayed nice and pink.

"Blue eyes…," she muttered, and the memory returned. "Did you see a man here? Oh, God, a *dirty* man with a grey jacket and blue eyes. Something else with blue eyes."

"No, I didn't. You must have butt dialed me? I heard Diego going crazy. I drove to your house then around the block thinking you would be at the park with Diego, and saw you on the lawn. You must have been passed out for a while! Did something hurt you?" Ben asked.

"Ahhh, noooo. Just scared I guess," Serah blinked. *Did she imagine it?*

"That guy was really creepy. Wait—you said some*thing*, not some*one*." She let the rest of her question hang in the air.

"Yeah," Ben sighed. "I did. Come on. Get up. Do you have a minute to talk?" He stood and reached out his hand to help her up.

Sitting in Ben's clean kitchen, Serah knew he liked to cook. Or at least liked to look like he did. Viking range, copper pots, *nice stuff,* she thought. Serah sat on a stool, head bent and stared at her palm rubbing the scars, waiting, while he pulled together items in the kitchen. With an almost silent sigh she threw her hands down, crossed her arms and stared out the window. The light inside reflected back from the dark night making the window a mirrored wall. She could only see herself. Annoyed at her reflection, she turned to look at something else. A few pictures were framed and hung on the wall.

Mom, Dad, brother, family trip. He had glasses then, that thought made her smile.

"What's up?" he asked noticing.

"Oh, not much," when he just cocked his head to the side, she continued, "I just thought, so you were actually a child once like the rest of us."

He smiled and asked, "Coffee, beer, or water? Or some version of each?"

"Umm. Water, please. I'm really thirsty for some reason." Serah noticed Ben had vintage signs on his cheery dark blue walls. *Coffee 10 cents,* one read, and *God, not guns. Wanted: Town Sheriff $20 a week, Apply within.* The kind of signs you would see in a small bar, in a small town, off a small dusty road in the Midwest. She wished she could go somewhere different and wake up to new sights, new sounds. She didn't even have a passport. Serah sighed again.

Ben set a tall glass of water down in front of her on the table, "It's the demons. From what I know, they are made up of a high proportion of salt content. That's what I've heard anyway, I can't see them. But apparently, my dear Seraphine, *you* can." He turned to set a dish of water down on the floor for Diego who was sprawled there panting.

"Demons...," Serah trailed off and started to laugh, but it died in her throat. Ben looked straight into her eyes and held her gaze. *He believes what he is saying,* she thought, stunned. She eyed her water and debated whether or not to drink it.

"Serah," he started. She turned to look at him and saw weariness in his face. Her compassion for her friend edged out the worry. This was Ben after all. They'd been best friends since they both walked into that LSAT study group five years ago.

"Serah, after we left Cuppa Joe last month, I decided to do my own research at the campus library."

Serah nodded and gave in to her thirst. Ben watched as she tilted the glass back and gulped it down.

Giving her a moment to savor the water, Ben remembered how he had returned to the university library several times to try to find answers.

"My university law library is one of the oldest in the country, so I figured it was as good a place as any to start looking. I spent a few days looking into the religious historical section. Talk about a maze of the esoteric," Ben shook his head. "I figured religion was the best place to start—the most educated for their time and most likely to write down knowledge that might serve us from long ago. I mean, we did kill witches and warlocks and wizards in disgusting displays of eradicating what we fear. Humanity, I mean."

"I found some very interesting historical texts that led me to believe I know who wrote that tome you found the library. History tells us of a sect of monks—Papar Monks—who lived on islands north of Scotland. They were described as wandering Holy Men who lived in the lands to the North. In the ninth century, they are said to have disappeared but leaving behind books. Large books of teachings that were found by Norsemen or Vikings when they started to settle the land."

Ben continued, "Papar meaning father, or Pope, they were considered men of the faith. These books are said to contain three things: The sign of the seventh seal, teachings about a race of demons that shall propagate on the Earth, and an inscription to the Seekers of the Truth," Ben took a breath as he remembered his search. Demon lore, historical documents, religious texts. Most nights leading him nowhere closer to any truth that could help. Until one, almost ready to give up, his search down the rabbit hole led him to the Catholic Encyclopedia a text that took over a decade or so to write in the early 1900s. Ben groaned when he saw the title page: volume one of fifteen. "Fifteen volumes?" He spoke out loud to the empty rows of stacks and stacks of books, he hadn't ever been this deep in the library and hadn't seen a single person in hours.

"I spent a few more nights trying to make sense of the index or find a tool that would help narrow my search. Finally in desperation, I tried Wikipedia which, thankfully, had an indexed version of the religious texts. Entering various combinations of words—Demons, Devil—I had no idea how would I come across the right article. It would take forever...," he trailed off. Serah sat wide-eyed, barely breathing as she listened.

Ben continued, "I kept searching because who are the craziest (and the smartest) people of each time period?" At Serah's blank look, he rushed on now excited by his sleuthing, "Radical clergy! I discovered a William Erbery, a radical Welsh clergyman who became a Seeker. I figured now I was getting somewhere. Erbery was around in the 1600s or so. Much more recent than the disappearing Scottish monks. I hoped I was right, and that he was a descendent of the original Seekers. So, back to Wikipedia I went. For a few hours I was grasping at straws writing in different combinations of words—demons, demons + religion, demons + Seekers—trying to find some kind of lead. Did you know The Seekers were also an old Australian rock band?" Ben chuckled at this, as Serah rolled her eyes.

"Ben, what the heck does this have to do with me?"

"I'm getting there! Besides a terrible Australian Band—yes, I listened to a few of their songs," Ben replied to one of Serah's looks. "Hey, it was late, and I was sleep deprived!"

He continued, "Besides being a band, The Seekers are ALSO an obscure, unorganized religion that branched off from Roman Catholics and was first recognized in 1620. They were burned at the stake, if they didn't recant. Some eventually became what is now considered the Quakers. Their motto? Searching for the truth, believing all organized religion was corrupt, only they could 'see' God's revelation," Ben stopped with a pleased look on his face.

"Ben, I appreciate everything you've done, but how does an obscure, unorganized religious sect from the 1600s help me now? Am I just going crazy? What am I supposed to DO?"

Expression dropped from Ben's face, knuckles turning white as his hand gripped his cold beer. Ben took a deep breath and a swig. He debated how much to tell his sweet-faced best friend.

"I have met only one other person with visions like yours. He is now dead," Ben shuddered as he remembered the grisly scene. "There is something rising in the world. Maybe it existed all along; I don't know, but it's out there now, and we don't know much about it, Seraphine. He, my friend Ethan, didn't ever tell me much. He didn't trust me enough. Only disturbing comments here and there, mostly when he was drunk, strange coincidences that unnerved me, so I rarely asked more. He did tell me three things that I haven't forgotten and still don't understand. Those with the mark and the sight can fight them. Dogs and cats can warn you of them—they seem to have a special gift to see and protect. And finally, that they always made him thirsty because of the salt," Ben paused to let it sink in. He wasn't sure he saw her breathe.

"He didn't call them demons. He called them shadows, sometimes spooks. He didn't have any knowledge, he was fighting blind, thinking he was slowly going crazy. We both did," Ben trailed off, closed his eyes for a moment, and shook his head.

"Ethan was obsessed with Viking culture. I'm sorry I didn't believe him more. It all seemed so out there. So...unbelievable," he winced as he said that last word.

Serah sat back against the wall and hugged her arms to her chest. Ben was quiet and watched patient, as she chewed on her lip. With a quick motion, she sat forward and brought the two legs of the chair that had been suspended in air down to the floor with a thump.

"WAIT. Are you telling me you've known about this all along? And NEVER TOLD ME?" Serah didn't even take a breath, "I thought we were best friends!"

Ben sat thoughtful his eyes on her face, *Please God,* he thought, *keep her safe.* "This all happened while you were grieving Jeremy. I definitely wasn't going to tell you about any of this then." He took a deep breath, "If you *can* see them, then maybe you can fight them, they seem to wreak havoc on the lives they touch, and, so far, you are the only person I know, living that is, who can do the first."

"Will you *please* stop saying that! For God's sake, it's freaking me out."

"For God's sake, and your own, Seraphine, you better listen to everything I say. Even to the hard parts," Ben's dark blue eyes looked across the table at her, sad but determined. "And we should all be so lucky to learn from others' mistakes and honor their sacrifice." The kitchen fell silent, except for the soft breath from the sleeping dog on the floor. Ben waited. A quiet minute ticked by.

Serah sat up straight in her chair and held out her palm with the scars toward Ben. The hair on the back of his neck stood up.

"Okay, Ben, I'm in. I want to help."

Ben smiled, "I knew you would say that." He turned and opened a drawer behind him, pulling out a stack of disheveled papers. "I printed out the pictures you sent me from the book and noted my theories of what the images and symbols could mean. I added in the religious research. Maybe some of it could be helpful."

"Wow, Ben this was a lot of work!" Serah grabbed the papers.

"Let's go over what I've discovered, and then, well I don't know what then," Ben sighed, closed his eyes, and continued, "then we each get a good night's sleep."

"Good night's sleep, yeaaah right." Serah whispered a lackluster agreement.

Ben sat down at the table next to her with a glass of whisky, "Sometimes a man needs a little whiskey," he answered Serah's raised eyebrow. Serah's other eyebrow shot up, with a sigh, he pushed himself up from the table and poured another small glass for her.

Smiling her Mona Lisa smile, Serah turned to the papers. "Okay, what did you find out? I'm dying to know."

"A lot of historical notes from what I skimmed from the religious texts. Historians cannot agree whether the Papar monks were real or imaginary—whether they were present at the time of naming, or whether they had vanished. The Catholic Encyclopedia is where I learned about Several Irish Christian Anchorites." At Serah's confused gesture, Ben explained, "Anchorites are holy men seeking seclusion from society. A sect of them were reportedly discovered to have lived in Iceland before the arrival of Norse settlers from Scandinavia. Which fits with the idea that this language is of Viking origin. Anchorites still exist, but their lifestyle is not…normal, to say the least," Ben paused again to see if Serah was still with him.

"Back to your book. The first page of Diego and Rubi seem to track with what I found out from my friend years ago about the cats and dogs. Ethan always had an affinity for them, felt they were good luck and protective somehow. I'm guessing it's to signify how important they are. Not sure if there is more to it; we will have to dig deeper. I wish Diego could talk."

"That's what I'm sayin'!" Serah smacked her hand on her knee. Diego jerked and popped his head up from the floor, "Sorry, bud, did you know you were special?" Diego's tail thumped the floor in agreement. "Go back to sleep," Serah added.

Ben continued as he grabbed another page, "Page two is a list of something, but I don't know how to translate the list. We have to figure out what kind of language this is. You said it's Norse, but it appears to be Norse-Viking. Something like that, but I'm just not sure. This stick type lettering is not one I've ever seen."

"Oh, just do this," Serah grabbed her phone from the other side of the table and tsked at the now-cracked screen.

"Must have happened when you fainted," Ben commented as he watched over her shoulder.

"When I *fell*," Serah said under her breath. Clicking through the photos, she found the page. Taking another screenshot, she edited it down to just one of the stick-like lettered words. Switching screens, she uploaded it into Google image. "Voila," she announced and turned the phone to show Ben.

"Younger Furthark," Ben stumbled over pronouncing the second word. "What the heck is Younger Furthark?" Serah typed quickly, "Younger Furthark, also called Scandinavian runes, is a runic alphabet and a reduced form of the Elder Furthark, blah, blah…in use from about the ninth century, after a 'transitional period' during the seventh and eighth centuries. Blah, blah…corresponds roughly to the Viking age," Serah looked up at Ben. "That fits with what you said about the monks right?" Ben nodded sharply and took a sip of his whiskey, making a face as it burned.

Serah laughed, "Sometimes a man needs a whiskey." She mimicked in a fake burly man voice.

"Gotta start somewhere, kid," Ben retorted, knowing how she hated being called kid, being only three years younger. Serah scowled and took a sip of whiskey, trying to keep a stone face but failed as she sputtered a little bit swallowing the drink down. "Damn, Ben, you actually drink this stuff?"

"Clearly, not really," Ben replied. Laughing, they clinked glasses and turned back to the papers.

Ben noted *Younger Furthark* on the paper. "I really want to know what this page means. What is this list?"

"There's no way Google translate would have a Younger Furthark translation would it?" Serah asked. Immediately, they bent their heads over their phones and went to work, using Google image to attempt to translate each letter of what appeared to be the main title of three pages. The work was painstakingly slow. Each letter corresponded to a "sound" and each sound was designated a letter. Turning back to the computer, Serah combed through articles discussing Norse languages, symbols and runes, the difference between Older and Younger Furthark, for at least an hour.

"Bingo," Serah said. Ben looked over from what felt like the most important word scramble of his life. "A philologist is a person who studies ancient languages. Had no idea. Did you?" Serah asked. Ben shook his head.

"Philologist," Ben repeated, stumbling over the new word. "Say that ten times fast." Ben laughed as she tried.

"So, all we need to do is find a Philologist, see if they wrote about Younger Furthark, and then ask them if they can learn how to translate this. Bennnnnnn, arrrrgh." Serah dropped her head onto her crossed arms in defeat.

"How quickly you give up, grasshopper," Ben answered and winked, as she slightly turned and peeked one eye out from under her bangs. Sitting up quickly, she grabbed the page of notes where he had managed to put together the title word of three pages.

"Appears we will have to translate it letter by letter. Good thing there isn't a lot of text on each page. Unless, like you said, we find someone who can translate it more easily."

"Demons and Weapons and Angels—sounds like Armageddon," Serah said, reading off the only words Ben had deciphered. Serah shrugged and tried to joke, "Jeez, could it be more intense?"

"I'm supposed to fight this list?" Serah shook the paper titled Demons toward Ben for emphasis.

"I thought we were best friends." Ben smiled gently, using Serah's words back at her.

His smile faded. "Serah, I promise you aren't in this alone." Her hazel eyes looked up toward his and nodded. Her teeth caught her bottom lip in that way he knew meant she was nervous; she held his gaze until he looked away.

Ben looked down at page three. "We need to translate all the pages. But to me this looks like ways to fight them? I don't know. Your rose bush weapon is here, which seems appropriate if that's the topic of this page."

"But wait, Rubi and Diego are on here too," Serah said.

"Yes, weapons of warning are also very useful in battle, sentries, warning systems, protection." Serah nodded along with Ben's words.

"Page four is intimidating." Ben pulled it out and held it at arm's length. "This wolf dog, whatever it is, is ferocious looking. There's a bunch of scary dogs in mythology. Cerebrus for Greek, but that was a three-headed dog guardian of the underworld. Garm for the Vikings, I'm pretty sure. So, my guess is this is Garm?" Ben saw Serah's look, and it was his turn to scowl. "What? I liked mythology in school."

"That seems it will prove useful, Nerdy McNerderson."

"Whatever! Be happy I'm here and didn't run screaming from this mess."

Serah turned solemn, nodding slowly. "Ben, truly, I am very grateful you are here."

Ben cleared his throat. "Okay, let's keep going, or we will be here all night. Diego needs his beauty sleep." Both of them broke into a laugh, as Diego let out a snore—as if on cue.

"What does Garm have to do with any of this?" Serah asked.

"I wish I knew; I really do," Ben sighed and shook his head. "Okay, page five, can you do that Google image thing for page five?" Serah nodded and went to work. Talking while she edited the photos down to individual images of each symbol, "So, I know that first one is Hecate's wheel, sign of the witch."

She quirked her eyebrow up and down. "One of the only memories I have of my dad is when I was about four years old. He asked me what I wanted to be when I grew up, and you know what I said? I said I wanted to be a princess or a witch. And since he wasn't a king, I knew I couldn't be a princess, so I said I guess I'll have to be a witch."

Ben smiled. "I can picture you, little Serah, wanting to be a witch...," he trailed off. "What do you think of it now?"

"I certainly don't feel any different, and, so far, it's scary as shit. Sooooo, I think I'd like to ask for the princess gig. Is there a parallel universe I can jump to where I'm a princess instead?!"

Ben laughed. "Maybe we will find one! You certainly are a princess about your coffee. Hey!" he shouted when Serah smacked him on the shoulder.

"Okay, ready to write this down? Here's the list of symbols."

Ben nodded and grabbed a pen.

"Hecates—wheel sign of the witch, Greek knowledge and life, Norse symbol for protection from enemies, defense of what one loves. Norse Helm of Awe—most powerful symbol of all. Well shit, why couldn't I have this scar? That one sounds cool," Serah commented as she read.

She looked up from her phone. "Did your friend—the one who saw spooks—did he have scars like mine?"

Ben paused and closed his eyes, trying to remember. "No." Opening his eyes, he shook his head. "No, I don't think I ever saw any scars. He did draw some symbols on both his forearms one Halloween with colored Sharpies, though. It actually turned out pretty cool, but none of them looked like any of these. Not that I can remember." Ben shrugged. "I'll see if I can dig up some old pictures of us from that party. Lily might have some; she had a crush on him for a bit." Serah perked up at the new piece of gossip about one of his law school friends. Ben motioned for her to continue with the symbols.

"Norse strength of will; Greek Oroboros eternity; circle of life; chaos, death, and rebirth. Ben, I had a dream about a snake the other night...," Serah said as she looked over at him, writing fast. She debated telling him that he was in the dream and the feeling that he couldn't save her, but decided not to burden him with what was only a dream.

"Ben." Serah paused, watching Ben scribble furiously, mumbling something about dogs and demons. "Ben. BEN."

"What??"

"Ben, if stuff really starts to go down, if I start to change…I dunno." Serah shrugged and shook her head slightly. "I don't know what I'm trying to say. Just…please remember me the way I am now, or before now. Normal, human, your best friend," her throat tightened on the last three words. Serah could feel her eyes start to fill with tears. Looking up, she tried to contain them. Keep them inside, keep it all inside—the fear, the longing, the rush of emotions.

Ben stared at her face. "I promise, friend. I will remember you as you are now, as I first met you when you walked into that LSAT class. I will remember when you took in Rubi and stepped out of your grief. I will remember you brave and sad and courageous and quiet and kind. I will remember all of it. I promise."

Serah didn't think she could talk. And if she could talk, she didn't know what she could say to that to do it justice. So, she settled on just two words, "Thank you."

"It's not boring," Ben whispered and smiled at one of their favorite sayings.

"It's not boring," Serah echoed, her voice coming back to her strong and clear. They high-fived as was part of the ritual and looked back to the papers covering the table.

"Do you think I will get allllll of these on my hand and arm?" Serah asked, knowing Ben didn't have an answer for her. Not now and probably not ever. She would have to find out herself.

Chapter 7

Serah and Diego walked home quickly that night from Ben's house. *Best to be quick before another encounter*, she remembered thinking, as she turned and jumped at every noise. Even a cute couple walking their dog was suspect, and she crossed the street to avoid them, despite Diego's wish to greet another friend. Serah bolted the door with a hasty sign of the cross. With no idea if that would be enough to keep her safe, she felt better nonetheless.

After telling Serah to get a good night's sleep, to which she responded with a roll of her eyes, Ben decided they should meet again as soon as the local Cuppa Joe coffee shop opened for the day.

"So, am I supposed to be some Demon warrior goddess or something, Ben?" Serah asked and then looked away, past the sunshine that bathed the charming outdoor patio, her eyes unfocused.

"I don't believe gods and goddesses exist, Serah," Ben laughed.

"I know, Ben, I know, but look at my hand!" Serah held her hand up to show the marks again as evidence.

Ben nodded at her scars. "There's a lot we don't know. We need to approach this like an experiment. Obviously, these *things* can cause you harm, since I found you passed out on someone's lawn."

Serah cringed.

"So, first we need to know how you can detect them. We need to figure out what we are dealing with here."

Serah nodded; Ben was right.

"Smart. Okay, well the animals seem to be able to see them pretty well, given those two nights. That night with Rubi on the bed and then Diego last night."

Ben nodded and started to type notes into his phone. "What else?"

"I can see blue eyes. I think they have blue eyes." Serah paused and closed her eyes, tugging on the memory of the night before.

"Ocean…salty air! I think Ethan was right—that they are composed of high salt content! That would explain why I remember it smelled like the ocean just before it happened! Annnd…" Serah focused hard. "I feel like it was low to the ground. Almost vapor, but then again not. It circled…like it was…hunting…waiting…" Serah's voice, already soft, trailed off as she came to the end of her memory. She shook her head, annoyed at the lack of clarity she felt. "Okay, so that's a start, I guess. I couldn't really see it until it was pretty much next to me."

"After you left, I figured out your Google image trick from last night and translated pages six and seven, for the most part. Page six was pretty easy, with only two symbols—Salt and Fire. Given that there are only two symbols on this page, they must be important. The final page is a picture of a, get this, Seraphim! 'An angel of the highest order of angels,'" Ben read off his scribbled notes.

"I have a friend who is graduating in international law and speaks about six languages; he's some sort of evil genius, I swear. Anyway, I have him looking at the pages and trying to help confirm the translation for us. I told him my friend is a librarian and needed the help for their historical document section. Not exactly a lie, am I right? He has such an ego, he didn't even question 'why him?'"

Serah smirked interrupting, "See, Ben—I'm an angel! You should be nicer to angels you know."

Ben laughed and rolled his eyes.

"Salt." Ben paused closing his eyes. "Wait. Salt mines. I remember reading something about salt mines. Interestingly enough, one of the largest and oldest salt mines is in Salzburg."

Serah sat, stunned; the coincidence was uncanny. *Mom's in Salzburg.*

"My mom. She is in Salzburg. Right now."

"I've read paranormal powers have been known to run in families." Ben didn't even blink at the revelation. "You never really talk about your mom." Ben shook his head. It was his turn to avoid eye contact, as he looked out the window.

"Ben! If that *is* my mom in Salzburg, she never even *told* me *anything* about all of this!" Serah was quick to quiet and said her next thought out loud, "Do you think she wanted to protect me?" Serah sounded amazed.

"Yes," Ben agreed with a sharp nod of his head. "I understand her reasons but disagree with her methods. You are vulnerable without knowledge," Ben frowned as he said this, showing his disapproval, and then smiled.

"Oh, no. Oh, no, nope. What is *that* smile for? I've seen that look before, BEN." Serah put up her hands then hastily gripped them together again, self-conscious of the mystical branding on her skin.

Ben huffed, "Serah, get a grip. If you are supposed to be some demon warrior princess, then hear me out."

"Princess? Whatever. I'm *not* a *princess.*"

"You need to set a trap." Ben started talking faster, as Serah's face filled with stubborn disagreement. "Set a trap, so we can learn more about what you are dealing with. This is the only way, Serah. You can't let it catch you off guard again like that. Don't be naive!" At that, Serah's mouth popped open and then shut with a click. She set her jaw and turned away for a moment to think, taking a sip of coffee.

"Okay." Serah took a breath. "Tell me how I should start."

Ben leaned in from his chair over the table. "They always return to the scene of the crime."

"Who does? This is not *Law and Order,* Ben. Seriously."

"I mean it, Serah. Maybe they have territory or favorite spots to soak up demon juice or whatever."

Serah crossed her arms as Ben continued.

"It would make sense. All creatures have something like that, right?" Serah gave a quick, reluctant nod.

"I think you should go back to the park. Alone. At night."

"That doesn't sound terrifying at all, does it?" she asked with a snort.

Ben nodded. "Perfect spot for 'fear' to live. Don't you think?"

"Okay, fine, I'll go back to the park. But seriously, Ben, why me?" she asked her best friend. "It should be *you.* You're the brave one. Not me. You always have been."

"Because life doesn't work out the way we think it should, Serah. You know that. Life picked *you*. I know you have it in you; I've always known that. It's you who has never believed."

Serah's eyes filled, and she pressed her lips together so tight it hurt. She swallowed back the pain and pushed her mouth into a small smile.

She couldn't meet his eyes, attempting a joke, "Maybe my headstone now has a chance of having *some*thing interesting written on it."

"*Demon warrior princess!*" said in unison. The two best friends dissolved into laughter, catching the attention of everyone within earshot. The sensitive strangers could feel it too—the power of a laughter that heals; the power to change a fate.

Chapter 8

Serah staked out her spot at dusk. She returned to the park where the encounter happened two nights before, leaving Diego safely tucked away at home with Ben.

Serah shined her flashlight at the small pile of rat droppings neatly piled on the edge of the street, almost perfectly marking the spot of the encounter. "See that?" she whispered loudly into her phone to Ben on FaceTime. "Same thing at my house when the animals went crazy on my bed. I had all this energy after that. Like we *moved IT...SOMETHING...*out. But it left behind evidence. It's like in the exact spot I saw it."

Ben nodded. "I don't think whispering helps when it's a demon, Serah."

Serah made a face at the screen. "Fine. Now what, Demon Master?"

Ben snorted. "I'm not sure. As you said, 'X marks the spot.' Find a place to wait and see what happens. You didn't believe me that they liked to return to the scene of their crime!"

Serah giggled nervously.

"Maybe, maybe we need something, like...like bait."

"What is bait to a demon?"

"Good question."

"Something dirty or smelly?"

"Bad people? Bad thoughts?"

"Rats? They seem like rodents of the underworld." Ben laughed at Serah's obvious disgust.

"Serah, you do realize that YOU are the bait."

"What? I don't want to be the bait! I never said okay to being the bait. I thought our plan was just to watch and learn?"

Ben sighed and rolled his eyes looking over at Diego and Rubi for help. The two friends debated what had been said while the last wisps of sunshine were snuffed out by the encroaching dark. Falling silent with the falling night, Serah took a bite of her protein bar, the only sound being the crinkling of the wrapper.

And they waited. One or the other occasionally making a comment, but each largely silent, thinking of ways to be ready for what was coming.

"Bennnn…it should have happened by now."

"Patience, Seraphina. How do you know? We don't know much yet. Don't give up."

The first hour dragged by. Serah noticed the comings and goings of the local rabbit family that liked to hop over to the park at dusk. She commented to Ben, "Peter Rabbit fam seems to give this place their blessi…Holy crap!"

"What? What! Seraphina!"

"Ahhhh…local cat kills Peter Rabbit baby and takes it back to his lair. Yikes. Is that an omen? I feel like a wildlife reporter who is being punished." Laughing nervously, they waited.

Two hours later, Serah sighed. "Well my butt is officially asleep and will never, ever wake Up. UGH. Stupid demons."

Serah rubbed her eyes from her spot behind a rosebush, as Ben nodded in agreement from his spot on her couch next to Diego who was listening intently. "Let's call it quits for tonight." Standing up, she gathered the few things she brought for the encounter: the rosebush weapon, some holy water (what Serah thought was holy water—*Isn't it holy if you believe it's holy?*), and snacks. Feeling defeated, Serah eased out of her hiding place and started walking down the now-darkened street, holding the phone in front of her to show Ben the view as she walked.

Serah saw it first. She drew her breath in sharply and clutched the phone. Crouched at the corner of a well-manicured lawn, it was circling, circling, circling something Serah could barely see.

"BEN!" Serah hissed a loud whisper.

"Whaaat?" Ben's head snapped up and focused back on the phone screen.

"Holy shit, holy shit, I see it…I think I see it, Ben. It's so…amorphous. Holy Jesus, Mary, and Joseph and their donkey! Holy shit!" Demon Fear's circle slowed, and it almost seemed to stretch; it had all the time in the world.

"It's Fear." Serah's whisper was rough out of her tight throat.

"*Fear?*" Ben repeated.

"Fear," Serah said, shaking.

"How do you know?" Ben asked in a loud whisper.

"I *feel* it."

She turned the phone to look face-to-face with Ben. Ben's eyes managed to get wider; Serah didn't think that was possible. She turned back to look toward Fear, fingers fumbling, attempting to turn the view of the phone around to show Ben. Hazel eyes met blue, and Fear hissed. The scream ripped through the air like an explosion. Serah dropped her bag, turned, and ran.

Fear followed her. The Demon's hiss grew louder, tagging along with the screams down the empty street.

Ben's voice caught up with her at the corner. "Serah! Dammit, Serah, slow *down! Stop! Talk to me! Serah!*" Ben could see the phone motion start to slow as his words broke through, and she slowed to a jog, then a walk.

"*Damn,* I hate running," Serah huffed, brought the phone back to her face, and saw Ben smile.

"Got you back. Good job. Get home." Ben sounded like a drill sergeant. Serah nodded and followed the instructions, half jogging, half walking the five blocks home.

"Ben." Serah gently pounded on her painted black front door. "Ben, it's Serah!" She pounded louder.

Serah took a step back when he flung the door open. "Are you hurt? Tell me what happened!" He leaned out the door, took a long look to the right and a long look to the left and pulled her inside. Serah stared, wide-eyed, at her best friend wearing only shorts and covered in colorful tattoos. *I knew he had a couple tattoos, but…*

Leaning both palms on the door, Ben closed his eyes and said, "My word is my will, you shall not pass. My word is my will, you are not welcome here.

My word is my will. It is done." Ben took a silent moment, pushed off the door, and turned.

"What happened?" He looked like a suspicious parent.

"I hate running. You *know* that." Serah reached out and grabbed Ben's arm as she doubled over out of breath, a grimace on her face. "It was Fear. Fear with a capitol F. Worst. Ever. Demon," she said, punctuated by deep breaths. "I did what you said, what we said to do! I tried to watch it, but the fear crept in, and I couldn't stop it. Worst. Ever. Demon. Dang, I left the bag of snacks! Hey, where did you figure out that door thing you did just now?"

Ben's arms remained crossed where he leaned against the door, unmoving.

"Uh, Ben? Say something, Demon Master, umm, wrangler? Sensei...?" Their laughter filled the room with power no demon dared to cross.

"Tell me what happened."

"It was HUGE," Serah started. "Well, no, it wasn't," Serah interrupted herself, trailing off.

"Serah, what did *you see*?"

"Welllll...like I could tell it was smokey. The air seemed different. I saw the eyes though!"

"Okay, okay. That's not really *seeing* them. Maybe like a middle-level intuition or something. I don't know."

"*Middle* level? Sheesh. Could *you* see it?"

"You started screaming, so I was distracted."

"What? I wasn't screaming."

"Yes, you were!"

Ben gently herded Serah into the warm kitchen. "Water?" he asked.

"Yes, please. You're not kidding about those salty bastards." She grimaced and licked her dry lips, adding a dramatic cough for emphasis. "Where did you learn that door-palm-mantra thing?" she repeated, now that he had time to answer.

Without turning around, "I've been researching. I'm terrified, Seraphine. I don't understand what is happening here. The only other person I know who understood this—or I think he might have—is dead. I'm ready to fight, but I hate the thought of you fighting without me. Alone." He stayed where he was busy in the kitchen, starting a pot of coffee for a potential long night ahead. Pouring her water, his shoulders slumped a little.

He looks tired, Seraphine thought. "Don't give up on me now, my friend," she said with a small smile.

Ben turned and met her eyes. "Never." He handed her the water, and she gulped it down. Setting the glass down on the table with a sharp ring, Serah said, "What's next?"

"Protection. First, you need to create a mantra for yourself. Or a few of them to use to protect your mind and your heart. We have to experiment with what works best."

"Like what you used on the door."

"Exactly. Mantras are most powerful when they are custom for the user, this I learned from my research. A few have been handed down through the ages, so they have the power of millennia of generations behind them." Seeing Serah's questioning look, Ben continued, "Like Amen, I will it so, Om. You know, one word repeated over and over again. The most important part is that they resonate with the user. You have to *feel* it. Feel it deeply. Otherwise, it's just a bunch of words." Serah nodded along as Ben continued, "The friend I told you about? He's translated two pages, so far. The Demon page," Ben took a breath, "and the weapons page. I really wish these monks had a few more weapons for us to try." He set the page down in front of Serah and took a deep breath.

"This conversation sounds absurd." Serah laughed a little, and Ben shook his head, agreeing but not happy about it.

"I want to arm you with knowledge and power, Serah."

"Sounds good to me, Ben. These guys scare me."

"That rose branch you felt called to grab after trimming? That was the start of your intuition. This power, I guess, it was a good call to listen to it as we see from the second image here. My friend said the words 'power' and 'protection' were repeated several times." He pulled out the page to point. "Here, this shrub is rosemary,"

Serah smacked her forehead. "Yes, that looked familiar!"

"And this is a compass with the description written 'Calling the Quarters.'" At Serah's confused look Ben explained, "I looked it up. It's a Native American practice to call in the help of all the spirts, ancestors, etc. They use it for many reasons—sometimes with wild horses that need to be tamed, which seem similar to demons to me."

"Sooo, I just wave my rose wand at it or what?"

Ben shrugged. "I'm not sure. I am guessing they become solid, or more solid, when they start to feed, if you will."

"Is that what we're calling it?" Serah shuddered.

"For now, yes. It's the only thing that makes sense. Why else do they care about humans? I mean look at this list of demons." He showed Serah the paper; someone had jotted down the list in English next to each one. The coffee pot beeped that it was ready. Ben hopped up, grabbing two mugs and pouring hot fresh coffee with a little cream into each. Serah had time to take in the list: *list of names? types?* She wasn't sure and didn't like it. Ben gently placed the steaming mug in front of her and watched as her eyes stayed focused on the page.

Horror

Rage

Apathy

Fear

Loneliness

Despair

Envy

Failure

"They are all emotions, intense emotions. Emotions that can lead to…well, you felt it firsthand." Listening, Serah swallowed her hot coffee extra hard. Ben looked down as his phone dinged with a new text.

"Sweet! He got another page. The page with just two symbols? He confirmed the writing for us. They are Salt and Fire. What we thought they were. Being the only two symbols on the page, they seem rather important."

"Okay, Ben, help me put this all together. What's the *plan?*" Serah gripped her mug, hoping it could give her the strength she had a feeling she would need. Looking around at her kitchen, she saw one of the favorite items in her décor—a simple print she bought recently at their favorite local coffee shop. "You can do this. Love, Coffee" was typed out in typewriter text on a white background surrounded by a simple wood frame.

"I can do this," she whispered, looking back down at her cup for encouragement.

"We need bait and a plan, so you are ready and expecting the encounter."

"Ready?" Serah snorted. "I'm not sure I'll ever be ready."

"You will be, I promise." Ben grabbed her hand. "Remember the rat poison; the rat droppings? That's what we are going to try first."

Serah nodded. "Tell me what to do." Ben leaned in and laid out his simple plan.

Chapter 9

Seraphine stepped out of her house and sniffed the air like Diego. It smelled of Demon. She could smell it, and the odor seeped into her pores. Every time they got close it was almost overwhelming. It smelled of salt.

Salt, a main component of all three: blood, sweat, and tears. *The stuff of character,* she thought. *The recipe of all emotions.* She heard Ben's voice in her head from a few nights ago. They had stayed up late discussing this plan: demon lore, Serah's options, and ideas on how to fight them best. With a final, "Information is power!" from Ben as he headed home, they both felt they had planned the best they could.

Tired of being caught unaware and afraid, *Ben was right,* Serah thought remembering what he said. *You need to get the upper hand, Serah. Let's set a trap, so the next encounter can be on your terms, and we learn more about them. Because it won't be long before you run into one again. These demons are all around us, it seems.*

The salty air, *it almost smelled good.* She knew then, when that thought passed through her mind, that she was created for this. She felt strong tonight.

She laid the trap a few hours ago, using poison. When discussing trying a demon trap, Serah had first questioned the need for rat poison, but Ben had a theory that the Demons loved it. Well, one did. The one who lived under her house. Serah and Ben put the pieces together while talking that night after the park incident.

Both thinking of the pet mayhem and the droppings found on Serah's bed that night a few months ago, they believed the demons left behind a sign of their presence; what looked like rat droppings. Unknowing at the time, Serah had called the exterminator to her house to deal with it. After seeing the droppings near the gridded access areas of the raised foundation, Bugs-Be-Gone left small bags of the poison to entice the critters to chew open, nibble on, and scamper away to die. Later, Serah noticed the poison was clearly eaten, yet the droppings continued. It was Ben who theorized maybe she didn't have a rat problem, but a Demon problem.

Serah remembered talking about Ben's plan: "Use the poison first; let's see how that works. The salt symbol from the book is confusing. Is it good for them or bad for them? Not sure, but maybe they manifest into a more solid form when they start to feed or create the emotions you feel. I would have your rose thorny thing nearby. We need to come up with a better name for this—or something sturdy, like natural materials. Keep Diego close. Obviously, dogs and cats are powerful and helpful. Have your mantra ready. Then you have to just see what happens. Be ready for anything, Seraphine."

It was a dusky evening when she turned the corner with Diego, taking out the trash, smelled the salt, and, sure enough, there on the side of her house it lurked. She stopped. Diego stopped and sat quickly at her side. He sniffed the air too. The demon was completely absorbed. Circling and purring, as it rubbed against the poisoned packet. No way to open it without the use of much emotion; it rarely manifested solidly until necessary to feed, to play. Serah was surprised to see it reach out a limb that slowly turned into a claw. Curved. Sharp. Useful. It reached out and lovingly traced a line down the center of the packet, its edge as sharp as a ten-blade scalpel. The package opened to disclose its contents, as if filleted. The purring and rubbing continued, as it sniffed and appeared to consume a pellet of the poison.

They have talons? Serah couldn't stand it.

"Stay," she whispered sternly. Placing her open hand in front of Diego's face to emphasize the command. He whined but lightly touched his nose to her palm. *Okay.*

She looked around and grabbed the shovel leaning up against the fence. Not sure it would help, but it made her feel better, cursing a little at her forgetfulness to leave the rose thorn weapon inside and not within easy reach. With her scarred palm out like a shield, she walked toward it. One step. Two steps.

"I am strong, I am strong, I am strong." Three times. *Always say it thrice, Serah.* Ben told her, *three times the charm is more powerful than you think.*

Two more steps and she would be almost on top of it.

And then what? At the lack of an answer, she felt the sweat start to trickle down her back; her palm lost its sure grip on the handle of the shovel. Shit. She knew Ben had never been in an actual demon fight; he could only tell her what he read—whispers of legends and a few cryptic conversations with his believed-to-be-demon-fighter friend.

"I am lucky, I am strong. This will pass. I will it so." The last line seemed to come out of nowhere, a version of Ben's mantra. It felt good.

It didn't see her. This was so different from the other times, where she was caught surprised. Last step. Serah turned back to check on Diego. He sat, vigilant, almost no breath escaped. His sad eyes watched her with so much faith. The sight of him made her pause. Demon blue eyes turned toward Serah. It coiled around her leg; the odor of her anxiety like a lovely perfume. She felt the pressure too late, and it yanked her off her feet. Diego barked loud; she heard him get to his feet to run.

"Diego, no!" She put her hand out to signal him and swept her hand over to face It. It recoiled at the sign. On her back, holding one arm out, she reached for the shovel, pushed to her feet—one leg pulsing, pain already. It didn't run but stared at her. It was Fear. Again. Fear taunted.

"*Keep moving forward.*" Ben's voice in her head. She swung the shovel. Hard. It made contact. Thwack! The vibrations burned up her arms. Surprised, *Ben was right; they become more solid as they feed.* Serah swung again and missed, as Fear danced out of range. Fear snaked its way up from her leg. She could feel its tingling path. She started her mantra, a respite from Fear's power.

"I am lucky. I am brave. This, too, will pass. I will it so." Serah used the mantra she and Ben created the other night; similar to one she tried to use on those long, quiet, lonely nights punctuated by panic attacks after Jeremy died. Thinking of that time in her life, Fear gripped her belly, and she was brought to her knees.

A prayer on her lips, "Please, please, please don't. Please."

Fear laughed. She was drowning. She couldn't breathe. Panic rose, as Fear edged up to her chest, her lungs, her heart. She was lost.

Diego waited no more. He sprinted up the path, growling and snapping and lunging for the creature he didn't understand.

"Courage," she heard herself say, gaining energy with Diego's help.

"This second, I will have courage. And the next. And then the next."

Turning the full weight of her words and thoughts toward Fear, "You are nothing. I am something. I am not afraid. I am not afraid. You are nothing. I am something. I am not afraid. You will pass, and I will *still.be.here*. I will it so." The panic ebbed. She was able to think clearly again, bringing the full weight of her scars' power and her mantras as Diego nipped at amorphous Fear. Serah started to feel filled with courage, drop by drop, second by second, until it filled her like liquid gold, and she stood tall. Diego howled and growled, as Serah held her garden shovel up over her head like a Viking ready for the final blow; her swing thwacked down on empty ground. Fear, not used to its victims having power to fight, decided to feed elsewhere and fled.

Serah laughed, falling back to the cool sweet-smelling dirt. Sweaty and tired, she laughed and laughed. Diego licked her face, and it was good.

Chapter 10

Year Two of the Demons

After setting the trap and Serah's semi-triumph, the demons kept coming. Sometimes there would be a week or two in between encounters, but they never stopped. They kept showing up with a frequency and pattern neither one of them could recognize. Ben tried to research and plan training sessions in between classes at school. Serah trained with him and at the local flight school, quickly using the lessons her mother purchased for her birthday and then buying more. Taking more shifts at the library to pay for more hours to fly, she found she loved it; she felt safe and relaxed in the air. Her flight instructor told her she was a natural. Everything he threw at her, she handled well. Never having been a natural at anything in her life, Serah was deeply pleased and proud.

"Try 'Calling the Quarters' next time we train, Serah. Now that I've had time to research, it sounds more powerful. Horse whisperers use this energy work to calm the horses and gain control over them. American Indians used it in ceremonies and before starting the hunt. I think it might help," Ben mentioned on one of their most recent planning sessions.

Serah walked into this session exhausted from a flight lesson a few hours before. The afternoon sunshine filtered in to warm the small enclosed patio that sat in the center of Ben's house. He sat on a small mat, so still she could barely see him breathing. He had gone deep. He called it the warrior's rest: to sleep without sleeping, while gaining energy equivalent to a full night's sleep. He tried to teach it to her as the demon encounters made her so weary, but like a lot of his teachings, it remained elusive.

Serah kneeled and placed her training journal next to her, filled with what they had learned: notes taken, ideas, insights. She kept the page open on 'Calling the Quarters.' This was her second try.

Standing, she faced east—the rising sun, the start of the day. She turned north, then south, and finished west; the sun sets, the day is done. Sitting down, she crossed her legs and chose the protection meditation to work on today. She was tired of the burning ache—like a dozen buzzing, stinging bees—the demon fights left behind.

Concentrate. Concentrate. Eyes closed, Serah tried to picture it. Her suit of armor. It was there like a shield around her. She had to be centered to make it powerful enough. Her nose started to itch, she reached up quickly to scratch it; her eyes popped half open, checking if Ben saw her move. No, she was safe. Serah settled back in, rocking a little back and forth on her tired sitz bones, trying to find comfort that wasn't there. *The only comfort is in your mind, Seraphine.* She heard Ben's voice again loud and clear. With an almost silent clearing of her throat, she started counting her breath. She needed help today to go deep. *Ten I am breathing in, ten I am breathing out, nine I am breathing in, nine I am breathing out.* Serah's breath got progressively longer and quieter, until it was almost impossible to detect.

She knew she made it to her inward safe space when she could see the girl on the lake.

There was a girl. There is always a girl. The girl on the lake. She sits holding a rose bush and a shield, looking downward deep into the depths of the water, sitting in a small boat on a vast, expansive lake. It is her, posture perfect, sitting up straight and tall in the boat, on the vast still lake like glass. The scene was so peaceful; Serah knew she could stay here, forever safe. Forever safe and strong.

A ripple appeared on the mirror that was the top of the lake. Serah watched with growing distress as Fear emerged, bit by bit, and slinked its way up into the corner of the canoe, reaching its icky tendrils up, slowly up and over the side as it slithered and pooled in the bottom of the boat. *The girl didn't see. THE*

GIRL DIDN'T SEE. Serah screamed at her to open her eyes. *OPEN YOUR EYES! FEAR IS COMING FOR YOU!* In the boat, the girl's eyes popped open, and they were blue—a bright, beautiful blue.

Diego barked at a squirrel as it tottered on the tip top of the wood fence lining Ben's yard. Serah gasped as she jumped, and her eyes popped open.

Ben stirred and sighed. "Seraphina."

"I know, I know. I'm trying my best, Ben."

"Trying your best isn't good enough. You have to play to win. Do you think the demons care about you 'trying'?"

"Do it again. Picture her. Become her: the warrior. See victory; you are the protector and defender of all of us who need you." Ben knew she wouldn't survive without being able to retreat to a safe zone inside her mind. Inside her heart. Finding that place demons couldn't go. Serah settled herself, back straight, cross-legged, relaxed. Diego was there, stretched out against a wall, sleepily watching, he was always nearby her now. Looking at him, she couldn't help the smile that spread across her face. His ear perked toward her as if her smile made a noise he could hear. Serah shut her eyes and held onto that feeling of peace; it warmed her like nothing else.

She could see.

There was a girl. There is always a girl. She sits holding a rose bush and a shield, looking downward deep into the depths of the water, sitting in a small boat on a vast, expansive lake. It is her. She is a warrior and a healer. She faces east— the rising sun, the start of the day. She turns north, then south, and finally turns to the west; the sun sets, the day is done. The light flows and buzzes around her like a suit of moving armor, as if thousands upon thousands of buzzing bees were ready to defend and protect. She holds the line, and she is strong, as final defenses have to be. There is nothing left after she is breached. She is sad but accepting of the burden.

Ben watched. He saw Serah's face relax and knew she found it. Now to teach her how to stay there, despite the outward cost.

Ten minutes, then twenty, then forty minutes deep. Each time she was pulled out, Ben pushed her to go back in. Faster, quicker, go deep, and stay there. "Learn the path, Seraphine. Learn your formula, like a free diver learning to stay under the surface for longer and longer in search of those precious, priceless pearls, training the body and training the mind, stillness and breath to connect to the power."

At sixty-six minutes, Ben winked his pride for Serah's success at Diego, who thumped his tail in agreement. Three hours passed when Serah slowly, cautiously stirred, as if coming out of a deep ocean abyss; the diver adjusting to new surroundings above water again. She let herself fall over on the mat, her head resting on the cool concrete. Eyes closed, she wanted to move; her body ached from sitting so still for so long. And she also didn't want to move—the depth of focus was an incredibly fatiguing workout for her mind.

This sucks, she thought, feeling a wave of self-pity travel through her. It always happened like this when she was exhausted. She could hear the train jangling across the tracks in the distance—two short whistle blasts sounded, and she knew it was passing the crossing a mile up the road.

Diego padded over. She could hear his nails click against the concrete, and, a second later, a cold nose and warm tongue was smushed into her face. Self-pity did not last long against that onslaught.

"Diego! Okay, okay, okay!" Serah sputtered and sat up laughing. She grabbed his head and pulled it into her chest. Her chin the perfect fit right between his muzzle and the curve of his forehead. Ben walked out with a steaming cup of tea, and she reached for it with greed.

She grimaced as she took a sip that was too hot to swallow. Serah set the drink down next to her on the concrete, fixed her ponytail, and eyed Ben. He was distracted again; it was unlike him. *Mr. Laser Focus,* she always said, *point that laser somewhere else for a minute, will ya? Sheesh.* Serah carefully sipped the tea and listened to a second train pass. She cocked her head slightly, almost like Diego.

"Another train?" She looked up at Ben.

"Yeah, there's something big going on in Mexico, so they are sending supplies down. Mass rioting, complete shutdown of social services. At least that's what I heard on the news. I wonder if the demons are gaining strength? Tipping the balance? Causing chaos? Not sure. Just not sure," Ben said slowly as he rubbed the cat tattoo on his forearm, back and forth. Serah watched. He shook his head at something she did not see and turned to look at her. He looked down at her sitting on the ground, sipping her tea as Diego lay beside.

Serah raised one eyebrow at his expression. It was her signature look, used often with many meanings. Ben couldn't help but smile. He squatted down to gently scratch Diego's belly.

"How'd it feel today? Stronger? More flexible?" Ben asked.

"Yeaaaah. Sorta. It took a while to get into it. I wish I could just step into it immediately. Go deep *fast*. I usually can when the demons are there. I know it's adrenaline helping, but I just wish I had more faith and knowledge that I could make it happen on my own."

Ben nodded. "Yes. We need to step it up a notch. I think you're ready."

"You *think* I'm ready?"

"Whether I think so or not is of little consequence. What matters most in life, as always, Seraphina, is whether *you* do." Ben stared as if willing, just this once, that all his knowledge, his strength, and his will could be shared with her.

"Okaaay. What do you need me to do?" Serah eyed him over the rim of her cup.

"Physical training."

"Like run?" *Oh, Lord, not running, please.*

"Yes. Running and gym training. Maybe I have been focusing too much on the meditations, the mantras. Mind and body must work together. Pain and fatigue force the mind to go deep, to focus, to turn pain into joy. You are a warrior, Seraphine. We must start acting like it." Ben stood at the end of his speech. He leaned down to give Diego one last pat on his head and turned to walk back into the house.

"Ahh...*pain*? Ben? Did you say pain?" Serah called to his back as he stepped inside.

"We start tomorrow," came the reply. Serah fell back on the concrete with a dramatic groan. Diego wagged his tail.

Serah dreamt.

She was walking down a cobble stone path that lead into a beautiful garden.

"Am I in heaven?" she asked, turning in circles to take in the beauty. She took a deep breath in of the soft smell of roses and trees and fresh air like she had never found before.

"No, this is not heaven. This is you, Seraphine." Serah turned toward the voice that came from behind her. A man sat under a beautiful Japanese Maple tree, fall colors mixed with spring blooms, butterflies and bees buzzing, mixing with hummingbirds. He sat with a raven on his shoulder and two more investigating here and there under the tree. The man smiled and patted a smooth stone next to him, inviting her to sit. Seraphine smiled back and felt herself float forward. The rock was comfortable, more than she could have imagined. She felt connected to the earth.

"Seraphine, my dear, you are a witch and warrior—a demon destroyer. You are Seraphim, descended from the angels of the highest order. You have the sight. You have the gift. You have power. The world relies on you to use it. It might destroy you, but the Seekers hope not."

"The Seekers?"

"The Seekers of the Truth."

"Why me?"

"Because it is so."

"That doesn't help."

"Yes, it does," the man said with a smile. Serah glanced up; his smile made her smile. It made her feel as if she could do anything, *be* anything. He handed her a piece of paper; it looked old. It shimmered from English to Viking to English, back and forth and back and forth.

The answers are in the quiet,
Listen hard, listen well.
The answers are in the quiet,
And the quiet waits to tell.

~ FROM THE BOOK SEEKERS OF THE TRUTH

"Are you a Seeker?" Serah looked up at him.

"I am not. I am something else entirely." The man chuckled and shook his head.

"Who…"

"Focus, Seraphine. This is not about me; this is about you. Focus," he said, the last more gently.

Focus. Serah woke, the word reverberating in her mind and whispered from her lips. She could hear the rain tapping on the windows and could feel it refreshing the Earth. Snuggling in under the covers for an extra minute she thought again: *Focus.* A smile crossed her face. She felt ready.

"She's not ready." Ben voiced out loud his concern to his silent and dark kitchen. He had searched online as much as he could. He desperately wanted to provide Serah with some real help—not just research and ideas but people who had the same Power and were going through the same metamorphosis, he supposed. That started him thinking about what it would mean for a Seekers group to be active today. *What would I do today, in modern times, to 'go underground'?* Ben knew exactly where he had to look next.

His phone beeped a text message. He glanced over, face illuminated by his computer screen, the only light in the room. It was Ben's law school friend Levi: *You up studying for Con law? Isn't he the worst??*

Ben laughed and nodded his head in agreement, texting back: *Yeah, we will be lucky to make it out alive. I'll be up all night.*

Me too. Need some company?

Ben looked back to his computer: *Not tonight. I'm just gonna gut it out as long as I can. Tomorrow, for sure. Cuppa Joe?*

Sounds good. Good luck to us both.

With a texted thumbs up, Ben clicked off his phone and turned to look at what was facing him on the screen. Ready to download and install? Click yes. The prompt blinked in the middle of his screen.

"Innocent looking enough..." he whispered under his breath and moved his cursor to click yes. "No turning back now." Ben watched his screen as a new browser software TOR was percolating through the bits and bytes to enable his computer to surf the dark web. He glanced at his note card of instructions.

Install TOR. Then go here: http://fygrbku36ok7.onion

DON'T GO ANYWHERE ELSE.

Be careful.

"Yeaaaah, be careful. Thanks." Ben took a sip of his beer, clicked to open TOR and type in the URL.

"I'll be damned." He took in the screen, his finger hovering over the "x" to close out the browser and shut down if he saw any indication of... "Of what? It's not like the bad dudes say hello first." Ben shook his head realizing he was talking to himself.

"I bet Siri is disappointed in me for going to the dark side. Is there a Siri on the dark web? Nope. Nope, I don't want to know. Stop talking to yourself for the love, Vondell," referring to himself in the third person, using his last name with emphasis like his college cross country coach used to yell across the track. "Stop pussyfooting it, Vondell! I know you have more in the tank! VONDELL, these are wind sprints for a reason!" How he managed to be heard like a mile away, Ben could never figure out. Shaking his head out of the memory of those long exhausting days, he focused back to his priority tonight: finding more answers for Seraphine. He felt like it was his job. *No, my calling*, he thought. It felt powerful and important and he wouldn't let her down. Not like Ethan.

Ben muttered, "Not like Ethan," shook his head, and started his search. He was searching for others; others like Serah. His translator buddy and all-around shady guy was the one who agreed with Ben's idea—to look on the dark web.

It was the oddest conversation of my entire life, Ben thought. *If I'm not counting the recent conversations about demons.* Both of them dancing around the real truth; neither fully trusting the true intent of the other. He remembered what his friend said, "If people want to remain anonymous, gotta go to the dark web, man. That's the only place you will find them. There's a Dark Web Facebook; it's a whole underground world. Nothing is tracked, its guaranteeeeed." Ben winced as his friend stretched out the word like a used car salesman.

Ben shook his head, "Facebook, always freaking Facebook." He typed in the website as instructed—all dark web URLs end in .onion he learned—and was surprised when it popped up. *This is too easy.* Ben's uneasiness grew. Quickly creating a new profile with a new name and photo of a local hiking spot he liked, he was in.

"Okay, let's see what we can find," he said as he typed in Seekers and crossed fingers of both hands and held them up, waiting for the search engine results. "Come on, dark web." He scanned through the list of possible groups. "No, no, no." He slowly continued. "Not the band. Why would you be on the dark web?" Ben chuckled and shook his head, continuing to scroll.

"Stop yer grinnin' and drop yer linen. Found 'em," Ben smiled, pleased he could find a reason to use one of his favorite movie lines. There they were. Seekers of the Truth. The photo was the same rune that Serah received as her first brand.

"I'll be damned," Ben said as he took a big gulp of his beer. The group was private. His cursor hovered over the "join group" button. *This is too easy,* he thought again. In one quick move, he clicked "join" with a beer in one hand and the other held up above his keyboard as if ready for anything. He waited. Ten seconds that felt like one hundred later, his screen went completely black then up popped a gif of huge blue eyes blinking slow. Below them a question typed out letter by letter: *What do you wish to receive by joining??*

Quickly, Ben set his beer down and typed, *Guidance for one who sees.* The eyes blinked, twenty seconds, sixty seconds, ninety seconds. Blink. Blink.

"Come on, come on!" Ben yelled at the screen. The giant eyes on the screen shut and didn't open again. Ben tried typing *Please, we need help.* But the cursor, the screen, would not respond. Ben put his head on his arms. "Please. We need help." His phone pinged and from a number he didn't recognize: *You must wait. We need proof.* Ben grabbed his phone and texted as fast as he could, cursing at the autocorrect as he typed: *Tell me what you need. Anything. She sees the demon. I already lost one friend. I don't want to lose another. Please help.*

Ben could see the dots of someone typing back. He realized he was holding his breath and took a big inhale, staring at the phone, holding it six inches from his face in a knuckle-white grip. The dots disappeared and no text came. Ben waited. He finished his beer and checked his phone; nothing. He started a load of laundry and checked his phone; again, nothing. He went through a workout circuit—ten pushups and sixty seconds of burpees, twenty-five squats three times each, and checked his phone; nothing. With a sigh, he grabbed his con-law book and tossed it on the table, opened his notes file on the section he needed to study, and checked his phone—nothing.

It's going to be a long night. Ben nodded in response to that thought, bent his head, and started to read.

Chapter 11

Serah liked to run at night, a simple four-mile loop around her quiet little neighborhood. Proud of herself, knowing how far she had come since she started, barely able to run a mile and now after only six months, she was holding steady at three miles on her run days, occasionally pushing past to four. Sometimes the demon effects required it.

Clearing her mind and focusing on her breath, Serah tried to release all thoughts of any demons, working hard not to call them to her, especially Horror. That one was the worst. Days after a Horror encounter, she would still be left with a cold aching numbness, a deep internal quake, a paranoia at every corner. Luckily, Horror was one of the rarer demons. Not like your run-of-the-mill Fear and Apathy; those she encountered often. She had learned to avoid places Horror liked to hang out: hospitals, the courthouse, jail. Basically, there was a one-square-mile section of downtown Serah avoided at all costs. Shaking her head, she went back to her mind trick of coming up with a compliment for every letter of the alphabet: A amazing, B badass. It helped keep her focused as she ran. Listening to music or a podcast was dangerous—she needed all her faculties to spot and avoid any potential trouble.

Serah felt good tonight. Her feet picked up pace as she rounded the corner, and her watch beeped Mile Two; Serah grinned. *Confident, Delightful, Elegant.* Serah snorted a laugh at the last two. *Ben would have something to say about that.*

Feeling as if there was a rope tied around her waist that a giant yanked hard, she came to a screeching halt and staggered backward. Taking big gulps of air,

Serah stared ahead of her in the gloom. *Oh my God, two of them?* Serah could feel the edges start to trickle in. It was Horror. *No, no, no. Why did I even think about them!* She squinted. Something wasn't right, not that anything was right with a demon. *Why are they acting so funny?*

The Horrors were weaving and swaying with no apparent sense of direction or balance. *Are they drunk? Can demons get drunk?* They hadn't noticed her yet, nor did she think they would, given how they were acting. One part of her wanted to stay and watch and see what might happen, at a minimum safe distance, of course. The more she could learn the better. The other part of her wanted to run screaming into the night. Like waves crashing on the sand, emotions rolled toward Serah with an energy she couldn't stop. She was frozen. Horror whirled and swirled about one hundred feet in front of her, dancing under the moonlight.

Surf the waves, Seraphine. It's been proven a feeling only lasts for about ninety seconds. If you can surf the waves, you can conserve your energy to act during the troughs, then surf again. Stay on top of it. Stay sharp. Especially Horror, remember that one has the ability to make people freeze. Don't let it.

Counting to ten, whispering each number with each breath she took in, her mind was blank. She only knew on ten she was going to move. Horror felt softer than usual somehow, maybe because they weren't alerted to her, not yet. "Niiiine…Ten." Serah immediately started backing up, moving arms and legs in unison; she backed up and started a wide circle around the pair giving them a wide berth, never taking her eyes off the threat. *Ninety seconds. Ninety seconds. Surf the wave.*

Turning to watch them to her right, Serah moved quickly but not fast. *Slow is smooth, smooth is fast,* she repeated a new favorite mantra in her head, taken from a mountain climber she heard on a recent interview. Once she had reached far enough on the other side of the two blue and white devils, she turned and started backing up again, walking backwards all the way down the block.

She saw it then—the smoke, the smoldering ruins of a house on the corner. Images flashed: *Horror relaxing in the once pretty flower box next to the flaming window that was quickly melting in the heat. Sirens and screams. Horror hopping back and forth between two of the crowd on the ground, the two family members* who were living the worst night of their lives. *Arms appearing out of the high window, holding a screaming toddler. The group yelling louder, "No, wait!" "Wait for the fire department!" "Yes, toss her to me!" "Do it now!"*

Serah could feel the shakes start. She hadn't known these neighbors living almost two miles away from her, but she knew them now. Horror had left their imprint on her soul. Frozen again, her feet felt stuck to the ground as she watched seductive tendrils of smoke wafting up from what was the leftovers of six lives. The corner of one eye twitched. Horrors were approaching, coming back to the scene of their feast, still slow and unsteady. *That's why they look drunk; they fed so much, it's like a drug to them. They are completely high.* Just then she caught it. Her vision narrowed and focused like a true hunter, poking around what looked like the remains of a crib: Despair. It was too much. Serah clutched her chest, turned, and ran.

Sprinting down her street, Serah ran as if Horror was chasing her, craning her neck to look back every hundred yards or so to make sure she wasn't being followed. She for SURE didn't want Horror to camp out underneath her house like Apathy did. The thought made her stomach turn so much she wanted to vomit. Her breath heaved due to her pace and also the thought. Counting down the houses as she ran past, *ten more to go, just half a block,* she rounded the corner to home. Running up her porch steps, Serah turned the door knob and pushed with a grunt as the force of the closed door stopped her forward progress; she forgot the door was locked. With shaking hands, she knelt down to grab the key she tied to her shoelaces, looking up and squinting hard to see down the dark street—nothing. They weren't moving fast in their drunken state. She guessed—hoped—they hadn't even realized she had been there. Nevertheless, best be quick to enter and secure her sanctuary. *Finally!* She got the key untied and slammed through the door. Leaning up against it, breathing hard, Serah unglued her fingers from the handle and opened her eyes to Diego and Rubi both sitting pretty and still as a picture in front of her.

Checking her watch, she managed to smile. "Personal best. How about that?!" Walking over to ruffle Diego's fur, Serah sat with a thump and a sigh, cross-legged on the floor in between them and pulled Rubi onto her lap. Diego plopped down next to her with an audible huff of happiness.

Her phone beeped; it was Ben: *How'd the run go?*

Serah shook her head smiling for real now. "How does he know everything, huh?" she asked Diego who thumped his tail in response.

Good, I guess. Ran into Horror. Two of them! Drunk maybe? It was weird.

Ben: *Where?*

House fire in my 'hood. Recent, I guess. Didn't know, was at work.

Ben: *Did you do the thing on the door? Don't mess with Horror.*

Yeah, I did. Serah lied and winked at Diego.

Ben: *Don't lie to me, Seraphina. Do it. Don't mess around with Horror.*

Serah groaned and ungracefully got to her feet, disturbing a comfortable Rubi who squeaked in protest, staggered a bit toward the door, feeling the blood flow back into her tired legs.

Placing both hands solidly against the door, Serah spoke the words, "My word is my will, you shall not pass. My word is my will, you are not welcome here. My word is my will. It is done." Diego barked, Rubi yawned, Serah flopped back down to the floor with her companions. Holding the phone close to her face she texted: *Done.*

Ben: *Good. Now get some rest. We will talk more about this drunk demon idea. It could be what happens if they overfeed. Not sure.*

Serah nodded to the phone. "Yep, great minds," she said out loud as she texted: *Okay, sounds good, thx Ben.*

With a final zombie emoji from Ben, which Serah knew meant he was going to be up late studying, the conversation was over, for now.

Serah turned to her furry family. "Who's up for popcorn and *Alias*?" Laughing as Diego jumped up and ran to the kitchen doorway—popcorn nights were his favorite. Serah pushed to her feet and followed.

It's going to be a good night, pushing all thoughts of demons, and especially Horror out of her mind.

Chapter 12

Serah sat in her truck in the gym parking lot—the Avoidance Ritual she liked to call it, a ritual that must be done, every time, it seemed. Six months had passed since that day at Ben's when he mentioned adding to her training protocol, and she had been keeping to a tight gym schedule ever since. Three days a week at the gym and running three nights in the evenings. Sundays, rest. Always wishing for more rest.

"Rest when you can, Serah. A warrior knows to take the rest when they can. The fights will still come, the time to rest may not." Ben told her that just the other day as they sat in their crowded coffee shop. She hadn't seen him in a while; law school was demanding more and more of his time and attention.

"Rest. Yeah, right. You know those pesky demons always getting in the way." She laughed. *This whole thing is nuts.*

She could see the lights of the main exercise room in her rearview mirror. It wasn't too crowded tonight, thank God. When it was crowded, she sat in her truck longer, prolonging the agony of knowing she would have to share: share space, share a machine, actually maybe have to talk to someone. *Ugh.* Working out was her own personal demon; she loved to hate it so. She had protested quite a bit at first, but as her body adjusted, and with persistence quickly grew strong, she knew there was a part of her that enjoyed the lengthy workouts. It was the only time she really felt sane. And for a little while after, life seemed to be okay.

Serah knew it served another purpose. In dealing with the demons, all the excess emotion slowly built up and was starting to make her feel crazy. Ben came up with a theory, based on his memories of his friend Ethan's behavior, who he believed was a demon hunter too, and how Ethan had died. Emotions leave traces, chemicals, and byproducts that slowly accumulate. *It was like a slow poisoning, similar to mercury or arsenic, but of emotions instead*, Ben explained. *And there's always a limit*. It appeared some can handle more, some less. He liked to compare it to alcohol consumption. Though Serah could handle more than most, she hated the feeling of being out of control, detested it. The feeling as if any moment she might lose it in front of a stranger. The gym also served a third purpose: her strength training and jogging regimen helped her to stay ahead of the Rage Demons on the run; they were *fast*.

With a sigh of resignation, she twisted the key out of the ignition, grabbed her iPod and gym bag, and headed in. She headed to the stair machine first. The stairs were brutal, and it seemed few gym goers had the willpower to last.

A man was already there stepping fast, working hard. Avoiding the machine christened with a half-eaten lollipop, Serah popped up next to a fellow stair stepper and started. Music and sweat, forty-five minutes later, she was done. Cooldown time. Nothing like that feeling. She was drenched; her shirt looked as if it had been dipped in a tub of water. Even nonsqueamish Ben refused to hug her hello after a workout like this.

It felt like heaven.

The steps slowed, and she checked her stats.

"Eight more minutes. Would you do eight more minutes with me?" The man next to her said. Serah looked over. He had a slight accent she couldn't place, and the most genuine smile.

"Eight minutes, no problem. These stairs are brutal. It helps to have someone gutting it out next to you, doesn't it?" Serah commiserated. She felt tickled that he had asked; happy to help a stranger in this way versus the distant goal of "helping humanity with their demons." Serah held back a snorted laugh as this thought crossed her mind.

"I ate a lot today. Ohhh, boy, young lady, I ate a lot. Tryin' to get to 720 calories burned, and then I'll be done. Just eight minutes if you can."

"Wow, you must have been here a long time! I don't know how you do it. Sure, I got eight minutes. Let's do eight minutes. No problem." She reset the timer and started in again.

"You know most people, I watch them. Some have never tried this machine before, and they get up here and last only one minute. One minute, before getting down and doing something else! Maybe twenty minutes for some here and there. Very few go for as long as we do. But you don't need to be up here that long, young lady—look at you!"

"I appreciate that, but you know how that goes."

"I sure do. I ate too much today. Mmm hmmm." They both tucked their heads and went back to climbing to nowhere.

"One more minute." The man held up one finger as he looked over at her and grinned. Serah smiled and nodded. She looked back at her screen, almost to a personal best. Not too bad. She looked down. There it was: the caution sign labeled on the machine. CAUTION! If feeling faint or dizzy or shortness of breath, get off immediately. This time she *did* laugh at that thought, *Shortness of breath...isn't that the idea?* With that they were done and both wiped off their dripping faces with their towels.

"Well, young lady, thank you. I appreciate the help," he said while wiping down the stair stepper railings as Serah did the same.

"Of course, I'm glad to. Always helps to have that extra push. I'm off to abs, have a good workout." Serah started to turn away as he spoke.

"Search for The Eight, Seraphine. It's always eight. Remember that. You do good work. Do not forget. Do not stop. You have the mark of the witch and a true heart. That is enough." He nodded and smiled. Serah stood silent. Before she could think of what to say, he strode toward and disappeared into the area with the large weight machines.

Eight? she thought. *Eight demons? Eight what?* She walked quickly toward where she last saw him, hoping for more information, desperate for more. *Please, give me more.* Serah hustled as fast as she could, trying to not look as crazy as she felt. Dodging the group of young boys trying to impress, stopped by the elderly couple holding hands and walking through the gym as if they had all the time in the world, Serah dodged this way and that, but the man was gone.

With a sigh she turned toward the ab machines to finish off her workout. *Ben would know what to do*, she thought and laid her towel down. Taking a deep breath, she started her three hundred crunches and let her mind try to wander through all the meditations, the knowledge, the demons, her most recent flight lesson, through her life for the past two years. *It's not boring,* she thought and smiled a smile that turned into a grimace as she picked up the pace of her hard work.

"Eight? Eight levels of demons? Eight ways to fight them? Eight what?!" Ben threw questions at Serah.

Serah held up her hands at the onslaught. "I dunno, Ben. That's all he said, and he disappeared, of course. Couldn't really tackle him in the gym now, could I? Don't look at me like that! I'm not gonna tackle anyone!"

"Okay, okay, fine…Eight is a powerful number in a lot of Eastern philosophies. Relating to the infinite and prosperity, Buddhists have a teaching: The Eightfold Path, also known as The Middle Way. This is the way Buddhist followers achieve the end of suffering. Which we have been using parts of in your training," Ben spoke thoughtfully, trying to gain more insight from the cryptic conversation.

"Well, all I know is I'm hungry. Who's up for dinner?" Serah asked, her patience often short when there were no answers to be had.

Diego barked yes, and Serah glanced toward Ben, who was muttering as he paced the patio floor. She placed her hand next to her mouth, crouched down next to Diego's ear, and in a theatrical whisper said, "If we go by ourselves, we can get a beer. Mr. Uptight over there would probably make us drink bone broth or kombucha or something equally lame."

"I heard that. Yes, you two deserve a night off. Go. Go on." Ben paused and looked over at the two. He cared for them so much. "It's Halloween, so be careful out there. Who knows what that means for the demons. It's our first All Hallows Eve where we actually know something. Maybe that's what I will research tonight, the origins of Halloween…" Ben's sentence faded off into muttering again with a half-hearted wave; he shooed them away.

I can't believe it's Halloween already. The year is almost gone. Serah shook her head on the thought, grabbed Diego's leash, and headed out the door before Ben could change his mind.

Chapter 13

Halloween

Serah stopped short just outside of Ben's house. The quiet street was quiet no longer. Serah and Diego could see ghosts and goblins, fairy princesses and Jedi masters trickling in what promised to become a flood of excited kids. Looking up, Serah could see two half-sized demons hopping from branch to branch in a nearby tree. She paused and Diego paused with her—together, unsure of what to do next. The demons appeared to stop and huddle together like two frightened children. *Baby demons?* Serah took a quick breath and realized she really didn't want to find out any more. Diego looked up at her and whined softly.

With a cluck and a tap on her hip to keep Diego with her, Serah marched toward her car, settled Diego in the back seat, and jumped in. The sun was setting; leaving a glare on her windshield as she edged her way from the curb into the street. Kids were everywhere. Most stayed on the sidewalk in groups, but some bigger, older kids were using this night as a reason to walk into the street and harass the drivers as they passed. Serah slowed to a stop at a four-way stop sign, motioning the other car to go. She paused and squinted, not sure of what she saw. "What the heck? Diego, did you see that?"

One of the baby demons floated down to land in what appeared to be a comfortable perch on a trick-or-treater's shoulder—a young pirate—now with a disturbing parrot to complete his outfit. Diego whined and looked out the front windshield, echoing Serah's concern. A honk from behind reminded her to get moving, so she slowly put her foot on the gas, watching the pirate wandering into the street with a vague look on his face. Serah gasped as she saw his eyes turn blue; he was making his way directly for her car. She slowed to a stop, rolled down her window just as he marched by, and with a flick of her branded hand, pushed the baby demon off his shoulder, feeling a jolt of emotion in the process.

"Holy crap! Like electricity, D!" Serah yelped to Diego, who whined. "I could feel all the emotions at once. It was weird…," she trailed off, thinking.

"Hey, lady! Get out of the damn way! Trick or treat! Trick for you, if you don't leave! Hahaha!" Pirate's harsh voice startled Serah.

"Sorry, buddy, I'm moving along. Stay safe out there."

"Stay safe out there," he mimicked in a high-pitched tone and started to reach through the window. Diego growled. Serah hit the gas, making sure no other pedestrians were around and drove as quickly as she could out of the intersection and down the tree-lined street. Navigating through the kids, parents, and demons, Serah was relieved when she finally pulled in at home. Grabbing Diego's leash, her notebook, and phone, she tugged him through the driver-side door, house key ready. Dinner and night off forgotten, Serah shut the door behind them as quick as she could. Turning, she placed both hands and all her weight on either side of the peephole. Using instinct and intuition, she threw all of her power with the words toward the door and beyond.

"We are safe. This sacred threshold, you shall not pass. This sacred threshold, you cannot pass. This sacred space, you cannot go. I will it so," Serah said as she leaned her head against the wooden door. She could hear the noisy street beyond.

"I will it so," she whispered. Taking a deep breath, she turned to see both Diego and Rubi sitting and staring. Diego's leash coiled around one leg; Rubi the cat watching, witnessing. Quickly Serah unclipped Diego and ran around turning off all the lights and drawing the curtains. The large front window, the window that made Serah buy this house, lured her to it like a bug to a light, like a demon to poison. She saw the window and knew instantly it was hers.

She walked over to the large love seat, one of her favorite spots in the house, curled up in it backwards, so she could peek between the curtains and stare over the sofa back out the window to the street—the world beyond. Her companions followed. Rubi jumped up to stand guard on the deep windowsill near the arm of the chair. Diego sat right beside her, keeping watch. A baby demon fell—floated down from the top of a large oak that graced Serah's front yard. It landed on her patio in a demon puddle.

Serah could barely breath. Rubi hissed. Diego growled.

Another joined it. Together they made their way toward the painted door. Serah's knuckles turned white as she gripped the sofa back. Closing her eyes she repeated, "We are safe, we are safe, we are safe, we are safe, we are safe. Sacred space you cannot go, sacred space, sacred space. You cannot go!" Her voice started as a whisper and ended up a yell. Tendrils of smoky emotion curled and coiled around miniscule cracks under the door frame. Serah's eyes grew wider. The powerful vapor appeared to change color, hesitate, and coil again. Rubi hopped down from her perch with grace as if she had all the time in the world. As if turned on by a light switch like a ferocious lion, she hissed, yowled, and swiped at the haze with her claws. Curved and sharp and filled with bravery, the delicate whisps of emotion-smoke shredded under the onslaught, seemingly sucked back into the baby on the porch, and the two danced away back into the mayhem of the street to disappear. Rubi turned and lightly leapt six feet from her spot at the door onto the arm of the love seat, much to Serah's surprise, and began cleaning herself as if nothing had happened. Diego thumped his tail in approval of her courage and curled up at their feet. Serah sighed her relief, sunk back down into the cushions, and pulled Rubi onto her lap, who promptly snuggled in. They closed their eyes and decided to sleep.

Chapter 14

The kitchen smelled of turkey. It was Thanksgiving Day. Serah ached for time alone to think, to think about a future she saw but couldn't reach. She took a long sip of her wine and got up to help Ben and his two closest friends from law school, Lily and Levi, in the kitchen. The three together were the smart crew that everyone wanted in their study groups, could always get the professors to laugh and loosen up a little, and were calm and at ease during the terrifying Socratic method lectures in class. Serah knew they had future plans of the three musketeers law firm, as they jokingly referred to it, and she had no doubt they would fulfill that goal and promise. *Maybe they would take pity and hire me to be the receptionist*, Serah thought with a mental laugh and groan.

"What's next?" Serah asked smiling, feeling at home and at ease for the first time in a while. It was a gift. But it was also lonely. Holidays always were a stark reminder of her own estranged family.

Ben's friend, Lily, turned and smiled. "One more pie to make! Buuut I think I didn't get baking powder. Baking powder or is it baking soda? Agh!"

Another pie? Serah was grateful to be included. She remembered when her mom took to traveling most days of the year, and holidays were lonely affairs sitting in front of the TV trying not to feel sad.

Serah laughed. "I'll make a run to the store, no problem. Write me a quick list, and I'll scram." Grabbing the piece of paper with a few scribbled notes and Ben's keys, Serah left Diego lounging in the kitchen looking very happy to wait for any morsel. Just a quick trip to the local neighborhood market, and she was back pulling in the drive. Serah shivered, pulled her scarf around tighter and hustled to get the bag of food and herself inside quick. She looked up and around the front yard, the neighborhood beyond. It was an idyllic setting; the sun was going down behind the purple mountains. Dusk.

"Shit," Serah whispered, realizing the time and wishing she'd delayed even for half an hour. That would have helped. But now she was out in it; a powerful time of day. Serah sniffed the air. No salt. Breathing a sigh of relief, she turned away from the sunset and toward the house. Then she caught it. Salty air. It smelled like the ocean. Almost, but not quite. Dammit. Her head snapped around quickly, but in the growing twilight it was especially difficult to see. *Just like they like it. Shit. Shit!* Turning in circles to try to locate what already saw her quite clearly and was ready to feed, Serah started to sweat. There it was, waiting near the base of the old oak tree that was the beautiful center of Ben's front yard. Serah grimaced and felt the first prick of emotion start to steal over her—it was Envy. One she did not encounter very often, and she didn't know why. Envy seemed so common in the world. Maybe all of the Envy demons were otherwise occupied. Shaking her head to clear it, she set down the bag of groceries and started her chant.

She faced east, then north, then south, then west, whispering as she went, "Air, fire, earth, and water, protect me now. I am your daughter."

Pausing, she cracked one eye open to see Envy moving closer. Envy was hesitant; it recognized the power of the chant and the power in the person. Serah held out her arm and watched it pause. She returned to her protection, going deep, envisioning the inward girl, the girl on the lake. The water was still, and she was calm; her breath slowed. Moving her arms in an arc in front, behind, and above, Serah cast her zone of protection. "Air, fire, earth, and water, protect me now. I am your daughter."

Envy approached, cautious, but still coming, clear in its intent. Serah waited. It was terrifying to wait until her protections had been tested; her mind screamed to get it over with. She took a clearing breath and went deeper. She knew she had to close her eyes to do so, and it was an agony to take her eyes off the approaching Demon. She could feel it reach her boundaries and test, one slow tendril. Envy was here.

Pushing her hand into Envy's center, she said, "You will not have power over me. I will it so." The ache started; she could feel her hand begin to numb. Serah tried to focus on the rest of her that felt fine. "I feel the earth, I see the sky, I feel the wind, look in my eye." Face-to-face with Envy made her shudder and pause. The girl on the lake looked up and reached out to help, frantic. Serah's eyes started to burn, Envy Eyes. Serah could taste metal—*Metal? Burning eyes?* Both were a first; it threw her off. The boat started to rock, and she was thrown in. Serah gulped. *This is not going well. Why can't I be more like Lily? Tall and blonde and beautiful. Always saying the right thing, smart and funny. Why can't I live a life like that?*

The thoughts poured in. The girl on the lake pulled herself back into the boat with a groan. She faced east, north, south, west. Serah moved with her. "Air, fire, earth, and water, protect me now. I am your daughter." Water! Grabbing the hose, she twisted it on, dousing herself and Envy. The shock of the cold was enough; Envy vanished. Serah sputtered and looked around aiming the hose at shadows.

Oh my God, I'm a mess. Looking down, she saw she was half soaked, a few oak leaves stuck in her hair and on her sweater. Freezing, she quickly returned the hose to its coiled spot and heard a cawing ruckus above her. Serah paused to look up. What looked like an audience of crows balanced on the high-tension line near the sidewalk, all looking down in her direction. *One, two, three, four, five, six...*Serah counted. "Eight crows...," she said out loud, remembering the man from the gym. *It must mean something. I better tell Ben...tomorrow.* Backing away from the crows and grabbing the groceries, she tumbled inside the door.

Greeted with a chorus of tipsy hellos, the three musketeers grabbed the bag and dove in with frantic preparations to finalize the delicious dinner and dessert.

"Wait. Why are you soaked? What happened?" Lily was the first one to notice.

"There was this dog that got out of his yard, I guess. He came tearing after me, so I did the only thing I could think of and sprayed him with the front yard hose. Thank goodness he didn't get the groceries!" Serah laughed and waved them off, with a chorus of "thank goodness" from the others as they turned back to finish cooking. Ben pulled her aside. "A dog? Seriously, Seraphine?"

"No, Ben, but what did you want me to say? Hey, folks I had my first encounter with the Envy demon and it went okay, I guess, other than being soaked," Serah whispered back. Ben shook his head and pointed. "Go grab a pair of my sweats and come join us when you are ready."

Dry and now sitting at the full dinner table, Serah looked around and raised her glass. "To family," she said. "To family!" the voices chorused. Glasses clinked, and Ben beamed as dinner went off without a hitch.

"Serah, I've been meaning to ask. How are flight lessons going? I'm so impressed at what you are doing!" Lily looked over, spearing another small potato from Levi's plate. "Hey! I was going to eat that," he protested. Lily ignored him, smiled, and nodded at Serah to continue.

"Honestly, Lily, they are going really well. Thanks for asking. I completed my day and night solos. The night solo was nerve-wracking; everything is so much different at night! I am scheduled for my check-ride in about thirty days, I think." Serah looked down at her phone checking the date and held up her crossed fingers. "So by Christmas, I will hopefully be a real private pilot." The whole table agreed this was quite the feat.

"You can fly us around when we are big shot lawyers!" Levi added. Serah laughed and nodded.

"Actually Al, from Executive Flyers Club where I'm learning, said if I continue to do really well, he would train me as an instructor, and I could get a job there. They don't have very many women pilots—none at the Flyers Club, so he thinks it would help business to have a female instructor."

"That sounds like Al, always looking for the money," Ben added.

"It would be nice to get out of the library and find a job; a career where I feel like there is a purpose. I don't know." Serah shrugged slightly.

"I feel really at home in the pilot seat," Serah said softly. "Like nothing I've ever experienced before." Her voice faded, then came back strong. "Maybe kind of like how y'all feel at home in the courtroom!"

Everyone laughed, and Ben piped up, "You can't handle the truth!" Lily and Levi joined in with a chorus of their favorite famous movie lines. Conversation slowed and quieted as the friends sipped their wine and ate homecooked food— the room filled with love.

Serah saw Ben glance at her right before he said, "Lily, do you remember Ethan?"

"Oh, yes, I sure do! He was dreamy. That dark curly hair and those dark eyes." Lily sighed. "I used to make all sorts of excuses to visit you in that dreary law office you worked as a legal assistant that one summer with him. Your boss was such a jerk! How did you even stand it?" They both laughed at shared memories of what Ben had to go through to make enough money for rent that year. He thought it would give him good law office experience, but it almost ended up making him quit the idea of law school all together. Only with the encouragement of Lily and Levi did he make it to orientation and then beyond.

"Did you ever get a picture of him by chance?" Ben paused, scrambling for a reason. He hadn't thought far enough ahead. "Ahh, I checked in with his mom the other day, and she was asking if we had any of him."

"His poor mama. How is she doing?" Lily's face changed from smiles to sadness.

"I think okay. I mean after what happened...I don't know if she will ever really be the same." Ben cleared his throat.

"What really happened, Ben? You never told us the full details of his suicide," Levi asked quietly, the wine making him bold.

Serah choked on her bite of turkey. "Suicide? That's what happened to Ethan?! Ahhh, yes, tell us the story, Ben." Ben matched Serah's glare with one of his own.

"Um, okay, not much to tell. And not a fun story for a holiday, but y'all want to know, so I'll tell you. He slit his wrists, and I found him in the bathroom. He didn't make it to the tub...but he tried," Ben said quickly and trailed off, leaving many of the details tucked safely away. The table was quiet.

"It was because of unrequited love with you Lily!" Levi grimaced as he attempted to lighten the mood.

The table laughed half-heartedly, and the laughter grew as the jokes started in earnest. "You practically dragged him into that back room and forced him to kiss you," the wine making everyone bold.

"I did not! He said he liked my eyes."

"Your ass, more like it," Ben added. "He was an ass man."

"You guys!" Lily protested. "We shouldn't speak ill of the dead."

"How is saying he's a butt guy speaking ill of him?" Levi wondered aloud, taking another big sip of his wine. "He was supposed to be making out with me! You stole him, you little witch." Levi grinned.

Serah's eyes were wide, looking back and forth as she followed the dinner conversation, not saying a peep, not wanting to interrupt this remarkable flow.

"And to your question, I do think I have a couple of pictures of him." Lily grabbed her phone and scrolled through. "That was how long ago? Three years?" Seeing Ben nod, Lily looked back down to her photo scroll. "Voila! Dreamy Ethan," she said, handing her phone to Ben. "There's a few on that day. You can swipe through or save them all for his mom. He looks so handsome. That was the day we went to the lake right before that party where he drew all over his arms in Sharpie. I don't know how he managed to do that so well on each arm. Was he ambidextrous, Ben? I mean, that's talent." Lily continued on as Levi added his own commentary regarding Ethan's physique. Ben was silent. He paused on one picture and enlarged it with his fingers. Passing the phone to Serah who was watching his every move, he didn't have to say a word. His look was enough. She snagged the phone and saw right there, slightly blurred and beginning to become pixelated but still clear to them both, was a healed brand on Ethan's wrist.

Serah mouthed the words, "What is this?" Ben shook his head and shrugged. It was not a brand Serah had, nor was it one they had come across in their research or the book.

"Lily, do you mind if I text these to myself, so I can send them on to his mom?" Serah quickly handed the phone back to Ben.

"Sure, sure, of course. Whatever you'd like. Give her my condolences would you, dear? Wait. She doesn't know me. Well, maybe Ethan told her I was the girl in the make out closet." Dissolving into red-wine giggles that were so hard to resist, despite the grim topic, Ben, Levi, and Serah all found themselves chiming in.

"Pie time!" Lily jumped up amid applause and cheers around the table, scurried into the kitchen and brought out her Dutch apple pie, warm from the oven. There were groans of appreciation around the room.

Everyone dug into dessert and the conversation turned to the latest horrible professor they had to deal with and future law firm plans, each interrupting the other with enthusiasm. Serah sat back stuffed, patting her stomach with pride. Demons, unknown runes, and rules forgotten for the moment. Sipping her wine, quiet and happy, her heart full. These times with her adopted family were vacations for her soul and her body.

Ben swirled his almost empty whiskey glass, wishing for answers. He sat alone in his dark, now quiet, house—everyone left almost an hour ago. In his favorite leather chair, one leg slung over the chunky arm rest, one hand resting on the cushioned back, the other held the whiskey. Eyeing it suspiciously, as if it was his enemy and not his friend, he tried to keep his mind focused on what to do next for Seraphine. He had logged on to the dark web a few minutes ago to check the status of his request to join the Seekers group, and it was still pending.

"Pending, pending, always f-ing pending." Ben sighed, swirled, and took another sip. Looking down at his phone, he saw what his latest research had turned up—another grim warning. From what he could gather, Ethan's brand was a rune that meant danger—suffering.

Ben choked back a laugh; he felt sick inside. *Spot on, universe. Danger and suffering. Spot on.* He could feel the memories start to press in. It did no good to resist. They would come anyway, whether it was now or tonight as he slept; the horrible visions waking him in a cold sweat. At least now he could pretend to be in a little bit of control. Closing his eyes, he pressed the warm glass up to his forehead and gave in.

He could see himself racing home, then charging into the house, then running, then slowly walking, then almost creeping down the hallway. Flashes of memories, flashes of visions, visions of what he didn't want to see ever again.

Ben supposed the memory at least paid homage to his friend who tried to fight, who endeavored to have a mission greater than himself, something Ben longed for, almost desperately at times. He could still feel the pattern the paint made on the wall, as he trailed his fingers down the hallway. Trying to keep in contact with something real, something solid, as best he could. As his pace slowed, his breath slowed to match. He knew he was not brave enough for what he was about to see, what he hoped he didn't have to see.

"Ethan?" Ben watched himself in the memory call out. It was a weak attempt. Clearing his throat, he tried again. "Ethan!" The silence filled Ben's ears and his heart.

"That was some party last night wasn't it, brother? I did the walk of shame, for sure. I know you had a few groupies after that number you sang. Legit, didn't know you had that kind of voice."

Ben winced as he remembered how the desperation for the truth to not be the truth crept up through his chest and into his throat; he sipped his whiskey to try to clear it. The rest of the memory rolled into his mind like a train chugging into a station. There was no stopping it now.

Turning down that last side hall, Ben could see the bathroom door was ajar; only a little light escaped. "Ethan? Come on now. Stop playing your stupid jokes." Ben felt like a robot, almost as if he was forced to continue. The dryness in his mouth made him wish they were sharing stories of their escapades over a beer, which is what they were supposed to be doing right now in fact. Instead, Ben saw his hand reach out from his body and slowly push open the bathroom door, wincing as it creaked long and loud. "Dammit, why didn't we freaking fix that, buddy?" One final step.

"Ethan." There wasn't a question in Ben's tone anymore.

He stepped into the bathroom to see the truth of what he already knew. Shaking out of the memory, he eased himself out of the chair to pour another glass. He twirled the pretty amber liquid in the soft dining room light. *I always thought seeing something like that would be different. More dramatic somehow. But it just Was.* He remembered telling that to the school counselor six months later. The memory swirled up again, and he let it take hold.

"Ethan, no. Damn you, Ethan." Ben stood still, stone faced and so still he had to force himself to breathe. A big gulp of air and the scent of blood. So much blood drowned his olfactory system, causing him to gag. The knife was placed neatly on top of the soap in the soap dish. Ben recognized it was the special fish filleting knife he wasn't allowed to use, because according to Ethan, "Ben you don't have any finesse. This knife is for *chefs*." They would both laugh, and Ben would head back over to his section of the kitchen to finish the salad.

"Ethan, WHY?" Like a soft cry of a wounded animal, Ben finally started to feel again. All the emotions rushed in, and apathy was pushed aside: fear at what he was going to have to do next, horror at the scene, despair at the loss of deep friendship, envy of others who never have to deal with this, failure at not recognizing the signs and helping, loneliness at the thought of being alone, living alone, going to that horrible place of work all *alone,* and rage, rage at the broken world, broken system, broken life.

Ethan lay partially in the bathtub and partially out, cut from wrist to elbow several times. It had been hard work. Work of Despair and Horror and Failure who sat on the edge of the tub drinking in the emotions that had rolled off of Ethan in tidal waves. In the final moments, the others arrived. All Eight ringed the tub like proud parents looking down at the body. It wasn't Ethan any longer, though it had just happened. The final wisp of emotion had emptied out of him just moments before Ben opened the door. Ben only saw Ethan. He didn't know the others were there. He could feel them, but he didn't know why he felt the way he felt.

Ben looked down the long tunnel of memory into the bottom of the whiskey glass. "I didn't know *anything*. I was such a *fool*." Standing up on that last harsh word, he slammed the glass down on the table and stalked to bed.

PART TWO

SamSerah – A Love Story

Chapter 15

Two Years Later
Year Four of the Demons

Serah's phone rang. The cat and dog protested as she reached out blindly toward her bedside table. She cleared her throat and answered with an attempt at perky.

"Hello?" She hated anyone knowing they woke her up. It always made her feel vulnerable and caught off guard. Catching a look at the time, she swore. Late for work. Again.

"Serah, Al is on a tear. He has a few extra lessons coming in, and you are late for your intro flight lesson," said Heidi, the receptionist at the Flyers Club where Serah worked as a pilot for the past eighteen months. "Don't pretend to be awake. I know you were sleeping."

Serah scowled into the phone. "Alright, I know. I knooooow. I'm horrible. I will be there in ten minutes."

"M'kay. I'll tell Al twenty, and I'll try to get the intro flight to go to Starbucks or something. He's kinda cute, actually."

Heidi hung up, yelling out to Al before the phone was cradled, "AL! Serah's on her way and this nice young man is gonna get me a Starbucks while he waits for our best pilot…" Serah laughed and hit end. She threw back the covers: *no time to dawdle,* she thought. Make coffee, feed everyone, brush teeth, grab coffee to go, brush hair—*Heidi did say he was kinda cute after all*—and she was out the door.

Seventeen minutes later, Serah breezed through the doorway at Al's Flyers, balancing keys, coffee, and headset in one hand—her aviator sunglasses on, wearing jeans, tennis shoes, and an old T-shirt.

Flying is a dirty business, but you can still look cute doing it, right? Serah told her instructor once. He had laughed and knew she would change her mind. But Serah didn't have to try to be cute. Fresh-off-the-farm-truck-girl complexion, wild hair, fit with muscles, and a bit bold, she was low maintenance—usually mascara and Chapstick, max.

Sam watched her from his spot by the sliding doors that led to the tarmac. *This was his pilot?* he wondered silently. He had to laugh at himself. *I'm sure she gets that a lot, from every asshole out there. Don't be an asshole, Gunner.* He watched Heidi point in his direction and nod. Serah turned quickly, tucked her headset under her arm, strode to him, and stuck out her hand.

Hmm. Good handshake, they both thought.

Heidi was right. He is pretty cute, Serah thought, distrusting him immediately.

"Sam? I'm Serah. Good to meet you. I gotta check out the plane really quick. If you want to come with me, I will show you what you would do if we started lessons. I have all that you will need with me here." She flapped her arm like a wing, gesturing to the headset.

Sam nodded. "Alright, sounds good to me." They turned to walk out the double doors that led to the hangers.

"It's a pretty day to fly," Serah added, making conversation.

"Serah?" Heidi called out. "It's your mom on the phone. She said it's important."

"Mind if I take this call real quick, Sam?" Serah said over her shoulder. She was already walking away, back toward the desks.

"Surrree. No problem," he drawled and smiled one of his polite smiles. Serah grabbed the phone from Heidi and rolled her eyes at the interruption.

Heidi made a shooing motion with her hands and whispered, "Be a good girl. Talk to your momma." Smiling, Serah picked up the phone.

"Hi, Mom. What's up?"

"Hi, Sugar." She sounded subdued. "I was wondering if I could come visit you? Soon?"

"Well, of course you can. I have a couple lessons here and there, but you can come anytime. Diego would love it."

Diego? Sam could hear the conversation; he tilted his head wondering who Diego was. *Probably a boyfriend. Just leave it alone, Gunnar.*

"That's great, because I have some news that I need to tell you about. Everything is gonna be okay, but I need to tell you first."

"Okaaaay. Can you tell me now?" Serah's brow creased as she pressed the phone to her ear, stepping further into the office area in an attempt at privacy that was not successful.

"I know you are at work, but I need to tell you. You need to know first," she repeated.

"Mom. Please."

"I'm sorry, Sugar. I...I have cancer."

Stunned, Serah leaned back against the counter and pressed the phone to her ear, hard.

"I'm going through more tests right now. So, everything could work out just fine."

"Cancer?" On that one word both Sam and Heidi looked up.

"Yes, but don't worry too much, okay? I want to stay positive and have everyone around me think good thoughts."

Serah paused, recalling when she would walk Diego on dark nights and think about how happy she was that her mom was back in her life, at least somewhat, much more than she ever had been before. How happy she was with her new job; proud of what she had accomplished and created for herself. Content that she knew her place in the world fighting the demons—and relieved that flying helped ease the demon effects. Everything was going so well for once in her life. She wasn't bored anymore; she had purpose and friendship. The only thing missing was a love life, but she would look down at Diego and laugh to herself. *Love life? Not enough time for a silly love life.* She knew Diego was all the love she needed; love for him filled her soul. She would walk and think of all that she had; she was lucky. Serah sighed and closed her eyes. *Too lucky. I knew it*, she thought.

"I understand, Mom. I do. I don't know what to say. What do you know so far?"

"Well, inflammation was found on an X-ray, and then a mass in my bladder when I went in for the PET scan yesterday. They recommend surgery, which will happen soon. Please don't tell anyone else. I only want to tell a few people right now, okay?"

"Okay," concerned, Serah closed her eyes again and agreed. "Okay, Mom. But you are doing okay?"

"Yes. I'm doing fine. I'm sorry to call you at work. I love you."

"Love you too, Mom. I'll call you soon, or you call me. I, I don't know. Whatever you need." Serah wondered what to say that would be right. Nothing felt right.

"Thanks, Seraphine. That would be good. Bye now."

"K, bye, Mom."

"Bye, bye."

Serah hung up the phone and stared: papers to file, stickers saying "kiss a pilot," flight receipts to input, all hanging from the office shelves.

Well, what do I do now? She slowly turned and with a half-sardonic smile, she looked at Sam. She knew with this news, she didn't trust herself to be focused enough to fly. Her flight instructor impressed this detail on her: *Always know where your head is at, Serah. If you don't feel 100%, stay on the ground. You can always fly another day.*

"You drink beer?" she asked him. Maybe his cute face could keep the shadows at bay for a while.

At his nod, "You and I are getting a beer. My treat. Raincheck on the lesson. The weather is crap anyway."

Sam looked out to a cloudless, sunny sky. "Beer it is!" They walked out of the Flyers Club parking lot, and he trotted a few steps to catch up.

"Where to?" he asked.

She jerked her chin across the street. "There's a place across the street—mellow vibe, salty folks."

"So where are you from? I mean originally." Sam couldn't place it, but he knew she talked a little different.

"San Diego." She looked at him, intrigued that he noticed.

At her look, he explained, "The way you said that just then, and hearing you on the phone…yeah, sorry, the office isn't that big…"

"Where are *you* from, Sam Gunnar?" Serah ignored his implied question for more details.

"Here."

"Whole life?"

"Yep."

"Why?" He looked a bit startled by her question. It was rare anyone asked.

"Family." He decided that was the best, easiest answer.

"A man of many words aren't we, Sam?"

"Nope." He looked at her and they both laughed.

"Actually, I lived in Southern California for a while—a few years, in fact. Loved it." He grimaced at the last part, but it was mostly true. "The ocean. I miss it."

"Yeah. It calls to me. I wish I could go back. Someday. Someday, I will sail around the world too. How 'bout that, Sam?"

"I throw up," he said and grinned.

"I am so disappointed; you're a vomiter. What a pity," she teased on a sigh and shake of her head.

"Beer helps though," Sam said earnestly, with a nod.

"Hallelujah. Beer helps a lot of things…," Serah trailed off as she realized how that sounded. But she didn't care; she didn't know him, and he didn't know her. She zipped across the street, dodging a few cars; Sam stayed close. Wing-walkers Bar was open, though it was barely noon. Sam was normally more fond of his drinks at night, but this was not the earliest he had consumed his alcohol, not by far. He remembered and then decided not to.

Walking through the door, he saw beautiful wood floors and a wood-paneled bar. *Definitely old school*, he thought. The aging salt sat at the bar discussing baseball, football, politics, how much better life was in the past.

Serah walked over to a table near the window. She always liked to sit outside if she could, but second best was a little corner of quiet with a view if she could find it. She saw the bartender look over and catch her eye.

"What kind of beer do you like, Sam?"

"Dark" was his simple answer. She signaled two "Black Dogs" then sat with her back against the wall. That is how he always liked to remember her. It wasn't a good day for her, which he was sad for. But sitting there, in the dusty filtered light, sipping a beer, leaned back against the wall, she was beautiful, strong, and so very real. *She had substance, layers*, he would think later, *rare*.

"Nice," Serah said under her breath. Sam could see her eyes looking over his shoulder up to the TV.

Without even looking around he responded, "Steelers or Browns?"

"Steelers." Serah almost blushed. She grinned, the first genuine smile he had seen so far.

"Who's on top?"

"Steelers, woohoo." She gave a little cheer and laughed, turning her attention back to her drinking buddy.

"I'm sorry. That's rude of me. I promise I'll talk to you. Well, during commercials, as long as you're interesting enough," she added.

Sam snorted into his beer. "Serah. You have no idea." He looked at her…*looked*. She returned his stare with one of her own, perked one eyebrow up, and waited.

Finally, "You know I heard somewhere that when people lock eyes for ten seconds, they are either going to fight each other or kiss," she said and stared with that eyebrow quirked, and he could hardly resist. Before Sam could decide what to do, Serah leaned back against the wall, took a sip of her beer, and smiled.

"When the devil smiles at you, you smile back. That's what I've heard," he countered and tipped his glass to her, smiled a crooked smile, and turned around to watch the game.

"Go, Browns!" he shouted.

"Hey!" Serah leaned forward and punched his shoulder. They both laughed and focused on the action on the field. Serah felt…light. She surprised herself; she couldn't remember the last time she felt this quiet inside.

"Second round's on me. And its halftime, so spill it." Sam turned back to her.

"Spill what, exactly?" she asked, pretending innocence.

"Spill the juice on Serah. You did invite me to have a beer, after knowing me for 3.2 seconds. That comes at a price, you know."

"Oh, I see how that goes. Well, what if I just lie?"

"Sure, go ahead. But I'm smart. I already know you like football, possibly only the Steelers. And you like the Steelers because someone in your family watches them or grew up back east. I'm guessing Dad, but could be uncle or brother. You enjoy beer, and I'm guessing by the way you drink it that you drink many other kinds of alcohol, but beer is sorta your go-to comfort alcohol in most situations. You are smart, and you fly a plane, which is pretty crazy awesome by the way. AND you think nobody really gets you…SO, lie all you want, Serah Macguire, but I will know." He set his glass down on the table for emphasis. Serah stared at him while he talked, inwardly a little impressed despite herself.

"Okay, slick, you want the juice? Here's the juice. My mother who has been mostly absent for the past decade and a half of my life just told me she is sick. Has cancer, mind you, and I think that maybe, just maybe, that means everything I thought was lucky about my life, really isn't. At all. My favorite color is blue, and I hate cats. So which part am I lying about, eh?" she challenged.

Sam paused to sip his beer. "The part where you sound surprised by the news of the cancer."

Serah looked at him. He was right, she thought. It pissed her off.

"Okay, points for that one. By the way Mr. Smart-man, I lied about hating cats."

She was about to say more. She wanted to say more, but the usual walls stopped her. Too much to tell. Too much to say. Too much crazy in there to let out, especially to a cute stranger she just met.

"Let's just watch the fuckin' game." She smiled to take the force out of the curse.

Sam chuckled. "Okay, let's watch the game. Fuckin' Steelers fan." He shook his head as if to say "what a shame." They both laughed, turned back to the game, and watched in comfortable silence, punctuated by sharp commentary on the plays. It was safe. It was easy.

It had been two weeks since her aborted lesson with Sam. Serah had spoken with her mother several times during those weeks; each time with better news. A second opinion was optimistic—there were options, manageable steps to be taken. She was going to come visit next week. Serah felt her good mood at the lucky news should not be wasted.

Sam, Sam. Hmm. Serah found thoughts of him tiptoeing around her brain often since that day. Unfortunately, another instructor had been rescheduled with his original intro lesson, yet she knew she had to see him again.

"Hey, Sam, I don't know if someone contacted you, but didn't know if you wanted to reschedule that lesson," Serah practiced in front of the mirror. *Terrible.*

She tried again. "Sam, this is Serah, Serah the Steelers fan. Ah, didn't know if you wanted to try to make that lesson this time…" *Getting worse.*

"Hiya, Sam, what do you say to rescheduling your intro flight?" Serah scowled at her reflection. *Laaaame.*

"Hi. This is Serah from the Flyers Club, thinking you might want to try again on that intro flight lesson." *Ummm. No.*

"Hi, Sam, this is Serah. Not sure if you rescheduled your lesson already but was hoping to connect with you and get you on the schedule." *Boooring.*

"Hello, Sam, Serah from the Flyers Club. I had a nice time watching the game and grabbing that beer a few weeks ago and was wondering if you wanted to cash in the raincheck on that intro flight lesson I owe you? Also wanted to say thanks for being there. It…helped. Talk to you soon." *Hmm. That one had promise.*

"Hey, Sam, this is Serah. I wanted to say thanks for watching the game and grabbing a beer with me a few weeks ago. It…helped. Was wondering if you wanted to cash in that rain check I owe you. You have my number. Talk to you soon."

Okay. There we go. Serah's reflection smiled.

Chapter 16

The trees listen. They know.
Secrets kept. Secrets held.
The trees listen. They know.
To the brave they will tell.

~ Book Seekers of the Truth

Serah ran on the footpath by the river. It was quiet. She didn't listen to music when she ran anymore; the only sound was her breath and the occasional bird or sigh of the trees moving in the breeze. Months ago, dead of summer, jogging down the path, iPod cranking, she turned a sharp bend in the trail and there was a snake stretched across the path. She had a moment to decide to jump—or wait. Waiting seemed smarter, and the snake smoothly cruised on into the brush. Adrenaline pumping, her run seemed a bit easier after that, yet for the remainder of that run she couldn't stop taking her earbuds out to listen to the rustles in the dense brush that lined the river and grew one hundred feet up the bank to the path. *Lots of places for Mr. Snakey to hide*, she thought, taking the earbud out of whichever ear was facing toward the brush. She would slow down and listen. But all she ever heard was her ragged breath and the wind and the squirrels.

Now months later, Serah didn't even bring her iPod, she liked to run and listen to her lungs work. She felt strong. She liked to listen to the wind and the stories from the ancient trees that lined the path. She liked to hear her paced footsteps, slower and faster, slower and faster.

If there was such a thing as magic, it would be here, Serah thought. She had this thought every time she ran this route, passing under a dome of trees, with filtered sunlight streaming down. It felt almost tropical, this area was quieter here than anywhere else on the trail. She always expected to see some magical creature, a gnome perhaps, peek its head out at her as she went running past. But, she sighed, never anything of the sort. Only Demons. It was depressing.

Serah rounded the corner next to the massive oak that stood fifty feet tall, as old and as wise as the river its roots were tangled up in nearby. Marking her halfway point, she stopped a moment to stretch and catch her breath, laying her palm on the trunk of the tree for support. Serah felt the hairs on the back of her neck stand up—human hackles, she liked to call them. Rage and Horror were the only two that ever elicited this response and before she turned to look, she knew: Rage was here.

Whipping around, moving fast, she lashed out first with her power, scarred hand and arm strong as an arrow deflecting the first onslaught of emotion. Her mind moved as quick as her body, taking everything in—how far, how much time, how fast was Rage moving—calculating her next step with speed. She knew she didn't have much time. Rage was *fast*. Her eyes saw Rage galloping toward her on talons of pain. Contorting her body, she tore her Camelback off and twisted open her spare water, blessing it and tossing it in Rage's direction in the same motion, same breath. Rage howled and struck out with its formidable weapons; Serah stumbled back against the tree. *Focus. Go deep.* Serah swallowed and attempted to conjure the girl in the boat on the lake.

Rage and Seraphim danced.

Rage sickened her. Unlike many of the others, it made her want to vomit with the force of its power. Rage's power packed a punch. Feeling her gut twist, she chanted, "I am brave, I am strong. This is my will. It shall not be undone."

Rage twisted too. It twisted and curled and tightened around her like a python of death. Trapped in its embrace, Serah felt herself weaken. Reaching for her backpack, she scrambled for the lighter. *I will set you on fire.* Down to her knees, Serah threw back her head and screamed. Reaching for a small branch of the oak, she snapped it off clean with her bare hands, and lit the edges of the leaves. The flames lit up her demonic smile. She was one of them too, she knew.

"I set you on fire, I burn you to the ground, I declare you to vanish, and forbid you around." She waved the now-burning torch closer and closer to Rage, a tricky feat as Rage was wrapped around her torso, making it difficult to breathe. Serah laughed and looked Rage right in the eye. Inhaling as if taking in everything that was Rage, fire lit her eyes. She was Rage. Lighting her shirt on fire, Rage screamed and vanished. Serah fell to the dusty earth, rolling to put out the flames.

I won, I won, I won, I won, I won. Serah yelled to the trees, laughing, "I won! Time to celebrate!" The urge for booze or beer started to trickle in. She recognized the familiar feeling that often came after the Rage demon, sometimes even before. Serah popped back on her feet with a lithe move Ben taught her from his martial arts class, and knew exactly where she was headed. With a quick dust off and ponytail fix, she turned and ran back down the trail; victory made her fast and light as she dodged shadows and puddles from the rainstorm the night before. Running away from Rage but into the fight.

Serah walked into the old diner that sat near the trailhead where she parked when she ran this trail. The door shut behind with a squeak. No one turned to look. No one cared who walked in for a drink in the middle of the day. They all sat at the bar battling their own personal demons. Serah smiled. Rage made her bold. Sauntering up to the bar, she caught the bartender's eye and ordered: gin, neat. It bubbled up inside, the rage. And it made her giggle a little—so much power, none of these fools would ever know. Shaking her head a little at the angry thought, Serah grabbed a stool at the bar and started to drink. She tossed her first shot back like a practiced sailor even though, in reality, she had only taken a shot two other times in her life. *I am different now,* she thought.

Signaling for another one, the bartender raised his eyebrows at this young woman who now graced his bar; a rare sight as his clientele tended toward the old, the angry, and the lonely. He obliged and also handed her a shot glass full of limes to ward off the taste. Serah laughed and pushed them away; she had no need for anything to take the edge off. She liked the edge. She needed the edge. She deserved the edge.

With shot number three, the bartender brought her a glass of water and the half-full bottle of gin telling her, "Have fun, but not too much fun, Miss. You look like you need it." Serah gave him a little cheers with shot number four. With a flip of her hand and head, it was burning a path down her throat. It felt good. Serah closed her eyes, reveling in the feeling that nothing could stop her; she was going to be okay. It was all going to be okay. She liked believing the story gin told her.

Shots five, six, and seven tore through her like fire. Serah squinted and tried to grab her phone that sat on the bar top; she missed it a few times and tried harder. Grabbing it, she scrolled through the texts: Sam, Ben, Work, UGH. She had no use for real life. Tossing her phone back onto the bar, she kicked her barstool back onto its two back legs, teetering for a second before crashing backward onto the floor. Serah howled with laughter. The other patrons glanced her way for barely a second, then turned back, absorbed in the movie they saw in their heads of their lives. No one cared about the drunk girl in the bar. The bartender sighed and walked over slowly. He leaned over the bar. "Miss? MISS? You okay? Can I call someone for you?"

Serah shook her head vehemently. "I'm okaaaay. I am, neverrr better." Her words slurred together like mush. Still chuckling a little under her breath, she rolled over to get up on all fours, working hard to stand as the floor tilted under her feet. "I got thisss. I do. Scout's honor." Holding up two fingers, then three, then making the Vulcan sign, giggling again. The bartender watched her with a straight face; he had seen it all before.

"Who can I call, Miss? No driving for you."

"Sam, I want to talk to Sam," Serah whispered and clutched her chest.

"Sam. Okay, Sam." He clicked through her phone to find Sam and hit call.

"No, no, no wait. I mean Ben…BEN. Call BEN, pleassse. Ben." Serah laid her head down on the bar.

"Nope, this is not good. Nope. Not good at all." The bartender pressed speaker and placed the phone next to her head.

"Hello?" Serah heard Sam's voice echo through the speaker and she groaned.

"Sam," Serah licked her lips. "This is Ssserah from the flight school."

"Serah! Hi! Can we reschedule?"

"Srrrurre, yep, we can. When iss good?" Serah closed her eyes with the effort.

"How 'bout tomorrow?"

"Tomorrow?" Serah repeated.

"Tomorrow?" Sam repeated.

"Tomorrow." Serah nodded her head on the bar, her ponytail flapping back and forth. Silence.

"Ummm, everything okay?"

"Yep, perffectlly. I jus, I jus' happen to need a ride."

"Okaaay, sure thing. Where are ya at?"

"The diner with lotsa gin."

"Ahhh okaaay, kinda early in the day. My kinda girl, my kinda day," Sam said. Serah giggled.

She took a deep breath and tried again, "The diner near the trailhead, River Parkway. Rage demon—oop, I mean ragelicious." Pushing herself up with both hands to a standing position, she grabbed the phone and brought it closer.

"I know that place. I used to run the trails over there. Okay, I'll be there in about thirty."

"Okay, thanksss, Ssaam." Clicking "end call" before Sam could ask any more questions, Serah signaled to the bartender again. "Coffffee. Coffeeee, pleassse, yep yeppers. Lotsa coffee. STAT." Serah giggled and waited for Sam.

Waiting at their lunch spot, Serah realized almost three months had passed since that drunken day at the Trailhead Diner. *How much had changed*, she thought, laughing that she was almost grateful to the Rage Demon, *almost*. It had brought her in touch with Sam. *Sam, handsome Sam.* She smiled as she looked at the time on her phone, *never on time.* Sitting and relaxing in the almost-summer-but-not-quite sunny day at their favorite restaurant patio, she didn't care; she knew she would wait for him all day. Plus, this gave her a chance to slow down and think a little. Her job at the Flyers Club had been hectic, spring and summer being their busiest seasons for tourists and intro lessons. She only had two regular students right now, but they were excited to fly as often as they could. Serah was happy with her paychecks and could feel the tension creeping around her neck, up to the back of her head and settling behind her eyes. Flying was a hard business, especially with newbies; she had to keep all her wits about her. She realized with a bit of surprise that she had not had any demon encounters in weeks.

Maybe it was Sam. Sam, my good luck charm. Serah smiled again.

She jumped as two large hands came down on her shoulders. "Hiya, babe! Been here long?" Sam set his motorcycle helmet down on the table with a thud and gave her a kiss.

"You're in a good mood." Serah blushed a little at the kiss. They had been taking things slow and easy; both busy, both bogged down by baggage, though each of a different kind.

"It's gonna be a great year, Sugar!" Sam beamed and Serah laughed, his enthusiasm infectious.

"Let's order, I'm starved. I just got done at the gym." Orders were placed and meals came quickly. They settled into an easy afternoon conversation.

Sam's phone buzzed on the table, on the right side of his plate. Serah tried not to glance over, but she couldn't help it. *Was it her? I bet it was her.* She grimaced at the gut wrench of jealousy, jealousy and insecurity, and looked back down to her plate. *At least he was honest.* Serah remembered Sam telling her about some of *his* baggage one night, after two flight lessons and coffee dates had turned into a lunch then a dinner, when it was clear hanging out felt more like being on a date than just a friendly connection—that he didn't want to take more intro lessons just for the hell of it.

Serah felt herself fall into the memory, while Sam texted the unknown person on his phone. This memory wasn't fuzzy. This one was burned into her brain. This relationship mattered to her, even though she didn't want to show that it did. This mattered like she was on the train of her life, rumbling into a station, and she had only a couple of minutes to decide to jump off and switch tracks or to stay on and see where she ended up. For some reason it felt like whatever she did, whatever choice she made, there would be no going back.

She remembered: Sam had cleared his throat. "Serah, I need to be honest." He paused and cleared his throat again. "I'm not the best in relationships. I have a tendency to wreck them." He forced a weak laugh. "I'm sort of dating, well not dating, but there's a woman. She's been in my life a few years, and it's twisted. I dunno, we have history. I want you to know, um...," Sam trailed off. Serah watched his face: *this is so hard for him.*

"I'm kinda broken, Serah. I don't want to hurt you. I really don't." Sam's blue eyes found hers, and she felt her gut twist this time with want—no, with need. She felt she needed this man in her life like nothing she had ever felt before.

"Ahh, young Sam, we are all a little broken." Serah tried to lighten the tension with a gentle laugh. Sam didn't smile back.

"I'm not sure I understand what you are telling me."

Serah stopped short of asking a specific question, hating the thought of scaring this man off or coming on too strong with too many boundaries and opinions. She took a sip of her iced tea to quench the flames of anxiety. She wanted him too much. *But I don't want to be number two on the list. I don't deserve that,* said the voice in her head. She shook her head and sighed. *Maybe it didn't matter. Maybe nothing mattered but enjoying the people who enjoy us, living life and sucking out all the juice we can, while we can. Right? Isn't that what we are supposed to do?*

"I just don't want to lead you on or hurt you," Sam repeated, his hands folded on the table in front of him. He pushed his plate away and leaned back in his chair, looking away.

"Sam." Her voice was always soft when it came to Sam. She waited until he looked at her. "I'm not a kid. We are two adults who enjoy each other's company. It doesn't have to be any more complicated than that." Serah smiled. "Besides, you better be careful. I'm easy to fall in love with. You'll see." She smirked and speared a slice of seared ahi off his plate.

"Hey! I need that protein. Tryin' to bulk up, ya know." He laughed, joking back. She looked at him with that smile; that smile that fascinated him. He liked her more and more each day. Fear, like bile, rose to settle in his throat. The smile slid off his face as he looked at hers.

"Don't look so serious, handsome. It'll be okay. Fortune favors the brave, right?" Hiding her nerves, it was a rally cry for herself as much as for him. She picked up her glass to cheers, and he clinked his glass with hers.

That conversation had been weeks ago now—no other mention of *her*, no other sign that he was interested in anyone else. They had spent, and continued to spend, so much time together that Serah soothed herself with the thought: *How could he even have the time?* Sitting there across from him even now, watching him text someone somewhere, she knew without a doubt there was no other place she'd rather be. *Plus, I have to be winning. I fly planes for crying out loud.*

Sam set his phone down—face down—on the table this time, an action which brought Serah rushing back to the present. *It was her. Why does he hide from me? I wish he didn't have to hide from me. Ha, pot kettle,* Serah thought with an inner hollow laugh, thinking of all she hid from him. *Seems fair.*

Shaking her hair back from her shoulders, Serah knew what she wanted. She wanted him, for as long as she could get him. She wanted to feel normal, to enjoy his company, and flirt, and fall in love. That last want had her gulp her drink a little faster. *Don't fall in love, Seraphine Macguire. Don't.*

With a laugh, and ignoring that voice, Serah reached her hand to touch his. "Want to try out that new wine bar after this? Or froyo! Let's get froyo. I haven't had any in ages."

Sam nodded. "Serah Macguire, you remind me there is still good in this world. Let's do both." He added, "We can take Diego for a walk after, to help burn off the love handles."

The love handles he doesn't have. Serah smiled. Laughing, they turned their attention back to their meals and dug in: to the food, to the conversation, and to each other. The questions and the doubts didn't matter—only this did.

Chapter 17

"I am lucky, I am lucky, I am lucky," Serah whispered to herself as she lay in a sleeping bag on the floor in her mom's small apartment. She closed her eyes tight and begged it to be true. The hospice nurse couldn't come by, and Serah had been left alone with her mom for over forty-eight hours now. Medications and catheters, forcing food; Mom never wanted food. It was swift, this cancer—swift and deadly. Serah didn't know what happened really. One day she was sitting with her mom in her sunny yellow kitchen, sitting and drinking coffee as they talked about the options. Things were supposed to be okay. That was five months ago. *Just five months?* Serah wondered, *Could that really be?* Most days she would look in the mirror and feel she aged five years in five months.

"I am lucky, I am lucky, I am lucky." Serah tried again, until she drifted off to sleep. The alarm jerked her awake only two hours later. She took a breath, threw the sleeping bag off, and pushed herself clumsily up from the floor. Rubbing a sore spot on her back, she walked down the dark hall.

"Time for your meds, Mom."

"Hi, Sugar. What time is it?"

"4 a.m. You sleeping okay?"

"I think so...I'm not sure."

"Yeah. How's your pain? The doctor said we could increase the morphine a little bit. Do you want more?"

"Please."

"You know, you hafta eat. Just a little protein shake." Serah shook the bottle a little for emphasis; her mom shook her head no.

"Mom. Please."

"Maybe later. Okay?"

"Mom, you say that every time."

Her mother sighed and closed her eyes.

"We need you to stay strong for chemo." Her eyes remained closed; her face pinched.

Silent, Serah got the medication together in jerky movements. Her mom swallowed a handful of pills: pain pill, laxative for the effects of the pain pill, antibiotic for the effects of the chemo, more morphine. She refused to take the antianxiety.

"Thanks, dear."

Serah nodded and turned to go. She didn't know what to do. She didn't know that she wanted to climb in bed and hug her mom all night. She didn't know anything anymore. She felt completely unprepared for this burden, this moment in her life. She felt cut off, adrift. Adrift from everything except Sam. The thought of him lit a flame of hope that was a drug. It coated these moments for her with a soft light that allowed her to go on.

"Seraphine. You should date. Are you dating?"

"Really, Mom?"

"You need protection. Are you flying?"

"Protection from *what*, Mom?"

"Protection. The flying will help some. Tell me you are flying!"

"Yes, Mom. Yes, I'm an instructor now, remember? I teach people how to fly. It's been two years now."

"Who are you seeing? Who?"

"There might be someone, but...he's still new."

"Who? Jeremy? I never liked Jeremy."

Serah stared at her mother in the hospital bed. The bed that, mother and daughter at first protested; there was no need for a hospital bed. The bed hospice delivered that turned out to be a godsend. The stupid bed barely fit in the tiny apartment bedroom smashed up against the wall and other furniture.

"Jeremy's gone, Mom. He died four years ago. You know that." Serah knew the medication was kicking in. "After him, it was...hard." Serah swallowed. "There's really been no one real since Jeremy." She whispered her confession.

"What do you see, Serah? What?"

Serah shook her head at the quick turn of conversation. "What? You mean who? His name is Sam, Mom. Sam." Thank God for Sam. The hope burned in her chest, and she could feel it like something alive, something bigger than her fear. The universe was watching out for her, and it would be okay. It would all be okay.

"Sam? No, no, no. What do you seeeeee?" Her mother started to slur her words. Serah watched as she drifted off to sleep. Hopefully to rest, to be stronger when she woke. The AC whirred on. The minutes were quiet.

"I can see demons, Mom. What about you?" Serah whispered to the sleeping woman who hovered in the in-between, the weigh station, waiting to be ushered across to the other side of the veil.

Serah closed her eyes and could see in her mind's eye the demon's lurking everywhere she went: Despair hopping around the large oak that marked the entrance to her mother's gated community, Failure lurking underneath the stairwell that led to her mother's small condo, Envy crouched near the pool deck, Loneliness perched ever present in the windowsill. Watching, always watching, but none of them approaching as if a stalemate, a boundary, existed; as if something more powerful was present—or about to be. The Demons watched and waited.

Serah swallowed and opened her eyes. "I can see demons, Mom," Serah repeated. "Can you?" The woman slept. The Demons watched. The room was silent.

"Time to change the shirt, Mom. Laundry day." Serah tried to sound cheerful. No response.

"I'll make a new protein shake today. It will be better this time, I promise."

Silence. Serah rifled through the clothes drawer, looking for a clean shirt for her mom. Soft, it had to be soft. Serah looked up. She stared at her mother's chest, squinting hard. *I see breathing. She is still breathing.* Serah sat down on the bed, exhausted.

"Betty Boop, Seraphine." The voice was scratchy. "The Betty Boop T-shirt. I like that one."

Serah looked down at the pink T-shirt in her hand. "That's just the one I grabbed. Perfect choice." Her mom smiled a little, then grimaced as she forced herself to sit up.

"More pillows?" Serah asked. Her mom nodded. Breathing hard, the outfit was finally changed, dirty one tossed on the floor. Serah brushed her mom's hair and tried to smooth it down.

"Got some flyaways, Mom." She smiled softly. "Maybe we could try a shower today? Got the shower chair in there now. I think that will help a lot."

Her mother licked her dry lips and tried to chuckle. "I think if my friends came over now, I would scare them off. I guess it's time to open that box." She pointed at the box in the corner. It had come by UPS the other day. A wig, one of the best the internet could find. Serah knew it was hard for her mom. *Always a little vain, in a good way,* she thought. She had heard, "Just a second, let me put my face on," many times before their estranged life.

Serah shook her head a little, thinking how most days she stayed in her workout clothes, running around and never having time to shower, let alone *put her face on.* She sighed, wondering if that was part of her armor. She never liked the attention makeup and cute clothes inspired. No one talked to the *maybe* pretty girl in sweaty clothes without makeup. She could hide there, and that was fine with her.

Everyone clapped as she blew out the candles. Serah's mom, Natalie, sat back with a smile. Serah looked around the table at the small handful of friends her mom had allowed over for a small birthday celebration. She was sixty-two and looked forty-two, even with cancer. Serah watched as her mother laughed and joked and even ate some cake.

She really is going to beat this thing.

Mom is going to beat this, and then we will fix what's broken between us. We will fix it, Serah thought as she cleared the dishes. She tossed the dishes in the sink and disappeared into the bathroom. The only space in the small apartment that was really private. She wanted her mom to have time to chat with her friends and Serah wanted to hear from Sam. Sitting crossed legged on the covered toilet, she dialed his number. It still made her nervous, even after a few months.

"Hey, beautiful, how's it going?" He answered on the second ring.

"Good. Really good actually. She's feeling good today," Serah's voice was soft with a tone of sweetness that he loved. She always seemed to sound that way when she talked to him.

"Great to hear, I'm so glad. You getting any rest?"

"Yeah...some...it is what it is, you know."

"Yeah." He chuckled a dry laugh. "I know." Serah often called Sam "The Terminator" because of his ability to keep going through lack of sleep, lack of food, stress, pain. It didn't matter, he was the strongest man she knew.

"The Terminator always knows," she replied. He loved it when she called him that. Loved it and hated it a little. It was a lot to live up to, and he didn't want to let her down. She was the type of girl that made him a better man. He'd told her that on their third date. Their relationship had progressed quickly from the almost disaster at the bar when he picked her up that drunken day near the river trail. Sam, impressed with her ability to hold her liquor based on what the bartender told him she drank, also felt good to be needed again—very good. *Too good,* he thought. Despite this, he asked her out quickly after their rescheduled flight lesson that turned into coffee, then lunch, then another flight lesson. Sam grimaced a little thinking of how so not subtle he was.

Even knowing the anchor he had on his heart, he was hooked. She amazed him with her courage and also intrigued him with her depth that he couldn't quite figure out. *Still waters run deep,* his grandma used to say. *Indeed, Grandma, indeed. Wish you could meet this woman.*

Their third date was almost another disaster—Sam remembered that night as they chatted on the phone. He had busted his lip open on a shotgun that afternoon, boys being boys. Friends had loaded it with the wrong ammo. One second he was thinking, *I get to go meet up with Serah tonight,* the next he was on the ground bleeding with a rapidly swelling split lip from an unexpected re-coil. He stopped the blood and went to meet her anyway; they went to cocktails instead of dinner, figuring chewing to be too painful.

He noticed her scars and thought they were wicked, but in a proud, re-spected way, especially when she said it was a pilot thing, like initiation rite. He remembered watching her walk back from the bathroom, helping a little girl, maybe four years old, along the way. She had crouched down to talk to her. He couldn't hear the conversation, but that image tugged so hard. Man, he wanted to kiss her. He wanted a lot more than that, he knew. It wasn't "let's just have sex." It was different—it was more real. He saw her with the little girl and had thoughts of kids and family and her and him creep in for the first time in many years. It surprised him, and then again it didn't. It seemed like it had always been this way with her, that she was meant for him—maybe fate. He didn't like to believe in such things, things that felt way too out of control for his liking, but with her it was different. Everything was different. It seemed like all thought of his past—of *her* from the past—it seemed like another life, as if the slate had been wiped clean and clear. Sam felt like this was a new beginning, another chance at something really good—deep down good. Any thoughts or concerns brought about by what Sam liked to refer to as his Public Service Announce-ment conversation were long forgotten.

"Busy day today?" she asked. Sam ran a Christmas tree farm, and Serah loved the thought of that. It was late summertime, and getting ready for the upcoming season was a constant process.

"Yeah, had one of the girls quit today. I think she was tired of getting shit from all the boys." Sam sighed. It never stopped. Keeping employees was one of the hardest parts of his job. Convincing his family to trust his ideas? That was even harder. He inherited the business from his dad and couldn't walk away. He loved working for his family but hated the business. It wasn't him. He felt he was slowly being pushed and squished into a box that most definitely didn't fit.

"Boys can be dumb," she said and they laughed. "But so can girls. I'm sorry you have to deal with that. Makes more work for you." She paused then continued. "It sounds echoey and quiet there though. Is that good?"

"I'm in my office. I need furniture." Sam laughed and looked around. Bare floors and a desk. A locker for keys and important papers, and usually his gun. A framed poster of a pinup girl sitting on a vintage motorcycle. His two Folsom Prison album covers, signed by Johnny Cash himself, were waiting to be framed and hung. There was a lot to do and decorating an office was not a priority.

"Punch any walls yet today?" Serah joked, but only slightly. His temper was under tight control, but work drama seemed to be his kryptonite.

"Nice," Sam laughed a little. "Not yet, but I'm missing you rubbing my head and keeping me calm. Especially after I meet with the guys today." He was always a little surprised that she was the only one he'd ever met that kept him calm. No matter the situation, she diffused the emotion. It felt like the bad stuff just got less...intense around her.

"Maybe I'll just pull out my gun and lay it on the table during the meeting," he added. Serah's eyes widened a little at that, but she knew his sense of the dramatic and, though he was serious about wanting to, she knew he wouldn't in the end. Sam was a little dark and she liked that about him. She liked it a lot.

"Well, Sugar, Matt is knocking on the door and I gotta go. I'm sorry. I hope you have a good day today. Text me later, okay?"

"Totally okay. Have a good day too. Try not to shoot anyone today."

"Will do," Sam agreed with a laugh.

"See ya, handsome."

"Take care of yourself, beautiful. Bye."

Serah looked at the phone after they hung up. It was only a handful of minutes, but it felt like she had taken a drug.

Thank God for Sam, she thought for the millionth time and carefully stood up on numb, tingling legs. She headed out the bathroom door to face the day again.

Chapter 18

"For you, Mom," Serah lifted the black leather flask and toasted. "It's your favorite." The woman in the casket lay silent.

"Ben made it, just the right amount of lime I'd say. Yes, yes, diet tonic," Serah sipped, then took a long swallow. "Tasty too." Serah leaned over and placed some favorite jewelry on her mother's bony hand, then turning her wrist over to check for scars, brands, anything. She gently tucked her mom's arm back into the casket.

"The mortician was worried, Mom. Said he tried and tried. He was so upset, the lady told me. Of course, I said it was just fine. Silly thing to be worried about. He couldn't make you look alive again. He couldn't even make you look like... you. He wanted to, he said. I gave him your favorite make up. That Bobbi Brown eye shadow. It looks so good on you. It does. He said the skin dried out so fast." Serah stared at the corpse and took another sip.

Everything just kinda collapsed, he told her.

"It was the salt, Mom. Wasn't it? The salt," Serah whispered. She sat down in a hard chair placed next to the casket for that purpose—the purpose of paying respects. Everyone seemed to know exactly what to do, everybody but her.

"It doesn't look like you at all. Who *are* you?" Serah's hoarse voice was horrified in that tiny silent room. She pulled again at the flask and felt it burn down her throat. A magic blanket to soothe for a minute, maybe even an hour or two. She clasped her hands and laid them on the edge of the simple wood casket, letting her head hang between them, remembering.

The hospice nurse was able to come the day after the small birthday party, and the day was shaping up to be a good one, all things considered. Serah was grateful. She sat at the small table paying bills and thinking up plans to keep her mother's spirits up. Serah stared out the windows to watch the pretty day.

"Goddamn hospice nurse, Mom. She told me too late. Too late!" Serah said to the small empty room.

"I think it's time, honey. You should come now," the nurse spoke slowly, and Serah didn't understand.

"What? What are you talking about? She was doing great yesterday. That's just...what?"

"Please come." Serah pushed back from the table and moved quickly down the hall. She looked back to see that the nurse did not follow. Pushing the bedroom door open with one hand, she crossed to the bed in a few steps.

"Mom? Mom," Serah called and leaned over, peering into her face. Her jaw was slack and open. Serah sat by the bed and grabbed her mother's hand. She waited for the next breath to come. She wanted to be there to help usher her through, to walk with her, to make sure she was okay and not alone. Please, not alone. She wanted to protect her. Protect her from any Demons skulking around to take advantage of the woman's weakened state. Protect her from Fear and Horror, from anything bad; no one deserved to feel that in their final moments. No one. Serah realized that she was also afraid. Afraid of what the combination of Demons and Death would be like; she didn't believe it would be pretty or nice. But when she looked around, she saw all the demons had fled—no sign left behind.

Serah waited, she listened. There was no sound. She watched the pink shirt. There was no movement. Her mom was gone. Serah saw it then, a piece of scrap paper torn out of one of her mother's many little leatherbound notebooks. Laid carefully on top of the little book, laboriously scrawled in black pen. Serah could see the writing was her mom's.

Burn ME.

Serah felt like she had fallen into a hollow well, far from anything she recognized, from anything that made her feel safe. She was cold and empty and tired. And filled with an enormous heaviness that was like an ocean inside.

"Damn nurse," Serah repeated. She lifted her head. "It didn't look like you even then."

"Knock knock." Ben's head poked through the large door's opening. Serah motioned him to come in. She handed him the flask and Ben took a big sip.

Thank God for Ben, Serah thought. Everything happened so fast in the few days after her mom passed. She was bombarded with mortuary to dos, friends, and requests. She needed an officiant and an obituary. She remembers repeating that over and over to herself in the quiet apartment after the coroner had left with the body.

"An officiant and an obituary." *It had a ring to it.* Serah caught herself on a sickening laugh. Right then she turned and picked up her phone. Ben immediately booked the next flight out and was there by evening.

Thank God for Ben, she thought again, as she watched her friend swallow another swig of gin and tonic.

"Not bad, my dear. Not bad at all." Ben turned to face the casket. "You made one hell of a daughter, ma'am. She's pretty goddamn amazing." For the first time in a few days, Serah's eyes welled with tears. She cleared her throat to keep it at bay.

"Ben. No scars. Nothing." Serah's voice didn't sound like hers, even to herself. Her shoulders slumped again. She saw Ben nod; he understood.

"Lots of people out there wanting to give their love to you, Serah. Come on out?" Ben asked gently as he turned to face the daughter. Serah reached her hand out for the flask and nodded.

"Love you, friend," Serah said.

"Love you best," Ben whispered. Together they pulled open the heavy door and walked out, leaving the fallen woman behind.

The service was beautiful—at least that's what everyone said. Serah stood in a receiving line nodding and smiling and shaking hands, giving a hug here and there.

"Your mother would be proud."

"Yes, thank you." Serah nodded

"She was a strong woman."

"Yes, she was." Serah smiled.

Many people she didn't recognize or know; only a few close friends who had helped put the guest list together. After a long hour, the line of guests slowed down to a trickle and then stopped. Serah turned to Ben, showed him the edge of the flask from her pocket. He nodded and crooked his head toward an alcove of the church behind the casket. Turning in unison, they hustled over to their spot to take a swig and try to relax. Serah pulled her mother's note out of her pocket and handed it to Ben. His eyes widened as he read it. He nodded, tucked the paper in his back pocket, and held his hand out for another sip. They didn't need to talk. In the silence of their friendship, everything was understood.

Serah could hear a quiet murmur here and there from the chatting groups of visitors who remained. She watched as the funeral parlor director walked into the large room, looked around, and beelined for the two friends. Nudging Ben with her elbow to get his attention, she jerked her chin in the direction of the approaching woman. Ben awkwardly shoved the flask in his pocket, flashed Serah a double thumbs up, and turned on a big smile.

"Look at those pearly whites," Serah teased under her breath.

"Ms. Macguire? Ms. Macguire?"

"Yes, that's me." Serah raised her hand halfway feeling like a kid in school again.

"I am so sorry for your loss. Excellent service."

"Thank you." Serah eyed the woman's attire, *neat as a pin.*

"Hating so much to rush you, and there is absolutely no rush. We will need all the flowers and arrangements cleared out when you leave as well. Rule of the house, I'm afraid. So sorry, so sorry for your loss. We do have another reservation for the parlor at two." She tapped her elegant gold and silver watch.

Serah checked her phone. "So we have thirty minutes?"

"Yes, yes. Well, maybe about twenty. That would be better."

Ben pushed himself off the large column he was leaning against. "I'm on it!" He ran to the front of the room and grabbed the microphone. "Folks! We have a special surprise for you. All these beautiful arrangements must go! You are the lucky ones who stayed long enough to get a free funeral arrangement—good for house warmings, good for visiting Grandma in the home, good for a centerpiece for family dinner tonight. Please step on up and pick the one you like!"

Serah winced and couldn't help but laugh. *Too much gin, apparently.* She noticed it felt good to laugh and loved her friend even more for it.

Turning to the parlor director, "Looks like we will be out of your hair in no time."

"Oh, yes, indeed, thank you." Wringing her hands a bit, she backed away slowly, as if this was how she was taught to deal with the bereaved. *Move slow. They are wild and unpredictable.* Serah caught the laugh that bubbled up as she waved goodbye to the retreating mortician. Walking to join Ben at the front, she saw one of the small tables littered with a pile of the condolence cards from each bouquet that had been taken. He was so focused on reading one, he jumped. "Jeez, you're like a freaking cat, Seraphine."

She laughed and shook her head. "Because of all your damn training! Whatcha got there?"

Ben handed the card to her to read. "Okay, so I haven't told you because I thought it was a dead end. I mean, shit, it's been two years, maybe? Maybe eighteen months? Whatever, anyway, I went on the dark web to find a group to help you. There *has* to be a group of people like you. There has to be and, if they wanted or needed to be underground, that's the place they would go. I had help from that shady friend." Serah's eyes widened at the mention of the dark web, and nodded. *Of course shady friend.* But she stayed silent.

"I didn't want to tell you to get your hopes up. There's a dark web Facebook of all things—Facebook! Can you believe it?" Ben tried to chuckle; Serah shook her head. He continued talking fast, "Anyway, so I found a group called the Seekers, which has to be it, don't you think?" Before she could answer Ben rushed on, "But they haven't let me in yet, my request to join has been pending for so long, I stopped popping into the dark web to check months ago."

"You just pop into the dark web?" Serah asked.

"Ahhh, yeah, yep. Anyway, did you read it?! It has to be them." On the small card Serah held in her hand, they could see the following:

If you are reading this, text the number 33333333, and we will verify you.
~ S.O.T.T

"I don't know what S.O.T.T. means. Just another code? I'm so tired of hidden messages. Find the eight, search for the eight," Ben muttered and sighed.

"Seekers of the Truth," Serah whispered.

"What?"

"Seekers of the Truth, Ben. It's them." She looked up to meet his eyes; hazel eyes met brown.

Ben fumbled as he yanked his phone out of his pocket. "Here goes nothing." Typing in the number in the phone number field, he paused. "What do you think I should say?"

"We are here," Serah offered.

"Good idea. Keep it cryptic too."

"Wait, maybe add, 'We got the note.'"

"Okay, okay." He typed it out and showed the text to her. "Good?" Serah nodded, and Ben hit send. They waited; both of their heads hovered over the phone. Nothing.

Ben expelled his held breath. "Gah! Answer us, you jerks!" he yelled, clutching the phone up to his mouth.

"It's okay, Ben. We knew it was a long shot. Let's go. I'm ready to go."

Ben looked down at his friend who looked smaller than usual today. He nodded and linked his arm with hers. They looked around; all the arrangements were gone except for one, a small bouquet of dried flowers. It was actually one of Serah's favorites. She loved the idea of beautiful evidence lasting a long time after the day faded into jumbled memories. Arm in arm they walked toward the exit. Serah grabbed the faded flowers in a quick gesture on their way out, the double doors glowing with the light of the afternoon sun.

Ben's pocket buzzed once, twice, three times in rapid succession, but he didn't notice. He continued out the door into the sun-dappled lot, breathing a sigh of relief for his friend; he was ready for her to be done with grief. They both paused as they stepped from shade to sun soaking up the warm rays after the chill of the building. It was time to try and enjoy this pretty day.

Chapter 19

Halloween

Serah was restless. Pacing, she watched the light fade from day to night. Dusk used to be one of her favorite times of day, before the Demons. Tonight was Halloween. The real demons mingled with the fake demons on this powerful night, and Serah hated it even more. Difficult, even with all of her experiences now, to know what was real and what was not, what to fight and what to pat on the head and give a piece of candy. She sighed and looked over at Diego. He hated Halloween, too, barking his head off at every noise on the street, every quiet knock on the door. It was definitely their least favorite holiday and now more so since Demon Time. Serah felt her life was measured BD and AD—Before Demons and After Demons.

Standing in one of her favorite spots in the house, she could see the approaching gloom as the light began to dim in her sunny kitchen. Serah weighed her choices. Option one: Sit in her pj's, watch the football game, and give out candy to all the cute kids who stroll by with their moms, dads, *families.* She said that last word in her head like a curse, jealous of the ignorant, happy families. *Didn't they know how dangerous this night was out there?* Option two: Get dressed, find a bar, have a beer, and be with other people who are also avoiding the holiday. Serah dropped her dish in the sink, from where she was standing and eating, and made her decision: *Bar. Definitely. Becoming a demon warrior princess makes me bold,* she thought with a laugh, surprised at herself and her decision, normally one for staying in.

"Okay, let's take stock. You look cute and people go to bars by themselves all the time." She talked out loud to Diego who thumped his tail in response. It was a lackluster pep talk, but she persevered and headed out to a local sports bar not far from her house.

Finding her spot for the night, Serah walked down the length of the bar slowly passing each stool. Baseball on that TV, baseball on this TV, the walk was almost a lesson in humility. All eyes were pinned on her: skinny jeans, black boots to her calf, a sweater that skimmed, and a black vest completed the look. She looked sharp, almost European, not from around here the other patrons would guess.

At the end of the bar was another flat screen. Serah squinted seeing a commercial, then fans cheering. *Bingo, here we go.* The football game, playing on the TV in a little corner of the bar with no one else around. It was almost perfect; twenty feet from a rear exit to where her truck was parked, good for a quick and stealthy exit when being alone at a bar proved to be too much. With this back up plan ready, she felt better. Signaling the bartender, Serah got her beer and settled in, noticing how she felt oddly at home in places like this.

"You watching the game?" a guy asked as he sat down on a stool at the corner of the bar.

"I'm watching the Steelers game," she clarified and glanced his way. A quick look, taking in a mohawk and dirty hands, was enough. Her attention returned to the TV.

"Yeah, I'm sorta a Giants fan, but I'm really a Niners fan! Man, they aren't doing so well this year though."

"Niners fan! Of course, you are. And you want me to talk to you? Niners." Serah scoffed and decided to play.

"Hey now, I know they are shit this year. That's why I switched to baseball. I'm a Giants fan!"

She laughed. "Oh, I get the Mohawk now. Does that actually bring good luck?

Mohawk man leaned back on his stool to better see the TV. "Hush!" He laughed and Serah smirked into her beer.

"Oh, come on, Miller! I can't believe you fumbled that!" Serah yelled at the TV. "Shiit." She took a sip of beer at the commercial and noticed he was watching her.

"Wow, a girl who likes beer *and* football?" her new friend commented. She had heard it before. It was nothing new, and it never changed; the only people who were impressed seemed to be those she didn't care about.

Serah laughed. "Yep. That's right."

He seemed to not be able to help looking at her ass. She sighed. *Really?* He grabbed her arm. "You look good, lady." That was all it took.

The Despair Demon lurked in the rear doorway, where an exit sign illuminated overhead. There was light, a lot of it; it wasn't a dark dingy place. But over there, Despair waited anyway. Blue eyes watching, it knew it found a conduit. It was drawn to those who couldn't fight it, and Mr. Dirty hands was perfect. Recent divorce, a DUI that followed him, debt, and loneliness. He was on the edge. Despair grabbed its chance and flew from its coil. Quiet, Despair always is, not strong like Horror or Rage, but stealthy, stealing over you until what you thought you knew was already gone, replaced with emptiness, desperation, and despair.

Serah's teeth clenched at his touch; her head snapped around to look at his hand. His nails tinged with blue. "Damn." Her tricep burned. Hot. Despair tried to take hold. She smiled sweetly at him through the pain. Slowly, hoping she didn't have to hurt him, she set down her beer carefully on the bar.

"My words are powerful, as is my will. You will not destroy me," she whispered with force almost spitting into his face, gripping his fingers, pulling them back one by one.

"Wha—?" He shook his head like a stunned animal and his hand dropped. Sitting back down on his stool, he almost missed the seat, and wiped a hand over his face in a tired gesture.

"I guess I've had one too many tonight. I'm...sorry?" He didn't know what he was sorry for. For being rude, for being a sad person, for being a victim of life. He was sorry for many things, and he would remember them all tonight.

Serah rubbed her arm and watched him carefully for signs. He took a long swallow and drained his beer, setting it back roughly on the bar. She grabbed her bag and slung it over her head, taking a couple sips of beer to steady herself. She had to move. Now. One last thing to try to help him. *Dammit. Dammit, shoulda known better on a night like tonight. Should have stayed home. Safe.*

"I gotta go—thanks for talking to me. My name is Seraphine." She held out her hand knowing what it would take to touch him again.

He stared for a minute, then attempted a grin. "Seraphine. I'm Mark. I come here all the time. I just walk on home, so stop by again soon. We can get a pizza." He shook her hand with a small smile.

"Yep. Sure, Mark. Nice to meet you. Have a good night." Serah swallowed despair and disengaged. Turning away to escape, she strode out the back door. It would come.

Serah couldn't stop. The tears started once she got in her truck. *Safe, safer from eyes, from people who see and ask but don't really care.* She couldn't hold them back. Her face contorted by such despair, it almost screamed agony, but there was no one around to see. She raced home in the dark, all the houses she passed filled with their people, sleeping sound, content. Serah hated them for that, and she was overwhelmed.

She dodged demons right and left, real or imaginary; she wasn't sure anymore. Her phone pinged with a text message, and she yanked it out of her pocket, slowing a little as she drove.

Ben: *Hey! The group—the Seekers—they responded. We are in! They say to be careful tonight. All Hallows Eve makes the demons a little more powerful. Where are you?*

Serah grunted a laugh and carefully texted: *I'm home. Safe. All good.* She pulled on to her tree-lined street and could almost see the brick of her front steps. *Close enough,* she thought.

Pulling in the drive, she grabbed her gear and ran toward the house. Ducking her head, ignoring the two demons perched on her favorite oak tree in the front yard, she heard herself whispering over and over, "My words are powerful, as is my will. You will not destroy me," as if from a long way off. "My words are powerful, as is my will. You will not destroy me. My words are powerful, as is my will. You will not destroy me." Soft, quiet, pursed lips and gritted teeth, she felt herself falling down a long dark well from which there might be no escape.

Serah flung herself inside.

Diego sat on the carpet by the front door. She was struck by how he greeted her, carefully, quietly. He always was very careful when she cried.

"Dogs can smell tears you know," she whispered into Diego's ear. "I read that once." He turned his head toward the sound to rub his face with hers.

"What do they smell like, huh, buddy?" Her eyes welled, and he lifted his head on cue. He stared, a sad but accepting look. She shrugged and smiled a small hurt-filled smile.

"Tears again. I know," she answered his look, and they spilled over, inevitable. With the tears come relief. It didn't always last long, sometimes minutes, sometimes hours. But that relief felt like an ocean of time.

Serah ran over to the shiny framed photo she kept on a bookshelf next to the fireplace. It was a photo of Mom. Smiling Mom, happy, so young. She always stunned people when she told them her age. She looked beautiful. Grabbing the photo in both hands, Serah stared hard. Her tears were silent; the pain burned so bad it made her sick, sick of it all. Finally, a noise escaped. It was despair in one note. A noise to quicken the feet of any late-night dog walker passing the house that happened to hear. It keened; it welled. On her knees, on the carpet, holding that photo, Diego approached. He ducked his head and together they cried. Tears are a relief from the despair. Until the grief creeps back in on soundless feet, like water stealing over the land. Patient and there. Despair Demon, always there.

Serah grabbed her phone and texted Ben: *Dogs can smell tears you know. I read that once.* Ben, for once, had nothing to say.

MARK

Mark stared at his empty glass for almost a full minute. The bartender noticed and walked over; he knew Mark. Mark was a regular, pretty easy going, not one for bar fights, average tipper. Not like the girl. She tipped pretty big. The bartender could always recognize someone else from the service industry by that, but for some reason, with her, he wasn't sure.

"Another?" He nodded his head in the direction of Mark's beer.

"Sure man, game's not over yet." With forced enthusiasm, Mark turned to watch the screen and moved over to Serah's vacated stool. *It is still warm*, he thought. Oddly, it made him feel better. She was pretty and actually talked back to him, joked around. That was rare. He wasn't so good with the ladies, especially not her type. *Kinda out of my league.* He snorted at himself. *League? How 'bout out of my universe.*

The thoughts came as he sipped his beer and pretended to watch the game. He would cheer when he heard everyone else yell, just to be involved, and stayed to watch the Steelers lose. Usually a decently happy, if not content guy, never one to want more than he had, never one to want to really reach for more, tonight was different. Tonight, Mark thought about his wife and his stupid choices, a refrain he often pushed from his mind. His thoughts circled like water in a drain, heading further downward. Mark swirled his glass and looked in, wishing for an answer like a Magic 8 Ball, though his questions weren't that simple. Emotion washed over him as he looked into the muddy liquid, grainy almost, not clear. Despair.

He threw a couple bucks down on the bar and nodded at the bartender as he pushed himself up from the stool. Exiting where Serah did, out the back door, he turned a quick left and headed down the alleyway home. He felt wounded, walking with his hands deep in his pockets. He felt his body ache. *No, not my body. My soul.*

"Where did I get that thought from?" he asked the quiet October night, but there was no one to hear, no one to answer.

A few rights and lefts, Mark zig-zagged down the back sides of dimly lit houses to get home. His blue-eyed companion, Despair, quietly followed, drinking in the emotions that poured from him. Mark's house was dark. *I should get a dog*, he thought. But there was no energy to muster up the feeling of what that would be like.

His mom always told him he was a failure. He failed at football. He failed at marriage. Thank God, he never had a kid; he would probably fail at that too. He failed at being an adult. Though not usually a heavy drinker, the whiskey bottle called. It was old, but he didn't care—dusty too. A small glass set out on his Formica counter did the job. He stood and thought, and stood and thought, and drank.

What is the point? Of anything? Not usually one to question things, he was not surprised these thoughts came. It seemed they had always been there.

I will always be alone. He swirled the liquid; it had no answers either. Only Nothingness. Despair. He wandered over and found himself standing in his bedroom at the spot where he hung up his work belt. He felt giddy at the thought of what he could do with his trademark tools. What painful things they could inflict on humans. On himself. Pepper spray. Taser. Handgun. Despair welled and felt like a fist in his gut. He was not a crier, so there was no release. There was only torment. Trapped with the weight of it, he felt his eyes burn. He grabbed his pistol. He's never had to use it in the line of duty. He's never had to kill anyone—never had to stare in the eyes of another human being and actually pull the trigger.

Maybe I should. His fingers slowly wrapped around the butt of the gun and pulled it out of the holster as if in slow motion, as if every action took such a toll on his energy. He could not do any more. The blue-eyed friend pooled on the floor at his feet and stared, drinking the air. It was almost full, but it knew what was coming and it was glad. Despair wouldn't have to feed again for a long, long time.

"I shoulda got a dog," Mark whispered in a voice that he didn't recognize as his. There was no one around to hear to know the difference. He closed his eyes and the images flash by. His mother's scorn, his mother's gaunt face, his wife, ex-wife (who believes she never loved him), the dead four-year-old tied to a chair left in the garage, the small body found behind the school, the burnt face of a drug addict who lit himself on fire. The images flashed, and he was overcome.

He looked down the barrel of his pistol. It's a long dark tunnel, just where he knows he will go, down a long and dark path with nothing but pain at the end.

"End this. Please," something whispered in his head.

He looked down the barrel, and he thought of her suddenly. *Seraphine.* Her eyes looked back from the barrel of his gun, and he thought of her lips. They were a beautiful shape. He thinks, maybe she will be there next week, and it gives him the tiniest flicker of hope.

"Seraphine," he whispered down the barrel of his gun. Despair froze at her name, froze and tasted hope. Hope is cold, so cold. Despair cannot bear it. But Despair has its own hope too. It knew what was coming, and so Despair waited still.

"Seraphine," he said it again. Despair flinched. Curious, bringing the gun with him, Mark walked to his computer. Clicking on the dictionary, he typed it in. He stared at the answer.

"An angel of the highest rank of nine orders of angels," he mumbled and set the gun down on the desk next to him. Despair howled a silent howl of agony and moved away on each word.

"An angel of the highest rank of nine orders of angels," Mark repeated louder.

"An angel of the highest rank of nine orders of angels!" louder still.

"A freakin' angel," Mark whispered and then he smiled. Despair fled into the night to be with those of its kind. It was over.

Chapter 20

November morning started with a beautiful face as Serah arrived at the coffee house for the union meeting. The same arguments were debated over and over, especially preparing for contract negotiation time: more pay, less hours, better benefits, more retirement. It never changed nor did management's ability to keep them at bay. They all needed their jobs. There was no way she, nor anyone else, could walk out or quit or take any other drastic measure that might have her boss Al, and ultimately the club's board, sit up and take notice.

Serah could find nothing to say. *I have to get up. I have to leave.* She eased from her chair and quickly walked to the bathroom. On the click of the lock, relief washed over her, and with it the tears. The Despair Demon she encountered a few evenings before was particularly powerful.

"Goddammit," she whispered to her reflection in the mirror. She looked and the face that looked back, eyes full of water and face full of pain, was almost more than she could handle. She gripped her hand over her mouth to muffle the sobs. She couldn't let anyone hear or see her loss of composure. Thoughts calmly stalked through her mind: *I'm going to be alone forever.* They reverberated around the empty canyons in her soul.

"Goddammit," she whispered again. Even knowing it was due to the recent demon encounter, these moments never got easier to take—they just seemed to get harder.

Turning on the water, she knew she only had a couple minutes. A couple minutes of this release and a minute to hide the evidence. Choking it back, she kept it down, working hard to keep the demon curse under control. She knew if despair got rolling, it would spew out of her like an unstoppable train. She had work to do and no patience for questions.

Splashes of water and more tears came, her breath short. She searched her bag for her de-puff eye cream. It was worth a shot. It worked magic in the early morning after too few hours of sleep, but tears of pain and despair—demon tears—were a different level. One dollop rubbed in with tears, a panacea for the eyes. She took stock; okay, another dollop. The tears slowed. They were swallowed down for another day, another time. Five minutes gone. Time to go and face it, face the life she had.

Good. I'm glad bad things happen to me. I deserve it. I deserve to never be happy EVER. Pain, always pain. Alone is good, alone is better, alone is necessary. The demonic thoughts of despair echoed as she turned to open the bathroom door. Her eyes closed as she fought. Needing one more minute, she started to turn back to the sink.

"Serah?" Heidi, the flyers club receptionist, quietly knocked. "Just wanted to make sure you were okay."

Serah cleared her throat to disguise the thickness. "Yep, just one minute," she brightly responded. Looking in the mirror, she practiced a smile. *Not bad.* She nodded at her reflection.

Serah tried to remember what it felt like to be happy. When was she last happy? A month? A year? *There's no way it has been that long. My stupid memory.* She forced her brain to dredge up the happy memories to remind herself that they existed. Her fading memory seemed to be a protection against the fallout from the demons but was troubling still.

Happy, happy, happy, she thought as she scanned her brain for any evidence. Diego and Rubi snuggling in on a rainy day. A smooth flight on a cloudless sunny day. Thanksgiving with friends. Small moments, real and genuine. Then she remembered, Sam. *It always comes back to Sam.* She sighed. The memory felt so right. A minute passed. Five minutes? And that was all.

"The universe," she would joke with Ben, "The universe is a bitch, but sometimes she is very, very kind." Serah looked down at her iPhone. The time registered. She had been in the bathroom for twenty minutes. Definitely time to go. Despair had eased. For the moment.

"Serah, what do you think? Should we ask Al what it would take for a $1/hr raise? Maybe we can charge more for the intro flights? He can send it up the chain, maybe?" another instructor asked as she walked back to the table.

"I think we should figure out how to make the raise most palatable for the big boss, send it up the chain ourselves, and spare Al the headache. We can always include him on the email."

"Sounds good to me, let's brainstorm."

"Sure, let's." Serah walked up to grab a refill on her tea.

Ninety minutes later, she walked out to her truck to enjoy the day. *Gym or run, walk Diego.* Her mind rolled through the important things to do today. *Survive.*

Mark drove casually through the quiet neighborhood in his unmarked car. He had been thinking of her pretty much nonstop since that night at the bar. He believed she had saved his life. Nodding along to the quiet music on the car radio, he rolled his window down to breathe the fresh evening air.

Seraphine, Seraphine, Seraphine. His mind repeated her name over and over. With each repetition, his will and his faith that everything was going to be okay grew stronger and stronger. He had casually asked the bartender if he knew her; if he'd seen her before.

"Who? The looker from the other night who looked like a spy?" The bartender laughed and shook his head. "Nope she was a new one. Not from around here, I bet," he added.

But she was, I can feel it. Mark knew, after fifteen years in law enforcement, to trust his gut. He didn't bother to disagree at the time, just sat on his regular stool and ordered his usual beer and watched the game, as usual.

I gotta get a new hobby. Mark sighed and stopped to let the couple out for a late-night stroll cross the street. A little bored, though that was just the way he liked his shifts to be, a little boring and a lot safe. He remembered a documentary he saw and replayed it over in his mind to pass the time. A bit of a history buff, an amateur historian he liked to say, Mark loved learning random historical facts. His most recent fact acquisition was about the train riding hobos of the 1930s and '40s. They used to mark houses with certain signs, a code for the other hobos to follow: Find work here, man with gun here, barking dog here, can sleep in barn, nice lady lives here. He liked that last one: Nice lady lives here. The sign was called the mark of the cat. Mark realized he was fond of believing in signs and symbols and the power they might hold.

The mark of the cat. He mused as he slowly drove down the tree-lined street.

"Report of three kids jumping the airport fence, possible bonfire in progress," his police radio reported the excitement of the night.

"Kids," he huffed and marked himself enroute on his computer.

Might as well cruise by, check it out. Nothing else to do. Mark drove the backway to the airport through the neighborhoods and entered airport property, accessing via the tarmac to park next to one of the private hangers. Driving a long, slow loop down the empty runway and around the office, then back toward the hangers, the night was quiet.

"S98 on scene, no visible fire or smoke. Will check it out on foot," he advised dispatch, as he rolled to a stop and parked. Taking a moment to peer into the dark, he sighed, grabbed his flashlight, and pulled himself out of the car. *I gotta get to the gym or go on a diet, for real this time,* he thought, tugging on his bullet-proof vest that got a little snugger and more uncomfortable every year.

"Copy, S98 on scene," dispatch repeated, as was protocol. Mark made his way around the back of the large hanger, where he would have a bonfire if he was a kid. *I don't blame them. I would hang out here too.* Swirling his flashlight around into the corners and up high onto the ceiling, he could see two small Cessnas parked inside the cavernous airplane garage. All appeared quiet. Exiting out the back door, Mark jumped. "Shit!" Not sure who scared who as he watched a large white tom cat scatter full speed toward the radio tower.

"Get it together, Jones." Laughing a little, he shook his head at his reaction. *The mark of the cat.* Taking a slow tour of the perimeter, nothing else was disturbed except a few moths attempting to bake themselves to death on the exterior security light. He could hear the radio tower hum—low and steady.

"Dispatch, S98, all clear at the airport. No sign of kids or anything else," he said, making his way back to his car and settling in.

"What the...?" he said under his breath, his hand hovering on the key in the ignition. He saw a young woman with a long ponytail run and gracefully jump up onto the low wall that marked the perimeter of this side of the airport. He could see she was breathing hard.

That's her. Mark squinted hard to see further in the dark. He watched her put her hands on her hips and look out to the dark sky beyond.

That's her! Seraphine. A nightly jogger, eh? He decided to wait and watch, feeling a little like a creeper. *I don't want to startle her* was his mental excuse. He pictured sauntering up to her with confidence to ask her a million questions or to simply tell her she saved his life. He wished he had the courage. The prospect of getting shot was easier to stomach than talking to her. Mark grunted a laugh and watched as she appeared to set her watch, turned, and jumped down off the wall picking up speed as she jogged down the airport street.

She must live around here. Does she really run that far? Mark was impressed as he realized the closest neighborhood was easily a few miles away. Without a plan, Mark held his breath and started his car, taking a slow drive out around the tarmac and out of the parking lot; his headlights found her a few blocks ahead.

What are you doing, Jones? He watched her turn left at the next stop sign, entering a quiet neighborhood he rarely had to respond to. Following the bobbing ponytail, he stayed the furthest distance he could, pulling over two more times and turning off his lights a couple of times to act like he was different cars pulling over and parking on the tree-lined streets. Her route weaved right, then left again, then took a long straight shot past the local elementary school. That gave him a more plausible cover. He could be night security cruising the school—his mind came up with all sorts of excuses in case she noticed him. Mark was careful, and she did not. Two more lefts and picking up speed for a final sprint. *Jeez, she has wheels.* Mark saw her come to a stop halfway down the block at a little yellow house with a brick-lined front yard. He watched her stoop over and do something with her shoelace. *Ah, a key,* he realized as he pulled over far down the street, hidden under a large weeping willow that graced a neighbor's yard. He watched as she did a few bouncing stretches at the top of her porch steps, then opening the door he saw a large dog run out and circle her a few times; he could even hear her laugh. It was a lovely sound. Mark closed his eyes and leaned his head back on the headrest. He was grateful he had met her even if just for a moment, grateful there were people in the world like her that existed. Grateful he had a second chance.

He wanted to do something to show his respect, *but what?* Mark waited. Still parked incognito under the graceful branches of the willow, he could see the lights switch on in various rooms of her house, then all went quiet and dark. He waited. He had nowhere to go, nowhere to be, no one who needed him right now. The radio and his small corner of the world was quiet. For now. Starting his car again, he coasted down the street and pulled over two houses down.

Grabbing his knife and his light, he heaved himself out of the car again. This time he felt like it was more important. He took his time; he definitely didn't want to disturb that dog. It was never smart to disturb the dogs—that was always asking for trouble.

At least it wasn't a pit bull. He thought of a few close encounters on the job; they never ended well. Walking around the grassy yard, careful not to step on any leaves, Mark avoided the front steps—too exposed with that large living room window staring right out into the street. No lights of a TV flickering either. *Good.*

He looked around; the neighborhood was quiet. Houses filled with hardworking people who went to bed at a reasonable hour, who rarely had the need for police or anyone of his kind. Easygoing residents who felt safe were less apt to be watching and wary. He made his way to just left of the front door, under the kitchen window, and decided to put it there. Pushing the daylily bush aside a bit and pulling out his knife, he flipped it open and started to carve. Delicately at first and then with more force to break through the many years of paint and just a little bit of the wood. He wanted it to last. Ready with the excuse of investigating a report of a suspicious person in the neighborhood and to show his badge if interrupted, Mark held his breath with each noise and kept working. Ten minutes later, he was done. Stepping back to observe his handiwork, he could hardly see in the dim streetlight that lit the house a few houses away. Not daring to turn on his flashlight, Mark grinned. *The mark of the cat. Now everyone will know. She's important.* He felt a little silly, but also felt lighter and happier than he had in a long time.

He hustled down to the sidewalk, flipping his knife shut, and stowing it back in his vest pocket. Once on the street, he knew he would be fine. He was supposed to be there; his job gave him permission to be out in the dark on the street late at night. No one would question anything now. Easing himself back behind the wheel, starting the car, Mark started to whistle. He knew without a doubt that everything was going to be okay. Rolling down his window a bit to let in the crisp fall air, the whistling filled the car. A tiny bit of the happy sound escaped as he drove down the dark and quiet street.

Chapter 21

Serah sat in the booth and played with her salad. She attempted to spear a cherry tomato but gave up after three tries. Sam looked up as she sighed and set her fork down.

"How's dinner?" He nodded toward her almost untouched bowl of greens.

"It's good. Really good, thanks." She smiled at him. It was a sad imitation of her former smile. God how he loved her smile, but not this one.

It's only been a month, Gunnar, he thought. He looked at her face; she was getting skinnier, he could tell.

"We should get away," he said, surprising himself, almost as much as it surprised her, as the words came out of his mouth.

"Away?"

"Yeah, like far away—Europe or South America. I don't know; somewhere we can get lost and soak up something totally different from here. Something different from the same old bullshit. I think it would do you—us—some good." His voice softened at the end. She looked out the window and chewed on her lip. He knew she was thinking hard about something. He'd pay money, a lot of money, to know; she was so hard to read sometimes.

"I'm not trying to belittle what happened with your mom or tell you to get over it. I just think that it would be good to see different things and feel...I dunno...amazed again at the things that are out there. Feel a different emotion other than sad." He flinched a little bit on the last part. *But it was true dammit,* he told himself.

"I know, Sam." Her soft smile warmed him. She always could acknowledge her humanness. He knew she thought of it as a failure of sorts.

Serah took a breath. "Okay. Where should we go?"

"Anywhere. Anywhere you want. I just want to erase that hollowness in your eyes. If only for a little while."

Serah stared at him. *I love him.* The thought walked quiet but firm through her brain. She stared at his strong face and his strong hands.

I love him, Mom. You sent him to me, didn't you? Somehow. You were taken away, but I was given him in return. A wave of peace and gratitude unlike anything she had ever felt surged through her. She felt as if she fell into an ocean of peace. Everything was going to be okay.

Everything is going to be okay now. The thought choked her on the strength of its emotion—the *relief.* Serah couldn't speak. She tried to will away the tears as he watched her face, waiting. Reaching out her hand, she grabbed his across the table and held tight.

Surprised, he asked, "Whatcha thinking, Sugar?" *Please tell me. Please.* He almost wanted to beg.

Serah paused. "That I can't wait to be somewhere amazing." *With you,* she added in her head. Sam smiled and squeezed her hand, hard. They both turned back to their dinners, discussing Serah's newest disaster of a student at the flyers club and Sam's horribly funny customer encounter at the tree farm. Dinner faded into night. The conversation never stopped until finally the lights dimmed in the empty restaurant. Both looked around and laughed, the last customers. They had done it again. With a wave and a hollered thank you at the few remaining staff, they gathered their things and headed out into the warm Indian summer night.

The next morning, warm memories of Sam still lingering on her face in a soft smile, Serah pulled open the door to her spare room. The last box sat staring at her in the middle of the wood floor. Sitting there quietly, it seemed to take up much more space than it should. Serah took a sip of her coffee and stared back. She could hear the click, click, click of Diego's paws on the floor as he came down the hall, then a nudge and a wet nose in her hand.

"Yep. I know. Gotta do it, buddy," she said as she grabbed his scruff and shook it slightly in greeting.

"Stay with me, will ya?" Serah laughed at the question. He was just a dog. *Shame on you. Just a dog? He's the love of your life,* came the next thought on its heels. Serah acknowledged that with a nod and looked down at her canine. Diego watched her as he always did—big brown eyes that never judged and followed her every move. She sat down on the cold floor next to the unassuming cardboard box. Patting the floor next to her, Diego moved over, circled once, twice, three times, and laid down with a sigh.

"The last box, bud. The last Mom Box." His head in his paws, he looked up at her words.

"Don't look so sad. It'll be okay. I promise." She sliced the tape with a pocket knife and pulled off the lid.

A letter, typed on thin paper. Typewriter typed it looked like. Maybe one of those old inkjet printers. Seraphine unfolded it slowly and started to read. It was from her mother to her sister, Serah's aunt. She hadn't seen her aunt in more than twenty years, maybe more. She'd sent a huge bouquet to the service with a hastily scrawled E on an otherwise blank note—and that was all.

Dear Evelyn,

It's been a few weeks, and I am sorry it's taken me so long to write. Seraphine is growing up so fast, she astonishes me every day. She asked me a question yesterday about cats. She has an affinity for the creatures, as well as dogs, which is a relief to me. She asked, "Mama, what do cats see?" I thought, at first, it was just a random animal question given that she is only five. But when I answered, "They see what we see, Seraphina," she turned those big, beautiful hazel eyes—her daddy's eyes, damn him— to me and said, "Oh. That's good. I'm glad Max sees the blue-eyed monsters too." Needless to say, I almost fell off of my stool. She is five, going on thirty. We must protect her. Send me what you know. She is everything to me, and

I will not have her ruined. Not like us. Not if I can help it. Dammit, this burden is too much for one family to bear.

I am sorry, Evelyn. It has been a long few weeks, and I am not myself. The emotions grow and I cannot seem to diffuse the effects. Are you in Salzburg now? I hope this finds you well.

Be strong, dear sister. Much love,
Natalie

Serah sat and felt the tears drip onto the paper. It started to blur the ink, and she quickly blotted the salty mixture away from the precious text. It was almost too much. She set the letter next to her and sloppily wiped her face. Serah felt a paw and claws push against her foot, gentle but insistent. She turned to see Diego watching her intently. It always upset him to see her cry. She smiled through her tears and grabbed his paw in a loving squeeze.

Thank God for Diego. She leaned down to kiss his nose.

"Well, bud, that was a good one. I *knew*. Who knew I knew?" Serah reached into the box again, hoping for another clue, as Rubi sauntered in on silent feet. Refusing the floor as any smart cat would do, Rubi jumped up onto the oversized love seat that could turn into a twin bed for guests—guests that never came—circled once and laid down to watch.

A few hours passed and Serah's legs grew tired on the cold hard floor. She poured over each item. There were many more letters, but most of them filled with benign, everyday stories told to distant family. At least that's what anyone would see if they read them. Serah couldn't decipher much of anything else. Some to her father, some to her aunt. It was maddening, except for the fact she could literally feel her mother's love contained in those words. Love in a lock of hair in a small envelope labeled "first haircut," in her soccer team photos, and in drawing after drawing of whatever she had scribbled out prekindergarten age; everything was carefully tucked away to save. It appeared to stop after she turned six.

"A piece of my freakin' hair, D!" Serah turned and laughed to her companion who wagged his tail in agreement of the loveliness of the gesture. Rubi just yawned, pretending boredom, however always on guard watching and protecting her human. Serah leaned back against the wall, weary. She pushed her hand through Diego's thick fur. Crossing her stiff legs, she pushed up off the floor with one hand to stand, finished. She leaned over, grabbed the box, and stood up aching.

"Man, I feel old!" She laughed a little at that and rubbed her lower back. A small piece of paper fluttered down to the floor, and she reached down with a groan and crackling knees to pick it up.

It was old and faded. Delighted, Seraphine realized it was a telegram.

I don't think I've ever seen one of these in real life before, she thought as she examined the date. October 6th? 1933. It was from her grandmother Eliza to a name she didn't recognize.

In Salzburg. It's here. Come as soon as you can.

Salzburg? What is UP with Salzburg? Serah held the note in her hand and stared out the window of the empty room. Turning the thin paper over in her hand, she saw a childlike design sketched on the back in what looked like pencil. It looked decidedly like a cat, albeit simple stick version of a cat. *Hmm, interesting. Did I draw this as a kid?* Serah wondered, laughing as she realized some kid, maybe her, decided to destroy a piece of history with their terrible art.

"Look, Rubi, a cat!" Serah held the paper up to show Rubi, who trilled and purred, then jumped down from the couch to rub her face over and over on Serah's leg. An old memory of Ben talking about salt mines in Salzburg years ago came to mind; she wondered why they didn't investigate that further at the time. *Too many questions. Not enough help.* Diego trotted over and pushed his head under her hand.

"I gotta go to Salzburg, D." She gave his head a quick pat and turned to grab her phone. Her fingers typed fast.

Hey. handsome Sam. What do you think of Austria?

Sounds perfect! When do we leave?

Soon.

Dinner? Tonight? We'll plan.

Excellent. xoxoxo See you soon.

Her heart beating fast, she set her phone down. *Research, prepare, plan,* she heard Ben's voice in her head. Thinking of Ben, she realized she should probably bring him in the loop. He had been growing distant lately since her relationship started with Sam. Maybe he was just giving her space. Maybe just busy with law school. Serah shrugged to herself as she grabbed her phone to text him.

Found some letters my mom wrote. Salzburg seems to be the place to go next to get some answers. Thoughts? Serah grabbed an apple while she waited and walked over to fire up her computer. Finally, her phone buzzed.

Ben: *Serah, I don't think you should go. Not until you tell him. He needs to be prepared. You need to tell him.*

"Ugggh, Ben! Why?? I just want to feel a little normal." Serah voiced out her frustration in her text as she typed.

Ben: *You know why.*

Serah: *I don't care.* Serah paused.

She added another text: *I love him, Ben. I really do.*

Ben: *Get some answers, Seraphine.*

Serah smiled.

Ben groaned and set his phone down on the kitchen table where he was studying; Lily and Levi both looked up.

"What's up?" Levi asked.

"Everything okay?" said Lily.

"Yep. Sorry guys, just texting Serah. She...ahh...she wants to travel with Sam, but I don't think it's a good idea." Lily and Levi shared a quick private glance.

"How come? He's dreamy." All three friends laughed when Ben countered, "Lily you think everyone is dreamy."

"True. I can't wait to get out of law school and actually have time to date again."

"By then you will be a hot-shot lawyer and have even less time. You will probably have to freeze your eggs." Levi added with a fake serious nod.

"Levi! Shut your mouth! These eggs will go down in history!" The three laughed again.

"Hey, where are those Cliff's Notes that you are using?" Levi asked Ben.

"I think they are on my desk. Let me get them," Ben said. *Thank you, Levi!* Ben thought as he hustled around the corner where his computer and desk sat in a little alcove near the bedroom. Ben logged in and quickly opened TOR. He rustled some papers to make it sound like he was looking for the notes, but he could see them sitting neatly on top of his desk. Navigating to dark web FB, he messaged the admin of the Seekers group: *My demon hunter is going to Salzburg. She will be alone. Need help. Backup? Something.*

The reply came immediately: *We have one stationed there. They will find her. We believe Austria is place of demon origin, many things to learn. Share intel.*

Ben replied: *Will do, thank you.* Ben quickly shut down his computer. Returning back into the kitchen, he tossed the notes down on the table and joined his friends, focused on studying tax law for an upcoming exam.

Time to get some answers, indeed, Ben thought as he opened his notebook. The three continued to study late into the night.

Chapter 22

Power as one can come undone.
Power as two will see it through.

~ Book Seekers of the Truth

Sam and Serah stood on a bridge, making faces into the camera, on their way to the city library. It was a chilly night in Salzburg—fall was here. The chill was much welcomed after a long, hot summer at home. Salzburg was an old city; the library itself was six hundred years old.

Serah walked through the massive ornate doors—quiet and respectful—and Sam trailed behind. She wished these walls could talk.

The things they would say, she thought. *The books—whose hands had held them? Were they old or young, were they educated, what did they believe? What magical moments did those people have with their books?* She wandered through the museum and looked at the glass cases of leather bound, silver-tooled and jeweled books, huge and heavy by modern standards.

"A time when books were respected. These have to be priceless." Serah pointed at the large leather tomes. Sam nodded; there wasn't anything to say. Times had changed, for the better, for the worse. They wandered through the quiet, cold library for a few hours, finding discoveries at every turn. Serah felt like she was in a labyrinth that held the answers deep within its center tomb. She wandered and wondered and remembered the last conversation with Ben before she left.

"*Ben, Salzburg is the place to go to find others like me, more answers on what is happening and why. I am sure of it,*" she told Ben excitedly.

Ben had more to say. "*I know, Serah, this is big. I agree with you, okay? But I found something in my research. In 696, all is hunky dory. The duke is giving gifts of salt and brine—St. Peter's Abbey is built. Exactly five hundred years later, it all goes to hell. The archbishop has the town and saltworks burnt down, Serah. They try again for a bit and then, oh one hundred years after that, the archbishop—hopefully not the same guy or he'd be crazy old—has his soldiers 'lay waste to the town' again. Lay waste. Not shut down, not move people along, but lay waste.*" Ben paused and Serah stayed silent. They both knew what that meant.

Serah sighed and gave in. "*I hear you, Ben, I do. Those demon monsters had something to do with it. But I've never seen more than one or two at a time. They seem to be selective, lone hunters.*" Serah's excuses petered out. She didn't have much more to say.

"*Yeah, but that's here at home. If you go to where we think they were made, where they were born? What made them? It's like you are walking into the hive where the queen is waiting. I just don't like it. I don't.*"

"*Ben, you have watched one too many horror movies.*" Serah's attempt to get her friend to laugh was rewarded by a thin chuckle from the other end of the phone.

"*Plus, Sam will be there, so I'll have back up.*" Serah could hear Ben's eyes roll at that.

"*Sam will cry like a baby when he sees one, that'd be my bet. Just watch your six, Macguire,*" Ben said. Her friend's fondness for quoting movies made Serah smile.

"*I will. I promise.*"

Sam took her hand, and she smiled up at him, shaking out of the memory. He looked at her with that serious face of his.

So much was serious, and then not. He was such a surprise, she thought.

We travel so well together. She is such a surprise, he thought.

"Time for dinner?" she asked with a smile. He was always hungry. She could linger for hours here, but she would rather be with him. *Don't get lost in lovey dovey land, Serah, this is serious. You must stay focused.* Serah shook her head, slightly ignoring Ben's voice in her head. Silent, the two walked hand in hand, slowly emerging from the library's museum full of old papers surrounded by brick and stone.

Someone built this, many someones. She could feel the salt of their sweat and tears, the emotion in every brick. It spoke to her. *There was love here too.* She felt safe, protected, a feeling that was a little bit like what Sam gave her most days.

"These walls are wise," she said and startled herself that she said it out loud. Sam looked over and nodded. "I wonder what makes some buildings feel that way and others not," Serah continued, a little afraid he would think her weird for these thoughts.

"It's the people," he said simply. "The people who live or work in them, most of the time, I think."

"Yeah, I think so too." Serah didn't elaborate as they walked through the heavy doors out into the city. The night was cold. They were the only ones crossing the bridge. Serah knew it didn't bode well for dinner options. They always ended up eating so late. She sighed; hopefully it wasn't another protein bar night. Stopping in a gloomy spot on the bridge, she made Sam pose in front of the beautiful city lights. Serah took a few pictures of him and laughed at the image.

"That's why no one talks to you at the gym!" The reason that she had come to this ancient city was forgotten; it slipped away like demons in the night.

"What? What'd I do? Do I look that bad?" He sounded genuinely chagrined.

"Noooo, not that bad, handsome man. But you have that serious *hard* look. Kinda how you look to strangers I bet."

"Wait. Stand over there. Let's take a picture of us with the night view. Think you can hold it steady?" Serah asked. Sam just looked at her and grabbed the camera.

"No faith," he joked. He snuggled her close and held her phone out and up. They laughed together as they tried to see both the view and their faces in the photo.

Once snapped, Sam clicked open the photos. "Let's see how good I did!" The image popped up onto the screen. Serah grabbed at it with a gloved hand.

"No. Please," she whispered.

"What?" Sam asked. "That bad? I don't think it's that bad. Jeez."

Serah could see the blue eyes over the top of Sam's shoulder, frozen in the image. The museum smelled salty, no wonder. It had followed them out. Followed *her*. She closed her eyes.

Ben's warning echoed, *"Serah, I don't think you should go. Not until you tell him. He needs to be prepared. You need to tell him."*

"Shit!"

"Ah, that's my girl. Curses like a trucker, but I still don't think it's that bad. Let's take another." Sam didn't see, he couldn't.

The demon behind them hissed. They were getting bolder. *Maybe it's just the European demons,* she thought and choked back a laugh that sounded more hysterical than sane. It blinked its eyes slowly. One. Two. She hated how they blinked, hated it to the core of her soul. So much, she wanted to rip its eyes out but didn't know how. She wished so hard; her body tensed. It sat on the railing, waiting. She wasn't going to let this happen. *Not tonight.* And they weren't going to get to Sam, not while she had a breath to speak her words and energy to lift her hands.

Serah's lip curled back, and she heard herself start to hiss, almost unwilling; it seemed to be torn from her.

Well, this is new. Damn, I wish Ben was here. He was her guide through these dark times. A light when she needed it most.

"Serah? What the hell…"

Consumed, Serah turned away from Sam and toward the demon. She stepped slightly to the side—her hands clawed—and then took a step forward. Almost ready to come up with an excuse to tell him, Serah didn't need to say a word, even if she could.

Sam fell quiet as a second demon, Failure, drifted up. All was forgotten, except the anguish. He was brought to his knees, his hand over his chest, clutched over his heart.

Serah glanced over and the demon was upon her. They grappled. She stared into blue eyes and felt hot, salty breath two inches from her face.

"Son of a bitch!" It was Loneliness. She was weak against it. Weaker. It tore down her walls. It made her shake. It made her curse her weakness. But there was no rage. There was no terror. It was emptiness that consumed.

Sam couldn't catch his breath. He saw. He saw things, things locked away, locked away for years. He begged for his heart. He begged for something to tell himself that he was good and worth it. *Worth what? Worth nothing.* He knew it. He knew it all along. He struggled to his feet, one hand reaching out, one hand still on his chest. Trying to hold onto his beating heart. He remembers *her* hand there on his chest, and it is good. It washes over him, yet it is not enough. Failure beats him back, blue eyes deepening in color as it fed. He couldn't really see, not like her, but he felt It. He saw enough. Sam staggered back and hit a wall. He slumped against it. It felt solid, real.

What is real here? he thought. He knew something was happening, something so wrong he couldn't make it right. Maybe before. Not now. Not. Now.

"My words are powerful, and so is my will. I am strong. You cannot defeat me. I am not alone. I am not alone. I am here, on this bridge, and I fight for those who cannot. My words are powerful, and so is my will." The words came out strong, yet she felt weak. Serah grunted at the force of the onslaught. She turned. She needed to help Sam. Without him, she was forever lost. He was her compass in more ways than she'd like to admit. *Dammit. Dammit. Dammit.*

"Sam! Sam!" Serah screamed. Loneliness had her by the throat, curled up like a snake around her neck. She felt it choking the will, the power out of her. She couldn't see past those blue eyes. Past the feeling that she was all alone.

Sitting, alone, watching Death herself walk up. There was nothing Serah could do. She was too afraid. She was alone.

Serah shut her eyes tight. The images played against her lids, scenes of agonizing loneliness. Loneliness showed her the vision: Serah's eyes popped open. She watched herself run screaming to the bridge railing only to toss herself over.

"NO." Serah grabbed her face, put one hand over her eyes, held the other out. The talismans to work their power. The agony of decision. She had to let go of Sam's hand to use both of hers.

Survive, she thought. *Just survive.*

"My word is powerful, as is my will. I am not alone. You will not defeat me. I am strong against your poison. My word is powerful, as is my will. I am not alone," Serah repeated. It was held at bay, but only just. It seemed equal—a draw—between her and It.

Ask for help, Seraphine. Just ask. Ben's words whispered across her brain.

"Who?! Who is out there to help ME?!" She spat in pity and frustration in Loneliness's face. It laughed and moved closer. Serah closed her eyes, reached around with one hand and felt for Sam. He was still there but barely standing.

He is strong, she thought. *He must be strong.*

She focused on Loneliness. "I exist and YOU do NOT!" It recoiled against the truth. She seized her moment, whipped her head around to whisper over Sam's shoulder.

"You are not alone. I am here. And you are strong. I need you. Sam, help me. You must fight." Her heart bled. Her moment was gone. Loneliness and Failure were done and ready to finish this fight.

Sam heard her as if echoing thru a tunnel. Her voice warmed him and made him happy. He had forgotten. He leaned back against the wall to stand. He felt wounded.

"I am strong," he repeated to himself in a whisper. The pain ebbed. Just a bit. Just enough. He felt it happen.

"I am strong. She needs me. I will not fail her." Loneliness and Failure backed up. Sam could breathe.

"Sam, repeat after me! 'I will not fail. I do not fail. That is my decision. I am strong.' Do it!"

"I will not fail. I do not fail. That is my decision. I am strong. This is what I say. This is my decision." He was able to stand up and open his eyes. He swallowed around the salt that choked. The demons blinked, surprised.

Sam's grandmother had told him stories—stories of some brand of ghost that took children's souls, stories of weakness. They went after the weak and the bad.

"Bad children, my love, and sometimes bad adults," she would whisper and tell him stories of men being carried off on silent hands, screaming into the night, begging for their lives. Stories of blue eyes blinking in the window, crosses hung, and prayers said in hopes they would ward them off. Stories of beings that were there, and not there, drawn in by the emotions of others.

"The devil works in mysterious ways, Sam, my beautiful boy," she said. "Best to be aware of those ways." He pictured his grandmother in her backyard raking leaves, gathering them up to burn. She would always put him to work, but she worked harder by far. She was strong. He could see her hair—almost all white, a little curly—and large, strong hands that could do a thousand things: plant, weed, bake, clean, touch a forehead to calm a fever.

"Sam." He could hear her laugh. "Sam, you are ten years old now, and I know none of this even matters. But someday, someday, Sammy boy, you are gonna see the devil standin' and smilin' at ya. Right AT you. So, you best be ready to smile back." She looked almost through him as if he wasn't there. He remembered.

"Smile back. I will Nan. Just for you." He respected his grandmother, but sometimes he just didn't understand her stories. She died a couple years later and his parents didn't think he should be at the funeral. He regretted that, even at that age. He regretted not being able to say goodbye.

All of this flashed through Sam's mind like a lightning bolt. He almost laughed. *Son of a bitch. Nan was right.*

"When the devil smiles at ya…smile back. You bastard." He smiled, and Failure turned and fled on his laughter.

Sam took a deep breath and coughed out the salty air. He realized the wall he was standing against was actually Serah's small back. She didn't leave. She hadn't left. He reached around and grabbed her hand. It was small and frozen. He almost couldn't force it around his. He couldn't turn to help her, but he would be her wall to lean on. By God, he would.

Serah could feel a change in the air. It was…less, somehow. The wind blew and, on the breeze, she tasted hope. She felt Sam grab her hand, and the hope surged through her.

"I *knew* it. I knew he was strong." She could taste her tears and they tasted good. They tasted of love. Loneliness hissed, which turned into a yowl as the tears slid down Serah's cheeks to land on It, sizzling and burning like acid. It didn't like it, didn't like it at all. Loneliness choked on her new emotion. It couldn't eat THIS. The tears burned their way through and, on that final note,

Loneliness was gone.

Relief flooded Serah, she sank to her knees, and Sam went with her. She took a moment with her face in her hands. Turning toward him, she saw he understood—at least some part of it. Victory. He grabbed her face with his hands and kissed her. Hard. They broke apart and laughed together in their success.

"Goddamn, I'm thirsty! I feel like I drank a bucket of saltwater," Sam exclaimed.

Saltwater tastes better, Serah wanted to say. Instead, "Yeah that happens after these…moments."

"Moment…huh. That's what you call it?" Sam smiled at her understatement. He had so many questions. She had so few answers.

"First things first. Let's go get a beer."

"Sounds like a great plan to me."

Serah smiled.

Chapter 23

Will is magic. Will is power.
Seekers must know, in that most sacred hour.

~ Book of the Seekers of the Truth

He grabbed her hand. She loved when he did that. It was a decisive grab that made her feel that was the only thing he wanted to do just then and couldn't help it. He just had to feel her hand in his callused hands that he was self-conscious of at times, but Serah loved them.

They walked silently away from the bridge. She was chilled from sweating during the demon encounter and pulled her hood up over her head to try to stop the shivers.

He could feel her shaking. "Cold?"

"Yeah," she said through clenched teeth, so they didn't chatter. He tugged her close.

He is patient, Serah thought. She would be shouting questions by now, wondering what the hell had just happened. Sam walked as silently as he could over the fallen leaves. Only wearing a T-shirt under his thin jacket, he was almost never cold.

Sam turned over the event in his mind. He hoped Serah couldn't feel *his* shake. It was internal. It was deep. There were memories there that he hadn't thought of in years. He had managed to shut them down. The pain snuck in at times, and it liked to hang out at the bottom of his whiskey glass, but he managed.

They turned past their hotel, too uptight a place for the beer they needed to drink. This thirst needed to be quenched. The salt needed to be washed away. Wandering down to the old town section of the city where they ate dinner the night before, they found the right spot. A restaurant with a loud, young crowd and thoughtful service, beer, and heavy German food for fortification. A tattooed server with dyed black hair pulled into a messy pony tail led them to a booth in the corner. She spoke perfect English.

"Two. Dark beer. Please," Sam ordered in broken German. She smiled patiently and nodded.

She mimed as she spoke in English, "Large or small?" with almost no accent.

"Large," they both said in unison. Setting menus down in front of them, she whisked away to bring them their relief.

Two long swallows of beer and a few minutes of silence passed.

He's going to think I am crazy, Serah thought and the panic bubbled.

She's going to think I am crazy, he thought and the frustration grew. He could sense that she was upset.

"What are you thinking?" he asked. Seemed like the best place to start.

"Lots of things." She grimaced. It was her usual attempt at avoidance.

"Tell me," he said. As if it was the only thing in the world that mattered.

"Sam."

"Yes?"

"Sam, there are some things you might not understand when I tell you. It might seem unreal. But all I can do is ask that you keep in your mind what you know about me. And I have to admit that I don't have all the answers to what I know are all your questions," Serah started. Sam nodded, patient.

"Do you trust me?" she asked.

That question surprised him. His answer surprised him more. "With my life." It came out of him in a way he hadn't expected.

"Okay then." Serah blushed, but she met his eyes. That was a lot, and she knew what it meant for this man to say that.

"A few years ago, strange things started happening. I lived a quiet life. Really quiet." Serah ducked her head to look at her hands clasped around her stein. She took a sip. It bothered her to tell these things to others, to others she wanted to keep.

"I have these marks on my hand." She uncurled her fingers and held up her palm.

"Yeah, I noticed that. You said it was pilot initiation...," Sam trailed off, as Serah shook her head acknowledging the lie.

"These marks, each appeared one day, months apart from each other. Fully healed. Out of the blue. From what I know, one is a Norse protection symbol and the other a Greek sign of the witch—Hecates wheel." Serah blushed again, still not confident in her witchy status. "But I don't know what it truly means. Only that it seems to help. It seems to help when things like what just happened on the bridge, happen. And they happen to me a lot." Serah paused. Sam waited.

"You know how you have picked me up from bars, and it looks like I've been in a scuffle, maybe even a fist fight? Doesn't that seem odd to you?" She wanted him to think she was this normal, everyday, simple girl. She hated that she wasn't.

"Yeaaaah. It was odd, as you put it. But you know me. It's not boring!" He laughed, trying to make light. Looking at her serious face, his smile faded.

"I am always glad to help you. It's nice to be needed. And it seemed you needed a friend—that you were going through some tough times. It was legit. I mean your job and then your mom..." Serah nodded, acknowledging his logic. At least he didn't think she was crazy. Not yet. Serah took another sip of her beer.

"Serah, you gotta just tell me. It's me. Sam. I can take it." He was right. He could take it, most likely more than anyone she knew.

"I fight demons." There. Done. It was out there. She couldn't take it back. No matter how ill it made her feel. Sam looked at her and swallowed his beer. It went down rough. His blue eyes reminded her of the Demon Despair. Serah blinked. *Stop it. He is Sam. You know him. It's not like with Jeremy before. It won't be. He is strong. He can fight.* Serah's stomach growled.

"Hungry," Serah stated. Just as Sam looked down and asked, "Hungry?" They both smiled.

He hasn't said anything. Why didn't he answer? Serah wanted to scream, her hands clenched and unclenched around the German brew. Patience was not a virtue Ben had managed to instill in her yet, though he tried.

"Well. I'll be honest, Sugar. If you told me that a few months ago, I might have chalked you up to the crazy list." She nodded; she knew his crazy list was long.

"But after what I just went through, if you're crazy, then so am I." Serah laughed and clinked her glass with his.

"Welcome to crazy town, Gunnar. Welcome."

"So, what do I need to know? Are there rules to this game? This fight? Seems I should know if I'm your backup."

She liked how that sounded. God, she had been doing this alone for so long. Trying to figure it out by herself for so long. She had Ben, but no one who had actually been in a fight with her; no one who really *knew* what it was like. The relief was tremendous, and it felt like liquid gold.

"The rules. I'll tell you what I know." Serah took a large gulp of her beer and dove in. "So far, we believe there are eight Demon Rules. One: They smell of salt, are made up of salt somehow, which is the basis of human emotions—tears. We think that's why they are drawn to salt and repelled by salt, in a way, too. Two: They seem to be able to influence people and events, feeding on the emotions that are created by their presence, enhancing them somehow. Three: I have only ever found them alone in a feeding/fighting capacity, but I have seen two 'hanging out together.'" Serah used air quotes, as Sam's eyes went even wider. "Yeah, I don't know what that even means. Four: They seem to have the most power at dawn and dusk. Wait, that's part of number three. Four: There are eight types of demons. Five: Weapons to fight them seem to be mantras and mindset/intuition, branding/runes like mine, connecting with the four elements, love." Serah paused, blushed, and took another large swallow of her beer. Sam watched and waited.

"Six: Dogs and cats seem to be witnesses and protectors. I know both Rubi and Diego have helped me on several occasions with the demons. Seven:

Typically, they have blue eyes, not like normal eyes. The demons don't seem to have an iris. Instead, they have a symbol or shape that possibly corresponds to the particular demon. We've begun to try to keep track of this. I need to work on being able to remember after a demon fight."

"We?" Sam asked when Serah paused to take a breath.

"Me and Ben. He's been like a trainer to me in this weird situation. I wouldn't be here without him," Serah trailed off in a whisper, knowing the demon effects would have overwhelmed her by now if it hadn't been for Ben and his teachings—his constant research and guidance. She shook her head a little at the thought of Ethan.

"Ben seems like an amazing guy," Sam said and drained the rest of his stein and tried to signal the server for another round. "You said eight, that's only seven."

Serah nodded and hesitated to tell him the final rule that she and Ben decided prior to her trip. "We believe they are ancient, that the demons caused the crusades. Not just some religious war, but that there's some sort of balance needed with the demons and humankind, and when it gets tipped, all hell breaks loose...and..." Serah closed her eyes. "We think they might have originated here. In Salzburg." She cracked open one eye to look at his face. Sam looked made of stone.

"Salzburg, you say. Here, in this cute little town in Austria..." Sam gratefully grabbed his fresh beer stein delivered to the table and plunked one down in front of Serah. "Well, Macguire, I give you points for ruthlessness and deception."

Serah gasped a little and grimaced. She rushed in to fill the silence. "Sam, I'm sorry. I should have told you. I know I should have. But honestly, all I wanted was a normal life. To be here, somewhere pretty and far away, with you. I..." Serah paused again. The beer made her brave. "I am falling in love with you, Sam Gunnar. Nope. That's another lie. I AM in love with you. I want you—just you. No one else." Serah stopped and stared at him without looking away. She was tired of hiding it, even if there were stupid demons and his murky past, a past that seemed to follow him even now. Even with all that Serah knew, it was time to be brave. *I am a demon hunter for God's sake.* Sam looked right back at her, and this time she didn't mind big blue eyes blinking in her direction.

Sam cleared his throat. "Someone once told me, if two people stare at each other for more than six seconds they are either going to fight or kiss..."

Serah leaned toward him, smiled, and whispered, "I'm sorry I took you to a potential demon hive."

Sam smiled and whispered, "I'm not." Leaning closer, softly touching his lips on hers, the promise of new love sealed in the sweetest kiss.

They sat in the smoky bar drinking another beer, eating a plate of potatoes with thick slices of meat covered in gravy, and talked. Sam had many insightful questions. Serah had fewer and fewer answers for him. After beer three, the room grew warm and the conversation grew fuzzy. She couldn't stop looking at his lips. She caught herself before she giggled at the thought of those lips and what she wanted those lips to do. *Giggling for God's sake.*

The freulein arrived, and they paid their bill. She wisely had left them alone, only to ask if refills were needed. She could tell the young American girl was well on her way to being drunk.

She scoffed, *American women. Can't hold their beer, embarrassing. But she was a sweet girl, and they were a cute couple.* She softened as she watched them walk out arm in arm. *He looks steady as a rock,* she thought. *That's good at least. Good stock.*

Together, they wandered through the cold cobblestoned streets of Salzburg. Old-fashioned gas lights were lit on each corner, dotting the sidewalks. It was charming to beat charm. There were only a few people out, and it started to snow. Sam tugged at Serah's arm. Serah turned toward him and then noticed a tiny snowflake drift down between their faces.

"Look, it's snowing!" he said, excited as a child. She tilted her head up to look at the sky. Sure enough, she was surrounded by softly falling snow.

"Snow?" she asked, watching the sky.

"Isn't it amazing how quiet it gets when it snows, Sam? Why do you think that is?" She looked back toward him, as three tiny snowflakes fell on her lips.

He was staring at her. "Shhh, Serah, I was going to kiss you...and the snow beat me to it." He laughed. At his words, the shot of adrenaline that sped through her was enough to warm her head to toe.

"Try to kiss me again. Please." She said so earnest that he chuckled and turned her face toward his. It wasn't like the last kiss on the bridge—or the one at dinner. This one took a while. They stopped and kissed every few feet back to the hotel. Wandering the streets, Serah was glad that he knew where he was going, because she had stopped caring.

They passed a bar playing soft music that spilled out from the open door; it looked so warm and bright inside. Sam grabbed her arm and they danced. A bit of a waltz, a bit of a twirl.

Maybe I'm in a movie, Serah couldn't help but think.

They made it: Hotel Sacher, home of the best little chocolate cake in the world, a secret historical recipe. *Perfect after a demon fight*, she thought. They ran inside, holding hands and laughing, past the stern Germanic bellhop, all laced up tight with his blazer and buttons. He quirked a smile at the two so obviously in love.

On the elevator to the fourth floor, Serah stared at the ceiling and glanced at Sam. She noticed he was doing the same.

Oh, my God. Is this really going to happen? Lucky, lucky, Sam has the key, she thought, knowing her hands would shake if she tried the lock.

Hurry, hurry, she tapped a finger on her jeans' leg, her only acknowledgement of impatience. *Keep cool, cooooool.*

The heavy door swung shut, and they were upon each other. They couldn't get enough. Clothes were tossed off. Tight boots and tight jeans, laughter at the silly clothes worn that were oh-so tricky and oh-so-not sexy to take off in a hurry. Serah shimmied out of her jeans after kicking off her boots. She unwound her scarf with Sam's help, and he unzipped her vest to toss aside. The sweater was pulled over her head quickly and tossed over a chair somewhere. Finally, just bra and panties, she stood looking at him. He had managed to yank everything off of himself.

He is delicious. God, those muscles. Finally, they were hers. She walked to him as he watched and ran her hands up his arms; she could feel it gave him chills. She held her face close to his and leaned in for a soft kiss as her hands found one of her favorite spots, those lovely back muscles. They fit perfectly in the palms of her hands as she wrapped her arms around him, fingers stretching toward the valley of his spine. He was strong. She sighed and leaned in. He had her.

If he only knew. Cool, baby girl, cooool. She smiled against his lips and it made him smile too. He opened his eyes, grabbed her waist, and tossed her on the bed as she squealed.

Thank God these walls are thick was the last thought that passed through Serah's mind that she could remember.

Tangled up, sweaty sheets, sweaty delicious Sam. He rolled over and pulled her arm over his side. Wide awake, she scooted to press the length of her body against him. She couldn't help but smile as she tucked in against his upper back.

He was hers. Finally. It was everything she knew it would be. She *knew.* They both fell asleep with the knowledge that neither of them had ever had a night like this before.

Serah woke. She was disoriented in the pitch-black hotel room, the blackout curtains drawn against the large window. Was it day? Or was it night? She didn't know and didn't like it. She realized she had turned away from Sam while she slept and reached to find her phone.

3:47. Ugh. It was night. They'd only gone to bed a few hours ago. Serah smiled remembering. She reached down to try to find her underwear on the floor; it was nowhere in sight.

Serah leaned back with a sigh. *I'll look for them later.* Turning over as her eyes adjusted to the dark, she realized Sam wasn't in bed. The comforter was down at the foot of the bed, but that was no surprise. The sheet was twisted and pulled. She listened; silence. A few sounds from the street below, a car, then nothing.

Serah felt looming panic, and she didn't know why. It was the darkness. It felt suffocating. Cloying. Choking. Not safe. *Bad, bad, bad. An empty bed is not always a safe place to be.* She got up.

She looked under the bed for her underwear, at the foot, and finally found them under the chair about six feet away. Pulling them on, she felt better, just a bit more ready. *Ready for what?* She wandered over to the bathroom and the light was off. It was dark. Turning the light on, she looked in. Nothing.

Finally, she called out, "Sam?" It sounded loud and grating in the quiet room. A bit frantic, she started to look around. All his things were here: She could see his wallet, his phone, his shoes. His luggage laying open on the luggage rack and jeans half out of the hard-sided suitcase. But no Sam.

Then she saw it. Droppings, by the door. Serah ran over and dropped to her knees. By the dim slice of light from the bathroom, she could tell what they were. Dark brown, pebbly, droppings. A demon had been here. She rocked back on her heels, her face in her hands. *Nonononono.*

Dammit! NO! She pushed to her feet, her eyes were wide, looking for something to do, somewhere to go, a plan, a solution. Trapped. She was trapped. She felt like the demon had stolen her dream.

DAMMIT! She almost screamed. *Calm down. calm down. Think think think think. You are smart, Serah. Think.* Serah walked over to the curtains and threw them wide open. They were high up, the city was lit, and the stars were out. It was a gorgeous view.

A gorgeous city. A gorgeous night. Serah looked through the glass. She stared hard. She could see her reflection from the lights staring back. Only wearing her black boy-short underwear, arms crossed, hair messed and wavy, her face stone hard.

Think. The adrenaline slowly wore off, exhaustion and fear found their way in. Her shoulders dropped as she turned from the window and walked as if wounded back to the bed. Curling up in a small ball, she pulled the covers over her, shivering, trying to get warm, trying to think what to do. Serah stared outside at the night and started to cry. Silent tears trickled down over the bridge of her nose and across her face and dripped into the pillow. The demon from the fight on the bridge was right. *She was alone,* she thought. *Always alone.* Serah collapsed into a deep exhausted sleep.

The Viking man loomed over the sleeping girl. He thought, *This was extremely unorthodox, getting involved, again, in this realm,* with a slight shake of his head. Yet he felt compelled. This Chosen One felt important to him. He shook his head again. *It wasn't supposed to be this way. I help protect and watch. That is all.* He knew his loyal companion disagreed. Garm liked to affect events; his intense hatred of the fallen one compelled him. One day, Garm and the fallen would meet again and woe to Nick on that day.

The Viking could see the traces of her tears dried on her cheeks. It made him sad. *Sad?* He looked up and around the dark room as if he was being watched. Hands held to his chest, he had not felt sadness in decades—maybe more. He knew he was treading on dangerous ground. This feeling meant he was breaking the rules. Reaching out, silent and gentle, he grabbed for her wrist; it felt so small and delicate in his hand. He knew without reservation, he had to help her. Maybe this was meant to be; maybe this, his free will to disregard the rules, was all part of the unfolding of The Plan.

With that thought, he expertly directed his powerful energy toward her and cast his spell, marking her with another powerful rune. He saw soft light trace a symbol on her wrist, and he felt her stir. Strength of Will, one of his favorite power symbols from his line.

He whispered lines memorized from The Text—the Seekers of the Truth—as they told it ages ago: *The moment you can do no more. The time when all is lost. You look, the darkness is vast. All Demons loom. This is a sacred time. For those who believe, the most sacred time of all. This sacred time amplifies power beyond known limits. Bend, Seekers, bend. Bend the universe to your will.* He ended with a Seekers' mantra, repeating it three times: *Will is magic. Will is power. Seekers must know, in that most sacred hour.*

The Viking's chest expanded, and power filled the room. With a silent pressure change of air that the nearby hotel guests would only feel the curious need to pop their ears, he vanished once again.

Serah woke a few hours later. Curled in the same position, her face crusty from dried tears. She felt lethargic, like swimming underwater. It was too hard to move. There were no good answers. At least none that came to her while she slept.

First: Shower, get dressed, eat. Second: Pack. Pack up Sam. She didn't know how she was going to manage all the luggage herself. But she would make it happen. She was afraid of what came third. If he didn't show up in the next twenty-four hours, she had to leave. She had to check out and make it to the airport without him. It was time to go home. But how could she leave without him?

It was one of their rules: "Must stick together," she whispered it out loud to the empty room. Serah swung her legs out of bed. First things first: shower. Her phone beeped. She raced to grab it. "Please. Please."

It was Ben. *Good morning, Seraphine. It's late here at home. Hope all is well.* She noticed her wrist and almost dropped the phone on the floor. Holding her arm up in the dim light of the hotel room, she saw her new brand. "What the hell," she whispered under her breath, snapped a quick picture, and returned to the message.

Ben, Serah texted back. *Sam is gone. I don't know what to do. Something is wrong. A demon was here, but it's like Sam…vanished. It's something we've never seen before. I have a third brand now. Woke up with it. Will send the pic. What is happening?? I'm scared. Tell me what to do.* She paced, holding the phone, waiting. One, two, four minutes passed. He would text back. He always did.

Get to the salt mines. Learn what you need to learn and come home. Be safe. I will research. Get home. We will figure it out, came his response. Relief flooded. Yes. He was right.

K. I'm coming. I'll be home soon. She hit send, set the phone on the dresser, and turned for the showers.

Chapter 24

Serah yanked on the white clothes. After donning the required coveralls to protect their clothing and also the historical site, she was herded into the train car with the rest of the group of tourists.

Dammit, I should have done this first, she thought. *But I just wanted to be normal, for just one damn minute. Normal with Sam.* Shaking her head at her mistake, memories from just prior to the trip came flooding back.

Sitting at her desk, sipping tea researching before the trip, she had found it: The White Gold. Numerous mentions of this white gold in all documents regarding Salzburg's history. And the history went back far. Almost to the beginning of our time. Records of settlers in 4000 BC who bathed in the salt springs of the mountain. In 600 BC, the Celts learned how to mine it and then soon came booming trade. Salzburg was built right on top of it. *I'll be damned.* Serah took a sip of her tea. *The white gold was salt.* Salzburg, the city of salt, was where it all started.

Waiting with the other tourists, Serah's fingers lightly traced her new mark, *strength of will.* Ben had done a quick search and sent her the information soon after her shower: *Not surprising the mark is Norse. Historians believe it means Strength of Will. A powerful and sacred rune according to Viking legend, but not the most powerful symbol they have from what I can tell. My translator friend found a few passages that refer to this symbol as 'the sacred time' or 'sacred truth.' Difficult to decipher, he said. Do you feel any different?* Serah had responded with a simple *no* as she sat on the floor in the messy, and empty, hotel room.

"Gather around me, gather around me." The small crowd's chatter grew silent as the guide waved and spoke. The jostling of the train car descending into one of the mining tunnels brought Serah back to where she was and why she was here: she needed some answers. She hoped she was ready for what they might be. She could see behind their guide spread a vast underground lake.

"Behind me is the world famous salt lake of Hallein. We are standing approximately three hundred meters under the Durnberg mountain. Above us is the Celtic village where our Salzburg ancestors mined this precious White Gold." He paused and moved aside to allow a sweet grey-haired couple take pictures. Serah looked at the others in the small group. One family—mom, dad, daughter, and son—looked like a picture themselves. Serah saw the brown-haired boy casually grab a handful of salted sand and sprinkle it onto his older sister's shoulder.

She would not like that, getting her cute pink sweater dirty, Serah mused.

They look so normal, Serah thought, and realized she couldn't remember a single vacation her family had taken. The thought made her ache with the knowledge that maybe she had never been normal after all.

One young man, Serah guessed he was in his twenties, carrying a pricey camera with aviator glasses tucked into his vest, finished off their group.

"Okay, everybody, please follow me onto the float, and we will continue the tour of the salt lake of Hallein." The group shuffled onto the wooden raft; Serah being the last to board. It made her nervous. She saw the float "operator" in one corner, holding the large pole that he used to push off the lake floor and move them at a slow, steady pace. His eyes were heavy-lidded; he was tall and rail thin. Pale too.

Just perfect for the boat ride to Hades. Grrrreeaaat, Serah thought. He seemed oblivious to the crowd but shoved off at a slight hand signal from the tour guide. Serah clenched and unclenched her fists. She tried to use her tools Ben taught. She went deep inside and saw the girl on the lake; she was sitting in the canoe as usual. But this time the girl was shaking her head. She was shaking her head and weeping. Serah's eyes flew open and she almost gasped. Looking up, she saw the float operator staring at her.

"It's alright, Miss. Haven't lost anyone yet," he called out to her in a clipped

Scottish accent.

Serah took a breath. *Act normal.*

"Oh, yeah? Well, thank goodness. How long have you been doing this? Two weeks?" she tossed back.

"Thereabouts."

She could see his eyes crinkle just a bit at the joke. She guessed he was rarely talked to by tourists—more of a piece of furniture or part of the backdrop than a person. She moved closer, carefully.

"I bet you know a lot about these mines," she ventured.

"Oh, yes, I know a bit of a story or two."

"Tell us a story!" The bored brown-eyed boy with thick lashes overheard and was ready for something more exciting. He was hard to resist, and the tour guide fell silent after finishing up the monetary benefits the salt mines brought to the trade system in the area. The group could hear the lapping of the water, the drip of the cave, and the creak of the wood below their feet. The guide waved a lazy hand for the boat operator to continue with a story.

"Well, Hallein village was a small village at the base of the Durnberg mountain and, back in the day, life was hard. It was cut off from most of the surrounding towns by bad weather eight months of the year, but the other four were beautiful beyond measure. With the salt trade a good one, the villagers were content to live here and make do." Serah could tell the crowd agreed with her: It was no hardship to listen to his soft voice and accent.

"However, those beautiful months came with a price, as all things beautiful are wont to do," the boat operator said and winked in Serah's direction. She didn't see, staring hard into the dark water ahead of them.

"For you see, a monster lived in the town with them," he said. "And each month, on the new moon, he visited."

"Cool," said the young boy and the young man in unison—the young man with aviator glasses blushed.

"The villagers could go about their duties and lives during the day, but as soon as that sun started its descent in the sky, they hurried a little faster, spoke a little quieter. They knew they had to be locked in their homes by dark." He had everyone's attention now. Even the guide's, who appeared to have not heard this particular story before.

"Half-man, half-ghoul, the monster would wander the town at night. Peering in windows and staring through glass-paned doors. Big eyes, they would talk about the next day, big blue eyes and devil's breath steaming on the windows. The villagers hid in their beds; some took their children into the cellars and locked them up tight for the night." He paused again and no one spoke.

"The villagers prayed hard. They prayed the talismans on the doors were powerful enough. They prayed they had done enough good deeds. They prayed they would be spared this night, just this one night."

"Talismans? What talismans? What kept them out? Do you know? Is there a record?" Serah's voice carried far over the dark green and milky water. The boatman cocked an eyebrow at her.

"The mark of the cat, my dear. And the mark of the witch."

His milky blue eyes bored into hers from across the barge. Serah folded her arms and stood her ground. Hazel matching blue.

"It was a crude sign, most often burnt into the wood of the front doors. Fire has added power and the intention of the sign maker, the most added power of all."

"Hey, that's cool! Is that part of the tour?" The young boy, Danny, pointed into the dark, toward the cave wall. It was filled with nooks, like a giant pigeon coop built into the side of the earth.

"Are those real? Holy cow!"

Serah squinted to see what his young eyes saw clear; tucked in most of the nooks were skeletons. Skeletons of different sizes, different shapes. Some looked like they had been tied with their arms over their head, still holding that position long after the ropes had turned to dust. Others laying prone on their sides, some holding hands. One looked to be almost tucked in a form of prayer sitting cross legged, head bowed, hands clasped. They were frozen pieces of time. Serah heard the mother gasp a little at the sight.

Then Danny saw something else. "Okay, how'd you do THAT? Hahaha! I thought this place was going to be borrr-ing."

Serah's pinched face looked over on the other side of the barge. The nooks were everywhere; skeletons filled her view. The underground mountain was filled with sadness and despair. She looked down at her arm holding tight across her belly. It was all she could do to hold herself together. She could feel it. She could feel *them*.

"How'd you run electricity down here to power the blue eyes?" Danny's father finally asked, excited like his son. Serah felt sick, but not surprised. She turned to where they were looking. Blink, blink, those big blue eyes blinked at them from an outcropping about ten feet above the water. The nook contained a skeleton protecting another smaller skeleton that looked like a child. The demon huddled and puddled around it. Despair. It was Despair.

When we die, it's still in our BONES, Serah thought. *Like an imprint. It's still there, and they can still feed on it after all this time.* She almost moaned as she clutched her stomach.

Stand UP. This is what you came here for. Be STRONG and get to work. You are the ONLY one who can protect them. It is up to you, Seraphine. YOU. Serah wasn't sure where that voice came from, but it was loud and it was clear—like a drill sergeant in her head. She clenched her fists and took three strides over to the boat man.

"Turn around, we have to go. NOW. You have to get us out of here." Everyone was still staring at the blue eyes. The Demon hadn't moved but was blinking slow, watching their approach.

"Ahh, my dear, you see that's where you are wrong. This is what they came here for." The Scottish accent was no longer sweet, but instead deadly in its charm.

"You brought us here? To be food for them? How *dare* you? There are *children* here!" She almost spit the words, her anger seethed. Seeing movement out of the corner of her eye, she turned. Despair was moving. It unfurled from around the skeletons and, in a graceful movement, tumbled off the edge of the nook. It fizzed into the water and disappeared. The next second, another set of blue eyes appeared out of the milky blackness. Serah knew it in an instant. It was Rage. She knew she had called it somehow. Her intention had been set and now it was on. She closed her eyes and tried…one, more, time.

"Listen, keep me. I have more power than they do. They are just…simple people. You know their depth of emotion at times bores the demons. They need more…spiciness. Right?" Serah guessed and the Scottish barge operator from Hades nodded. "Yeaaa, lass. You are most certainly correct. But it is too late now, you see." His eyes almost looked sad, and then he smiled and nodded his head toward the other side of the barge. Serah looked; the molten form of Rage was curling its way up over the edge of the barge. She blinked. A second pair of vaporous fingers stole their way up and over. Then a third.

"It's too late, it's too late, it's too late," he whispered over and over and over. "Three, a whisper of demons makes three."

"Shut *up*," Seraphine said, taking three long strides and shoving her hand into the last demon's face. It hissed and fell back from the power of the mark.

"Woah, what the heck is THAT?" Serah knew the group couldn't really see the demons. They looked more like a haze of fog than anything to them. The fact they could pick out the blue eyes surprised her, maybe because of the added power of this place? She would have to think about that later. Serah turned her head to avoid the splash from the salty water and looked smack in the face of Fear.

Fear was reaching for the blonde girl. Serah remembered what Ben learned from the new group: *Children were a delicious snack to the demons. Their emotions were more pure but short lived. Like the strongest, purest hit of heroin. It didn't last long, but while it did…my oh my. Adults were more tainted with additional impurities, but their emotions lasted much longer.* Serah saw Fear hesitate at the girl's shoulder and then reach around to her mother. Before Serah could really move, the feeding had begun.

The woman clutched her jacket and her purse, white knuckles. Serah recognized the stance, arm wrapped around her body as if to hold her soul in.

"Dinah? Dinah?" The woman shrieked for her child.

"Right here, Mama." Dinah stepped forward and laid her hand on her mother's arm.

"I'm here, too, Mom," said Danny. The woman's eyes darted back and forth between them both. Serah watched as Fear curled around the mother. She would be no good to them if she became catatonic. Serah noticed Fear avoid the girl's pink sweater. It almost flinched every time it swirled by.

The salty sand, Serah thought. *It had to be it.*

"Danny, grab your sister's sweater and toss it to me."

Serah wanted to move quick. She could see the woman's eyes begin to glaze over; she started to rock a little back and forth. Serah didn't want her to have any lasting damage.

"Honey? Honey?! What's wrong? What's happening to you?" The woman's husband turned to the boat operator. "Sir, please head back. Something is wrong with my wife, please." The boat operator shook his head and smiled. Like the baby demons that emerged only on All Hallows Eve, a small white demon was pooled at his feet like a dog.

"Danny!" Serah said.

Danny jumped. "Yeah, okay, gotcha. Grab my sister's sweater." He shook his head a little; he felt kinda fuzzy. He stumbled, grabbed onto Dinah's sweater, and yanked.

"Hey!" she protested, but it was weak. He grabbed the cuff, pulled it off in a twirling motion and tossed it to Serah.

"You, sonofabitch," the man said as he turned from his wife to focus on the boat driver. Rage. Serah could hear it in his voice. She stalked closer to Fear, molten lava at the mother's almost catatonic feet. The woman had a grip on her daughter's arm; Serah could see Dinah flinch.

"You, sonofabitch," the man spat as his hands turned to claws he aimed at his perceived target.

"You, sonofabitch, take us back. Take us back NOW."

"I wish I could, sir. I really, really do. But it's not going to happen. Not this time," the boat operator answered, unperturbed. The man shook his head back and forth like a bull. Spit flew, eyes fuzzy, Rage had its claws in deep.

"You take us *back*, or I will *kill* you. I will tear you apart with my bare hands. I will tear you apart and laugh as you beg for your life," the man slurred with fury and stepped closer to his victim. Serah lunged for Fear and wrapped it up in the pink sweater. She grappled with its amorphous shape, feeling it ooze around her and touch her skin. She closed her eyes and choked back the dizziness. The onslaught of stomach-turning panic was almost too much. In one quick motion she turned, pivoted, and tossed it overboard where it appeared to dissolve back into its original state. She hoped she had time before it appeared again. Serah turned to watch the man yell something unintelligible and lunge at the Scot. Two large steps and he was on him. He grabbed the rail-thin boat operator and tossed him into the churning milky water. The small white demon followed him into the lake with a soft hiss.

The man took a few heaving breaths but did not calm. Rage twirled under his legs like a cat eager for more treats. The man turned back to the group, and Serah knew he would be searching for another target.

"I breathe in pain and anguish. I breathe in rage and fear. I breathe out peace and light, love and comfort. I breathe in pain and anguish. I breathe in rage and fear. I breathe out peace and light, love and comfort." The tour guide was chanting. It sounded Tonglen, Serah thought—a method Ben had just started to teach her before she left on the trip.

Despair sat at the tour guide's feet. It toyed with him. Reaching out a long tendril to touch the man's foot, sending him into a spasm of sobs between chants. No time for Despair. On the hierarchy it was less important. He would survive. Rage first. She had to finish off Rage.

With a quick step, she reached out and touched the mother with her powerful palm.

"My word is my will. You cannot defeat me. You are strong and unafraid. What you see, you will face with certainty. You are a mother; you are created to be brave. My word is my will." Serah whispered quickly and pushed out her light into that touch as much as she could. Then she turned, took a deep breath as she thought, *this is gonna hurt,* and dove for Rage. She grabbed and held on. She tucked her head, pulled her knees in close, wrapped her arms around Rage, struggling to maintain her grip. She locked her arms together at the wrist and her legs at the ankle.

OhmyGodohmyGodohmyGod. She burned. It was acid. Acid on her arms, acid on her legs and face. It was then that she knew Hell.

"I breathe in your pain. I breathe in your anguish. I breathe in your rage. I breathe in your fear. I breathe out peace and light. I breathe out love and comfort. Pain. Peace. Pain. Peace. Pain. Peace." The words sounded far away, as if shouted from a canyon rim and she was on the other side. Serah tried to concentrate. *FOCUS!* She turned inward. She saw the inward girl in the boat that was her. She watched her take a knife and start to cut. Over and over and over again.

Serah gasped. *Nononononononono.* The boat with the girl in her mind, filled with blood. She slipped on the sticky slippery mess. It spilled over into the lake, until it ran red and thick.

The light, bring the light. She opened the sky, trying to pull it in. It flickered. It pushed. It faded away. Serah grabbed and raked the bottom of the barge with her fingers trying to claw her way out of the vision. Her nails split and broke as she held onto what felt real and what was not, skin ripping open, bleeding.

"I breathe in your pain. I breathe in your rage. I breathe in your fear. I breathe out peace. I breathe out light. I breathe out comfort. Take it. It is meant for you." Serah could hear the words coming from the other side of a long tunnel. She tried again and grunted with effort. The sky opened; the light flickered like an electrical short attempting to make a charge.

So tired, so tired. Give in. Give in. Give in. Give in.

"Peeeaaaaaccccceeee." The tour guide drew out the word into one long syllable.

The sky opened. Serah breathed. *A little relief. It's coming, baby girl.* She looked up, ready, open. It was only black. The sky was black. There was no light. Rage laughed.

Noooooooooooooooooooooooo. The bloody inward girl on the lake threw her head back and screamed. Serah was helpless and did the same. The group, almost in unison, clapped their hands over their ears to muffle the tortured sound.

The sky was black. The demons laughed. Serah passed out.

"Young lady. Young lady, are you okay? Ummm...are you awake?" Serah heard someone say. *I wonder who they are talking about,* she thought a bit lazily. The voice sounded like the guy with the camera.

"Miss? Come on, Miss. We need you to wake up now." *That was definitely the tour guide,* Serah felt a tug on her arm. *Wait a minute. Are they talking about ME?*

Serah's eyes felt glued shut. She struggled for a second and lifted a heavy hand to her face to help force them open. She squinted and looked up. She found herself on the ground in the middle of a circle of faces peering down at her. The faces all started talking at once.

"Are you okay?"

"What happened back there?"

"That was so COOL!"

"You know we could all sue."

"I got some great shots…of…something."

"Dear me, I feel woozy still."

"I need a drink!"

Serah put her hand out. Ouch. Her head hurt. *I second that, sir. I need a drink too.*

Rage Demon, Serah sighed. With her eyes still closed, she half sat up, resting on one hand. Serah turned her face to the sun. It was a bright, clear day. She opened one eye and peered out with a grimace. One eye met two, the thoughtful tour guide watched her. They locked eyes and he reached out a hand to help her up; Serah was grateful to accept.

"Miss. I believe you and I have a tad in common, Miss," he whispered in her ear. She nodded, hesitant to believe it. The crowd around them was still loudly discussing the option of a suit. The wife disagreed and wanted to just go home. The husband was loud in his need for finding someone to argue with, or a bar, whichever was easiest.

"Any bright ideas what to do with them?" Serah waved her hand to denote the tour group.

"Why, of course," he winked and turned to the cackling crowd, his hands up and open to gather their attention.

"Folks. Please, folks. Thank you for coming on the tour. We are very glad that it was such a hit! Our technicians have been working night and day to really make the experience unforgettable."

"Wait, what?? You mean that was part of the tour? That's crazy! What about the boat driver? I pushed him in the freakin' lake!"

"Yes, well that is unfortunate and doesn't usually happen, but, as we speak, he is drying off in our employee quarters and getting ready for his next performance."

"But the poor girl," the woman gestured at Serah. "She passed out!"

Before Serah could speak the tour guide rushed in, "She is doing fine, and regrettably didn't inform us of a former..ah..brain injury that reacts to bright lights and close spaces. She will be speaking with her doctor later today."

Serah tried not to laugh as she nodded along with the story. The group was silent, staring back and forth from Serah to the guide. They could find nothing else to say. As they tried to remember the depth of what they felt and saw, it was already fading. They reached for the memories of the event and were met with not much more than a vague disquiet. It didn't feel right, that's for sure, but they had no idea why.

"Folks, let's head back to the office where there are some coupons for delicious restaurants nearby waiting for each of you. Please enjoy this beautiful day on your trip under the protective eye of the Durnberg mountains." There was a general nod of agreement, most vigorous from the man who needed that drink.

"Come, come follow me." They followed like sheep ready to keep the day as a fun story to tell their friends when they returned home. Serah leaned up against the stone wall of the small building and sunk down into her coat. She watched the guests troupe inside behind the guide and felt almost like they were hers... her flock.

My flock? That is an odd thought. She smiled at them to show she was okay and winked at Danny as he passed her with a big grin of his own. The street was quiet and the sun was warm as she waited for the tour guide to return. They had a lot to discuss. She hoped he would tell her something she could use. Something powerful. She was ready for something, anything, to even the scales.

"Bye now, thank you. Yes, it was quite the ride wasn't it? Oh, the boat operator is just fine, he's at lunch now, in fact. Yes, please do enjoy your trip." The guide followed the last of them out, the sweet old couple even smiling thinking of telling the kids about their mini adventure today. The guide came and stood next to Serah and waved at the group as they headed off in different directions. He paused as the last one rounded the corner.

"Wait," he held up a hand just as Serah opened her mouth to speak. She couldn't stand it, she had so much to ask.

"Come inside," he said as he turned and held the door open for her. She pushed herself off the wall and followed. The corridor was long and dark.

How does everything in Europe look like this? So lucky, all who live in a place where the word "tract home" seemed unfathomable. He walked ahead of her into an office and flipped on a light as he spoke. Serah couldn't remember his name, though she knew he had told them when the tour started.

"I've been here five years. We finally got a chance to post a guide here that was one of us. It was a big moment. Unfortunately, it hasn't given us as much information as we were hoping for." Serah peered at a framed certificate on the wall. *Thomas. Thomas McGrath.* Serah wondered again who this group was. Ben spoke of his dark web Seekers group on occasion but didn't seem to know much more than it existed. Maybe Thomas did. That would be nice; she felt so alone.

"Yeah, I graduated from University of Scotland. The tour guide with a degree," he noticed her looking at the frame. Serah turned to see him shake his head.

"But it's not really our fault that we are...different." Light gray eyes met hazel.

"How long?" he asked her.

"Less than a year actively, but things started happening a few years ago."

"Ah, just a wee baby warrior in the fight," he smiled brief and soft. "Hi, call me Tommy, Seraphine." He stuck his hand out to shake hers over the large, medieval desk.

"Serah. Nice to meet you. Really glad to meet you actually." They both smiled and Serah felt at home.

Tommy turned serious, "I'm sorry, Seraphine. I am sorry to see your pretty young face here. Truly I am."

Serah waved her hand as if to brush a fly away, petty annoyance that belied her true feelings. "It's okay, really. I'm here now. It cannot be changed it seems, no matter how hard I try." She was not surprised he knew her given name. She wondered when surprises would be fun again.

"No, it cannot be changed," Tommy whispered in agreement.

"Do you believe in the Devil?" he asked, making a motion with his hand to get her to answer.

"Well. I guess so. I mean I was raised Catholic, so it's not something I ever really questioned you know?"

"Good. Because I believe he's real and he believes in *you*."

Serah blinked and thought of all the crazy things that had happened to her lately, "You cut to the chase, I like it. So let me do the same. It would have been helpful if this group you speak of, if this group could have, oh, I dunno? *Told me, helped me.* The Devil, Tommy? What are you guys doing out there? Why is no one talking to each other, what does all of this even mean?!" Serah was so sick and tired of being in the dark feeling like she was learning everything on her own, with the learning curve being to basically learn or feel like you want to die.

Tommy nodded, "Yes. That is something that is sorely lacking. The world has grown so fast, so *much*. I've been told that during the Middle Ages the group was strong and had masters and apprentices. They knew who had been chosen. These chosen ones were sought out before they could be killed; they were sheltered and taught. When the dawn of the renaissance, they thought it meant they won. They got complacent. The word, the truth, was not passed on, and slowly the knowledge started to die out."

"Before they could be *killed?* I guess that's a good reason to stay silent," Serah huffed a laugh and crossed her arms.

"Killed by Nick, the fallen one. His legion would travel in bands following rumors, 'questioning' aka torturing and interrogating for information, marking houses to kill those who had the sight. The group had to keep it very secret. Whole family lines were slaughtered, the sight the power is believed to be passed down from the mother to daughter, sometimes and sometimes not. There have been cases of boys with the sight, though more rare. Crusades were not about religion as we were taught in school, Seraphine. They were fought between the demons and the Seekers."

"Thomas, please tell me what to do," Serah almost begged.

"I will tell you everything I know, Seraphine Macguire." And they talked. They talked through the afternoon, Serah scribbling down as much as she could. Tea was made, and Tommy kept talking.

"We are descended from the monks of Papar. They left the islands north of Scotland many years prior to the Norse." Serah nodded, Ben had learned of the monks, she knew this part.

"My family line has always been involved with this. It has been that way for centuries. Some lines are like that and some are fractured. One appearing randomly in the middle of a line that has seemingly no relation to the monks."

"My mother was one, I think."

"Yes, it comes from the maternal side, sometimes skipping generations, but usually that's how we can trace it."

Serah paused, "She died and never told me anything."

"Often that is the way, an attempt to protect through ignorance. It does not usually work well," he said with a bit of sarcasm.

Serah almost snorted, *Understatement of the year.*

"Seraphine," Serah looked up from her notes. "You are powerful. More powerful than me." Serah started to protest, but he waved her off.

"I am different from you. I have my power, but it is in a different form of intuitive. I was taught, and I use my Tonglen to fight them, but it doesn't destroy. It just protects and mitigates. You, my dear lass, have the power to destroy." They let that statement hang in the air. Serah didn't know what to say.

What the hell do I say to that? Oh, goody?

"That doesn't sound...great."

His grey eyes took stock, "It is never 'great' to have the power to destroy. It is a responsibility of the utmost. You are being trained I assume?"

"Yes."

"Have you seen more than one demon at a time yet?"

"Sometimes two, but usually just one," Serah swallowed remembering. "When my mom died, I saw...I saw a lot, but they didn't seem to be active, if that makes sense," she finished her voice thick, the words stuck. Tommy nodded.

"They seem to respect death. It's a holy time for all of us, even them it seems." After a thoughtful pause, he continued, "Demons are more powerful in groups. Obviously, beware the Whisper of Demons. When three or more gather, it is a sign of respect for the hunter, however none alone have been able to meet that power with victory. None that I have heard of anyway. We had the pleasure of meeting a Whisper today. Together, on the barge. They know your power now, Seraphine."

"A Whisper?" Serah whispered the word, "three or more, got it." She forced her hand to continue to write. *Three demons at once, alone. Holy shit balls, nope. No, thanks.* Serah knew without Tommy's help today, she would have been lost.

"Do you know about the animals?" Tommy moved on like a train, hoping and needing to download as much information as he could.

Serah startled by the quick change of subject, "Animals? Ah, no, I don't think so."

"You have some I presume."

"My dog, Diego. Cat, Rubi."

"Good. They will help you. Cats are half-in, half-out. They are comfortable with the night and the shadows that pass through it. Treading around on silent feet watching, always watching. They are the keepers of the records, recording the comings and goings of those from the other side—as well as the humans who encounter them. Cats have been witnesses to these events since the time of the First Choice. Their memory is long and unwavering. Unfortunately, few still alive have the skill to access this information. So, in time, the knowledge will pass into oblivion, as the line between this world and the other grows more pronounced—more of a barrier than a gate. In time, no one will remember what it means to even see a ghost, to encounter a demon, but they will still exist and soon the balance will tip.

Dogs are in our world. They are the protectors of humans. They are there to bring peace, protecting their humans from most often unsavory contact with the other side. Many now are scared themselves. Anxiety causing encounters to go awry. Unexplained, the numbers of Dogs Who Know are dwindling out of existence."

Serah wrote as fast as she could. She remembered the letter from her mom that mentioned the animals. What Tommy said made so much sense. He sipped his tea waiting for her to catch up.

"I had this realization on the barge. The salty sand on the girl's sweater seemed to repel them. Why does salt affect them if that's what they are made of?"

"We believe it works like a magnet. The two poles repel each other. Born of it, but repelled by the crystal structure of salt. Salt opens all channel gateways in the body to allow the light in and demons can't handle that. Astute observation,

Seraphine," Tommy steepled his fingers and waited for more.

"Have you ever had anyone...disappear?" Serah asked.

"Tell me," he sounded urgent.

"I was with a...friend on the Salzburg bridge and the demons appeared to us. He fought them with me, and fought well, from what I could tell. He...helped," Serah closed her eyes.

"A loved one."

Serah opened her eyes, "Yes. He disappeared. He just vanished. That night we went to sleep, and when I woke, he was gone."

"He is in his parallel universe. He has been caught by *him*." The way he said that made Serah flinch.

"Him?"

Tommy looked at her for a long time. "The one who fell."

"Ummm..."

"It is a universe of the fallen."

"Fallen angels, Seraphine. There are nine orders of angels. Dammit!" he pounded the desk hard, Serah jumped.

"The education is so lacking. What happened to us? Nine orders of angels...," he muttered, his frustration palpable. Serah decided to remain quiet.

"Seraphine. YOU are an angel. Or a piece of one. We don't know for sure yet. Go and study this. You MUST understand what you are first. Understand and know yourself and THAT is where your power is. That is where ALL of our power is. It is always inside us. Waiting to be used." Serah just stared, wide eyes.

I am an angel? She shook her head a little and decided to leave that alone for now. She certainly didn't feel angelic. No way.

"Okay, back to Sam. How did he get there? It's my fault we were there and got attacked. I never should have put him in that position. I have to get him back. I HAVE to help him. What do I do? Tell me, please."

"He was there of his own free will. None of us cause these things. We believe we cause them. We carry around the guilt nonetheless. Free will, Seraphine. It always is free will. He was there because he wanted to be. Make no mistake." Serah remained silent as Tommy continued.

"It's quantum physics really. We are all made of the universe. 5% of all matter we can account for. The other 95%? Dark matter, dark energy. It's *unknown*. We are made of the universe, Serah. We are all stardust in this form that was chosen by God, or by science, no matter what you believe. We are born from an exploding star that God created and our science has explained. But it doesn't get it all quite right. We don't have all the answers yet—that is the way of growth. But the fact remains, we are pieces of stardust. From you, from me, from the brick in this building, to the birds that I hear outside my window."

"Quantum physics is such a new science, yet it is the closest thing we have to explaining this. Our matter vibrates at a certain frequency. It has been discovered that atoms can actually be in two places at once. Atoms are actually fairly large chunks of matter, when we really get down to it. And just by *watching* them, we change their behavior. They are stardust, Seraphine—just like you and I. They recognize that in us, and they dance." Tommy sat for a minute and smiled. It was clear he loved this topic. The magic of the quantum realm explained so much, and yet, still they had so much to learn.

"Sam is caught between what we can see and what we cannot. He is here, and he is also there. He is two places at once. We cannot reach him physically, not really. But we can *influence* the dance he is in, if we try." Serah was transfixed. She hardly understood a word but it was the most information she had received so far from someone who understood. Someone who understood and knew what she was going through. The relief almost made her cry. The relief in the knowledge that Tommy existed—that he is alive and a resource for her. She is part of the team.

I don't have to be alone anymore, she thought. Tommy tried to explain more.

"Think of this, Seraphine. Our heart beats in our chest. The source, as some would say, of our life. The electrical frequency of our hearts can be accurately measured several feet from our bodies. Think of that. *Several feet from our bodies.* My heart is communicating with yours right now. My brain, if we knew how to access this information, is taking in your frequency right now and understanding it. We sit three feet apart. That is nothing. Our stardust is dancing with each other and we don't even know what it is saying. Or do we?" He smiled soft and extended his hand.

"You are not alone, Seraphine. None of us are. That is the tragedy of the human race. Thinking we exist alone in our own space. But that is not the case. We are all connected. And now you and I are connected even more so," he held out his hand and she took it. She could almost feel it vibrating. The dance of stardust.

Holy shit.

"Sam is still there. He is not alone. Reach out to him and draw him back to you. Draw him back here where he belongs...if this is where he belongs that is. Reach out and save him. You can save him, if you try. Be careful with the power of your mind. It is the most powerful spell we have. We can use it for good or for evil. Make sure you are acting from a sense of clear purpose," Tommy said and could tell Serah stopped listening after the words, *you can save him*, exited his lips. He shook her hand a little to gain attention.

"Remember, Seraphine: free will. He may not *want* to be saved. He has to want it. He has to reach a hand out to you for you to grab. Do not fall into the trap and waste time if he cannot be saved. There is much for us to do before..." Tommy stopped.

"Before? Before what?" Serah interrupted.

"There is much for us to do." That is all Tommy would say. The room grew silent and cold. Serah untangled her hand and reached for her tea. Cold. She shivered. Her watch beeped. Her flight departed in three hours; it was time to go.

"Is your teacher Benjamin Vondell by chance?"

Serah nodded, quickly gathering up her notes and small pack, "Yes, how did you know?"

"I had the chance to connect with him in a dark place on the web where we hide." Tommy paused and murmured, "He seems very devoted."

"Ben's my best friend. I wouldn't be here without him," Serah's eyes crinkled as a grin took over her face.

They quickly exchanged emails and phone numbers. Tommy hugged her, "Good luck, Seraphine. A lot of the fallen are in powerful places now. Everyone must be extra careful, including you and your Ben. Remember: You are descended from angels. Always follow that path and things will work out." He wasn't sure if he believed that anymore; his faith had been shaken, tested, too many times. But seeing this young, bright girl stand in front of him, he was driven to believe anew again. She was so strong, and she didn't even know it. Tommy shook his head and sighed as he watched her walk away, then turn and wave, bright and shiny energy, radiant love.

That's what it was, he thought. *She radiated love.*

We can do this. Source, creator, we can do this. Just give us time…please, give us time, was Tommy's final thought as he turned away and closed the door.

Chapter 25

(The In-Between)

Watch the Ravens
Listen to the Trees
You are here, in the In Between.
In Between hope
In Between knowing
In Between coming and In Between going.
The road you must follow
A choice you must make
When you think you are ready, the train you will take.

~ UNKNOWN AUTHOR, ORIGIN: DARK AGES

S am walked down a road. He knew it was a road; it looked road-like, a sin-gle lane. He looked around and was reminded of England. Rolling hills. Pastures. A few trees. He had no idea where he was or how he got here. He still smelled of her. The thought of her waking up alone, thinking he left; that thought made him panic. She had to know something happened. *She had to.*

It wasn't cold. Salzburg was cold, so he had to be somewhere else. He looked down and realized he was wearing a longish black leather jacket with a sweatshirt hood. T-shirt, jeans, boots. Okay, so he was dressed fairly normal. He reached up. Sunglasses on his head. He reached to his neck, chain on, and his silver cross belt buckle. Check, check, check. No wallet, no keys. *Shit. She had to know something happened.*

"Damn, what a night," he started to smile, kinda proud of himself as he remembered. But he looked around again, "Focus, Gunnar. Christ's sake." He realized he was talking to himself out loud, but there was literally no one to hear. It reminded him of the movie *28 Days Later*. Spooky. Spooky quiet. It was then that he wished for his gun.

He looked around: no street signs. Nothing. Just a road. A road through the hills. *Shit, this doesn't feel good.* He topped another rise and saw a fence. It ran along the road to his right, seeming to start out of nowhere. *What need for a fence?* Two crows sat on the first post. Three arranged themselves near the second. Two more cawing at the ground. He looked up and could see one more crow circling above.

"That's eight," he thought. It reminded him of the rules Serah told him. Eight rules. So far anyway. Eight rules that she knew of. *Not good, Gunnar. Not good.* The fluttery heart of panic took hold and grew.

He felt like he was in a movie. Sam started to whistle. It felt a little lame, but maybe someone, or something, will hear it and investigate. *Is that good or bad?* Sam wondered.

I'll keep walking forward until it feels like the wrong thing to do, he decided. For now, it felt right. Onward. The fence continued. One of the birds followed but the rest stayed behind.

"Crows are creepy," Sam said out loud. "Never thought about it before, but they are creepy, creepy birds." He could see the road bend toward the right and head into a small grouping of trees. The fence followed. Sam neared the trees and slowed. It was dark, some light filtered in. The trees were large, old. He briefly wished he had one of those motion detectors from the movie *Aliens*, but, he reasoned, they never did seem to do much help except add to the panic of the approaching alien hoard.

Okaaaay, Gunnar, let's keep it real now.

The trees didn't extend too far and not long after entering this small forest he saw a man leaning up on a large fence post, casual; looked like the cowboy sort with a big hat, chin on his chest almost like he was asleep.

"Stop yer grinnin' and drop yer linen, found 'em," Sam couldn't help it, he found himself whispering a favorite movie line.

Sam slowed as he approached. He could see the man was turning something in his hands; his head was down, attention absorbed. An older man with tanned, darker skin. Sam was curious. He rubbed the back of his neck with his hand—his nervous gesture. Though he didn't think things could get more weird and uncomfortable, he could feel his body radiate tension.

"Time to play, Gunnar, game face." Adrenaline surged at a long-lost football term he used to use. *Time to play.*

"Howdy," Sam decided on cordial and dumb. Dumb often disarmed and made people careless. The man continued to look at the object in his hands, but he smiled. Sam waited. It was hard to wait. The seconds ticked and Sam fought the urge to whistle: whistle or punch him. The first would be better, the latter would *feel* better, but that would give him away.

Sam noticed what the man was playing with a Rubik's cube. He hadn't seen one of those in a decade, maybe more. The man's hands moved fast. He twirled and turned and hissed a little when he caught a mistake. He had one row of yellow. A full red side. Sam saw another row of yellow click into place.

He's pretty good, Sam felt ridiculous waiting. *Enough.*

"Sir, I do believe I am lost. I'm not really sure how I got here, believe it or not, and I would kindly appreciate some help." The man with the big hat slowed and stopped his fingers that were engrossed in their game. He raised his head and finally looked at Sam. He smiled. It was a nice smile.

"Well, I guess my little game can wait. It's lucky I was sitting here playing my little game, almost as if I was waitin' for you to come along, eh? Lucky." He spoke slow, black eyes stared out of a darkly tanned face.

"Yeah, it does seem that way," Sam replied, hesitant. Why did the man suddenly seem familiar to him? Certain he had never seen him before, but he couldn't shake the feeling—it stuck in his mind like glue. The man pushed himself off of the fence line and stuck out his hand toward Sam. Sam grabbed it and they shook.

"Pardon me for my manners. I'm Nick. Nick Fandaen." Sam recognized a slight southern accent—smooth, lilting.

"Sam. Sam Gunnar."

"Sam, Sam Gunnar, you look like you might have traveled far? Where are you from, my boy?" Sam hesitated to provide the real answer. *I don't trust this guy.*

"California, currently traveling," he said, deciding a version of the truth was best. Traveling could mean anything, and he wanted to be deceptively vague.

"California?! Yep, you sure are a long way from home…California." Nick shook his head seemingly in wonder at the notion. Sam didn't know what to say. He had to get home; he had to get back to…her. He couldn't let her think he had left. She passed through his mind, a vision of her wrapped up in the sweaty sheets, sleeping. Peaceful.

A faraway look passed across Nick's face. His eyes seemed to briefly go out of focus, listening to something inside: a memory, a voice, something *else*. It always irritated Sam when people did that. He didn't talk just to hear himself speak—he was fond of saying.

Nick focused back on Sam with a strong smile.

"Would you be able to tell me how I get to the nearest city or airport, please?" Sam asked, Nick's smile irritated.

"Well, gosh. Now that is going to be tricky. See, Sam, there aren't really any cities around here. No actual airports," Nick's fingers made air-quotes as he said airports.

"The best idea is to follow this road here. About a thirty-minute walk, there's a nice little boarding house that rents to strangers. Get a room and get some rest."

Nick's accent grated and Sam's patience thinned, "Well," he used the man's word. "Well, I just can't really do that unless it's a last resort, I'm afraid. I'm trying to get back. I need to get back." Sam struggled to stay calm; he tried urgency. *Maybe this man will feel sorry for me and help me out.*

"Last resort. Sounds pretty serious," Nick nodded a few times, then smiled again.

Shit, Sam thought, *he is creepy.*

"Sir, can you tell me what city I happen to be in?" back to dumb and helpless, maybe that would do the trick.

Nick smiled, "Nope. No, I sure can't. You are In Between."

"I don't understand," Sam's panic mounted. "What is the name of this freakin' city, town, what-the-fuck-ever place I am in?!"

Nick smiled, "Oh, Sammy boy, that's a good question. A darn good question. Well worded too."

Sam turned and started walking. He walked briskly in the direction of the boarding house, *Not that it will be there*, he thought. *But this direction was as good a one as any*. He quickly left the man in the big hat behind.

Shaking his head, his mind was racing through all he could remember. He remembered the bridge, the beers, the evening with Serah, falling asleep quickly, her pressed up against his back, and then waking up to walking.

Think, think, think. He felt dazed—like coming out of a deep heavy sleep.

But how long had he been dazed? Why couldn't he remember more? What happened during the part he was missing? Shit. Shit. Too many questions tonight, last night. Today. He was tired of questions. Goddammit, he wanted answers. And he didn't think he was going to get them anytime soon. He looked over as Nick appeared at his elbow, walking with him, a concerned expression on his face.

"You like Garth?" Nick asked. A finger thoughtfully placed over his lips. Arms crossed as they walked side by side, he looked like he was genuinely concerned for Sam.

"Garth? Ahhh. As in Brooks?"

"Yep."

"Of course, he's, ah, pretty well known. One of my favorites actually," Sam tried to be polite after his outburst.

"Excellent. There is a song you might be familiar with. It's like Mr. Brooks says…It's better than pushin' up daisies," Nick smiled. Sam could barely contain his irritation. He wanted to punch that smile off his face. He tried to figure out what the hell Nick was saying.

"Well, sir, I admit I'm not too sure what you mean," Sam restrained.

"I'm being obtuse, I apologize. I'm just saying that being here, regardless of where *Here* is, is better than 'pushing up daisies' or, if I need to explain further, the In Between is a lot better than being dead," Nick smiled.

Sam didn't know what to make of that. After a minute, "Yes, sir, I suppose it is."

I need to get the fuck out of here, Sam's panic mounted; he swallowed it down. Their footsteps echoed slightly, the only sound as they walked in silence. Walking in silence down a lonely road, a road to nowhere, and nobody. Sam felt lost. He never felt that way with her. He hoped she was okay. He knew she was tough and she was strong. She didn't need him. Didn't seem to. Maybe he should just let her go. Nothing ever works out anyway. He always fails. He always runs. The only time he didn't run from love, he almost died inside. He couldn't do that again. Never again. A part of him felt like he *did* die. He wouldn't give her the power to do that to him.

What a bitch, she was trying to control him by being too perfect. Tricky. She was very tricky. Women are always fucking tricky.

Wait. This is crazy. Why am I thinking these things? Sam felt crazy. Crazy here in crazy land with crazy man Nick. Nick with the stupid fucking smile.

His smile, the thought made Sam pause.

"Nick, I appreciate you taking the time with me. I know you must have so many things to do, you know standing along a fence playing with a Rubick's Cube. Must mean you are a pretty important man. Lots of people to attend to, a lot of important decisions to make. So, you know, I just wanted to tell you how much I appreciate you tagging along while I walk to the next town," Sam gained speed as he talked. He sounded annoying to his own ears and pressed on.

"I hope this isn't taking time out of your really important day," Sam looked up and smiled. Sam's smile dazzled.

Nick's face drained, his smile faded and faltered, he looked almost pale. Sam's smiled broadened as he noticed the reaction. He was getting close to something; not an answer, but something. Nick gathered himself visibly.

"No…no not at all, Sammy boy. I'm here to serve you. Whatever I can do to help you, please just ask me for help and I will give it," Nick's smile returned.

"Tell me where I am."

"Well now, Sammy my boy, I already did. You are in the In Between. I can't really say more, it's against the rules."

"Fuck the rules. I am not your boy. I am my mother's son. You. Are. Not. Real. I feel sorry for you, stuck in this miserable, boring place," Sam started to laugh. He laughed stronger. He laughed louder and louder until he was holding an arm across his stomach, slapping his leg. The tears started; he couldn't stop. He could barely open his eyes. His laughter echoed.

Nick opened his mouth and hissed. He hissed, stopped himself quickly and glanced around. Sam didn't hear; he could only laugh and laugh. He remembered laughing with Serah over beers and a football game. He remembered her hysterical laughter when he told her the story about his friend Max and smelly feet; her laughter when he reenacted scenes from a movie to keep the grief of her mom at bay. Memories of her laughter filled him up and he laughed with her face in the forefront of his mind. His laughter slowed, then stopped, and he wiped his eyes. When Sam finally looked up and looked around, he found himself alone.

"Smile at the devil. Thanks, Gran, you were right!" Sam spoke to the whispering trees; he won that round. Feeling victorious, he started out again. His boots made a distinctive noise on the road. Every now and then he would chuckle, remembering. The feeling lingered until the silence settled over him and Sam's chuckles stopped. He ducked his head, hands in his pockets, and set his pace. It was quiet and he knew he had a long way to go.

"Hey, Seraphina, how are you?" Ben asked a tired Serah, after all her bags, including Sam's luggage that she managed to haul back from Salzburg, were tossed into his car at the front of the airport.

Serah turned to look at him, "Exhausted, but excited. There is a team out there, Ben. I met one of them. That means we are not alone. That I am not alone."

"I did some research on the notes you sent me. Quantum mechanics, really, Serah?"

"Yes, I am very very lucky to have you Ben," Serah replied. Her serious tone made Ben pause for a minute, but he continued.

"And this is operation *Rescue Sam*? I *knew* he couldn't pull his own weight." Ben stopped. "I'm just glad you are okay."

"What we think we create, we are all connected," Ben repeated from Serah's email to him from Salzburg after meeting Tommy. "It's in all the literature. Everything I read talks about some version of this idea. Still hard for me to fully believe. Yet, it makes sense that quantum mechanics is the science that connects all the dots—that explains it ALL," Ben rushed on to explain more.

"Okay, the science behind quantum mechanics is that particles, when alone, act in weird ways. Alone meaning in a vacuum, no light, frozen down to almost absolute zero. They are observed to be 'delocalized' aka in two places at once. One of the big questions is what would it be like to be in two places at once? How would a human consciousness handle it? From what I can tell, science is a long way off from even realizing any of these answers, but the research so far fits what you are telling me. You said the room was pitch black; it was almost frozen cold when you woke up. I'm guessing by-products of Sam being 'delocalized', for lack of a sexier term. So, he still exists, but in a sense, he has to choose which timeline—which universe—to reside in. Our brains cannot process the information of two events: two lives happening at the same time. At least these are my assumptions."

"That is profoundly weird," Serah's only comment, as she listened.

"And it gets weirder. Our new friend Tommy is right. This idea of the quantum world, allows for the fact that we believe everything is all interconnected. But it goes deeper than that. The connections to all the things around us literally define who we are. Right now, Sam defines himself by this other 'space'. We define ourselves as being *here*. Wherever here actually is. So, as Tommy said, the very act of our thoughts—our observations—can influence what people define as who they are, what they see, and what they hear. It can literally define *them*. The big question is, can we have an effect on this process in our brains? Our energy vibration? All of this happens on a level that we don't even realize. It's incredible, really. If you can get the clarity and power over this process, this *influence,* I can't even begin to imagine the implications. First and foremost, you would be able to reach out to Sam and help him. If you wanted," Ben glanced over at Serah as he said that last part.

"Tommy mentioned I needed to 'reach out to him and draw him back. Draw him back here where he belongs' but how would I even start? What would I even do? He said we all have free will. That it's up to Sam to even want to be saved," Serah shook her head. "Maybe he doesn't even want to be with me, in this weird world of mine."

"You have to know, if you believe this yourself. You can't really move forward if you don't." Ben waited for Serah to jump in with enthusiasm as she usually did, but the car remained silent.

"I really don't know, Ben. I'm so tired. I wish I could just be *normal*. I don't want to learn about parallel universes and quantum mechanics. All I want is to love a boy and have him love me back, play with my dog, and enjoy my life. I'm so tired of being alone."

Serah didn't see Ben wince at that word, as she reached over and turned down the radio. Leaning her head back on the car seat, she blinked her eyes dry from the long plane ride. She shut them to try to think; think and decide what to do next. She promptly fell asleep. Ben drove down the empty highway toward home in the silent car. It was up to her to decide what to do next.

Chapter 26

"Stop moving and sit down. Man, you are wired today," Ben watched Serah pace, then drop her hands from where she was holding them in a ball at her chest. She looked at him and plopped down on her mat. The soft morning light filtered into Ben's patio between the leaves of the trees that stood tall and silent just outside the windows.

Weary. That word popped into her head.

Weary. It repeated itself like a gong.

Ben saw her close her eyes but not before they welled with tears.

"Serah, you are creating your own universe right now. A tired and sad and frustrated universe. Take your pick, pick all three. It is yours—you own it." Ben paused. "So, dig deep and stop it," he pushed.

"But I'd be faking it," she responded with her eyes still closed. She had controlled the tears, *bonus.*

"No, it's called imagining what you want your future, your present to BE. Imagining and then creating it. Faking is just what it *feels* like at first. But if something doesn't exist you have to imagine it first, to create it. What world would you create? Tell me."

"A world without demons," she whispered.

"Good. What else?"

"A world where I can be loved."

"Yes. Keep going."

"A world that lets me sleep more," she smirked a little at this, getting into it.

"Let's not get crazy now," Ben smiled when Serah opened one eye to glare at him. "Yes, that's a great goal and great reality to create. Sleep is where we repair. Sleep is where you gain your power. Sleep is where you learn. But that is why we meditate, to create that while we are awake."

"Ben, can I do this? I mean, really?" Both of Serah's eyes were open now, bright green today, unlike their usual hazel, pinned on his.

"You could quit. You could hide. You could turn away from what you see and close your eyes. Is that what you want to do?" Ben asked gently. Serah held his gaze. Then sighed and shook her head, biting her lip she looked down at her hands.

"If you want to try to keep Sam on this timeline with you, you don't have another option, Seraphine Macguire. You really don't. But I am here, and I will not let you fall." Ben's heart beat on these words. His heart that was communicating several feet from his body. His heart that reached out and enveloped the tired girl in front of him, enveloped her in warmth, in peace, and in protection. He pushed that energy out and reached for her.

Serah sat shifting her weight to get to that comfortable spot where she seemed to sink just a little, right into the floor. Everything was connected. Her molecules now mixing with the mat, mixing with the wood, mixing with the earth below. If she concentrated hard, on good days, she could almost feel the earth breathe.

She could hear Ben speaking soft and slow the words to draw her into the right space. It was easier at first to concentrate on someone's voice and let the rest drift away.

"Picture him. His face, his walk, his stance, his weight in the world. Watch him watch you. Where is he? Put yourself there."

"He's walking down a road. Somewhere far away. Somewhere old." Serah knows she speaks but did not realize she had this answer to this question. As if she stood far away from herself. She felt a curiosity, but it was removed, a *watching*.

"Reach into yourself, your core. Build a rope, a tether, a lasso. It is you, your energy, your light."

Serah looked down, in her mind's eye she could see the inside girl—the inside girl in the boat. The girl in the boat was standing. Tree pose. It was a powerful and balanced pose; muscles tensed. The girl reached in and pulled out silvery strands of beautiful energy. It was her. She maintained her breath and sunk deeper into the floor.

"Toss it out. Toss it to him like a net, like an anchor. Ask him to grab hold."

Serah scrunched her face in a small scowl, "He is moving away...fast...I cannot reach him no matter how hard I try...he is...he is on a train now. He is in pain."

"It does not matter if he is on a train, or an airplane, or standing still. Past and present and future are an illusion here. It is all one time. At any point, events unfold and branch out in pathways like branches on a tree in all directions. Reach it out. Toss your rope around him and tug. You are calling him to you."

Serah's hand reached out in front of her mirroring the girl in the boat who was deep inside. Her broken and scabbed fingers and nails, reminders from her tussle at the lake, made Ben flinch.

"Your hand reaches out. It's not touching anything but air. How do you know that your hand exists? Conjure up the feeling of the palm of each hand. Feel the warmth, the power. Surrender all resistance to physical suffering you can't avoid. Fear, anger, regret slip away because past and future don't exist except as stories in our minds."

"Got him. I think..." Serah pictured her silver light wrapped around his left hand. That is all she could reach. She tugged...she asked...*Come to me. Please, Sam. Come back.*

"Now let go. This is important. Let the rope fall and let it go. It is his choice now. You've done what you can."

Serah struggled. It felt so good to be near him, even in this way. She could see his face, and feel his skin. She wanted to take away his pain. He sat in the wool chair on the train zooming away from her. She could feel it.

"Serah. Let GO. It is not up to you."

The silver strand of light fell away and she was tugged back to the inside girl in the boat on the lake in the starry dusk. She gasped at a last flash of vision; the picture changed.

"What is it?"

"He sits on a low brick wall. There is a young girl...with my name." Her eyes popped open. She didn't even have to move her head; she was already looking straight at Ben.

"What does that even mean?"

"Well...I think it is a very good sign, Seraphine Macguire." The garden patio was silent. Ben smiled.

Sam made it to town, a ghost town as far as he could tell. His teeth crunched on the thick dust of the road, he spit one more time and stopped walking. He looked up and down the Main Street and chose the movie theater, seemed like the best option among no options. The door creaked as he pulled it open.

I swear to God if a zombie comes walking out, I will not be surprised.

"Hello?" he called into the deserted expanse. Brown and gold and green, the carpet looked almost new; he could smell fresh popcorn. A head popped up and bobbed above the candy counter.

"Hello!" It called to him.

"Are you open?" Sam asked, *brilliant question, Gunnar.*

"Why yes, yes we are, please come in. I just made popcorn would you like some?" said the enthusiastic head.

"Ahhh, no. No, thanks," Sam replied just as his stomach growled. *I'll be damned if I am going to eat anything in crazyland.*

Sam started toward the counter and let the door fall shut behind him, "I'm a bit lost and looking for a way out of town. Can you help?"

"Most people are my friend. Most people are," the girl behind the counter nodded with a look of sympathy.

Man, that sucks. Even here they gotta wear horrible uniforms, he thought.

"Can you tell me the quickest way out? I, ah, don't have any money," Sam wasn't used to being in this position.

"Well, that's okay, sir. Your money isn't good here. We take other forms of currency." Her ponytail bobbed with her cheerfulness as she told him that.

"That's, ah, great. Really great. Okay. Soooo, quickest way outta town?" Sam persisted, he decided to leave the question of what type of currency alone, he didn't want to know. Blonde ponytail paused and her blank face concentrated.

Must be a tough question, Gunnar.

She grinned and asked, "Have you tried the train station?"

"I sure haven't. Can you direct me, please?"

"Yep! Just head out those doors, hang a left, follow Main Street four blocks, I think, and it will dead-end right into the main station! Trains run pretty often, but I don't know the schedule. I'm sorry," she looked genuinely sad about that.

"No, no. That's great. That's perfect, thank you. Thank you so much," Sam turned and started for the door.

"Popcorn for the road?"

Sam paused, his hand on the bar of the door ready to push it open, "Um, thanks, but no, thanks. Hey can I ask…what is the name of this town?"

Blonde ponytail smiled, "You are anywhere, Sam. Anywhere, in any town. Some call this the In Between. You are at a crossroads. You get to pick. Travel safe, Sam." She held up her hand in goodbye and Sam could see a wheel-like scar on her palm. He stared at it for a second, then turned picked up his pace, and started to run.

Sam boarded the first train that came and settled into a seat. *Anywhere is better than here.* He looked out the window at the countryside flashing by and he remembered.

They were sitting on a little patio, drinking coffee out of delicate cups, watching the sun go down.

"Can I ask you a question?" She doesn't turn her head, just quietly sips.

"Of course," turning to look her way. "Uh, oh. It's one of those questions," he tries to joke. Her mouth quirks but that is all he will get.

"I need you to promise you will be honest. Don't you dare try to lie," her voice is soft and calm. A tone of sweetness he loves. He doesn't hear it often, but he can

always notice when it changes. She is open. Vulnerable, but truly herself.

"I'm always honest with you," he starts. Defensive. He is scared. She looks over at him, her hazel eyes above the rim of the cup searing his face. The 'thousand-yard stare' as he has nicknamed it. She sets her cup down slowly to disguise her trembling hands.

"Please don't shut down on me. Please. This is important. You can shut down in a minute. But please just listen."

He nods, expectant. He waits.

"If she showed up here—tomorrow—said she wanted to try it again, that she wants to make a life with you? What would you do? What would you want to do? Would you take her back?" The words were powerful. He had given her this ammo of knowledge many months ago. He recognizes it. He almost wants to laugh. He always knew he was the destroyer of relationships without even fucking trying.

He pauses. She waits.

"I don't know," he finally says, and she believes him.

"I always thought I would. But now, I really don't know. You have changed me," he continues quietly. Her look he cannot decipher. She flees again inside out of reach. Out of his reach, he corrects in his head. Some can reach her. A few.

"Thank you for telling the truth," she says. Picking her coffee cup back up, she takes another sip and turns her eyes back to watch that sun ease its way down behind beautiful hills.

"Why do sunsets look so much more amazing far away from home?" she asks with a small smile. He stares at her. He cannot tear his gaze away. Her lips. That mouth. Her eyes. A terror grips him. He does not know why or where it is from. Fear's chilly hand is there winding around the muscles in his throat, making it difficult to speak, to think. He clears his throat. She meets his gaze and he cannot bear it. He turns to watch the sun blink out for the day, starting its travel toward his home.

"They look more amazing because of you," he thinks and wants to say. But he refrains. He is stuck.

Instead, "I don't know, but they sure do. I guess we will just have to see them all," he smiles and grabs her hand tight. She smiles back, her Mona Lisa smile, silent. Together they sit, quiet guardians of their broken hearts.

Shaking his head out of the memory, he tries to figure out where he is—where he is going. Instead, all he sees are frames of his memories flipping by like a stop-motion camera.

Salzburg on a cold bench, lying in bed, laughing head on her belly, a bike ride to town, a hot tent, a muddy hike, kisses in the rain, laughing always. Only once, her tears. Only once. So much strength. Her hands on his face.

The scenes flash by in rapid succession. He watched this part of his life go by so fast, yet it seemed like so much more. Bigger. Longer. It was everything to him. The film stopped and was replaced by the view through the train window. Bleak and starting to get dark, it pained him. He wanted to run away from this, he hated, no he detested this pain, this vulnerability.

"Dammit," he felt tortured. "What's next, Gunnar? What the hell are you gonna do next?" He said out loud to the empty train car. The train's relentless motion bears him away, onward.

He leaned back against the chair, shut his eyes pulling his cap down. No one to bother him. The back of his neck itched against the scratchy wool chair. She told him a story once about scratchy wool chairs she had to sit on for many years of her life. He rubbed it away with a hand, "Son of a bitch. Scratchy wool. She is everywhere."

Time to run, Gunnar? Maybe. Maybe not.

Sam woke, startled out of sleep. He sat up quickly, the memory flooding back.

I am at a crossroads. The thought kept repeating itself in his head. He looked out the window to a dreary day. The train was pulling into a town; he leaned close to the glass as he recognized the scenery.

Is this some kind of a joke?

He was home. The city buildings that fought with the large pine trees were such a welcome sight, he wanted to cry. As the train slowed, he turned to grab his bag which was sitting politely on the seat next to him. He didn't have it before, but it was his, he was sure of that; the small nick in the leather handle, the luggage tag his grandfather gave him that traveled through WWII with him. It was his. He reached into his jacket pocket and his cell phone was right where it always was. Sam shook his head. It was like this was normal and, yet, not. His mind was fuzzy. Memories had already started to fade like an unsettling dream fades with the shock of the alarm.

The train pulled into the station and stopped. He ducked down to look out the window and saw a few passengers disembark. Everything looked fine. He snagged his bag with one arm and started off the train down the steps between cars.

"Sam!" Sam's foot came down on the pavement just as he heard his name. He pivoted toward the sound. Scanning the crowd, he saw his brother Matt. Matt waved his arm standing out of the way at the edge of the platform near the station. Puzzled, Sam slowly walked up.

"What are you doing here little brother?"

"I'm picking you up, what do you think I'm doing here? Hanging out waitin' for the ladies?" Matt laughed and grabbed for Sam's bag.

"Where's Serah?" Sam asked. Matt gave him an odd look as he shouldered the small bag. "She's at home. You called and said once back in the states you guys were going to take the train here on to home. It is almost Thanksgiving; things are really picking up at the lot. It's good to have you back." Sam knew there was much more to that statement than Matt was letting on. Working in their family business, they each had their roles: Matt was more of the brawn, Sam the brains, and their dad was often difficult to handle making some twentieth-century decisions that were fine a decade ago, but weren't now.

"How was the trip?! Did you drink a lot of beer? Tell me about the Fraulines!"

Sam laughed at Matt's enthusiasm and started in on a story, "Well one night we were in this little town of Salzburg, it started to snow, we were dancing in the street, 'cause there was no one around." Matt made a noise at the cheesiness. Sam continued," We found this great little bar right off the small main road. They spoke perfect English! I didn't have to look like a douche trying to use my high school German." The brothers laughed and turned to exit.

"So, this HUGE beer, right? It's a stein called a liter, we drank at least one each. Serah was blitzed. I'll admit it was a lot of beer for me too. The food was amazing, our hotel had this famous chocolate cake, it was like a brick of chocolate. It was so good..." Sam continued his story as they walked away from the puffing train, getting ready to resume its journey again.

Home, well sort of. Sam stood in the doorway of the big empty cabin, one of three buildings on the north property; this particular one he claimed for his own years ago. Far away from any noise, situated the furthest north in The Pine Forest, as they called it—720 square acres they owned to farm trees, and the closest to the dirt road that wound for days up into the mountains. He was sweaty from an afternoon on his bike. It was the only medicine he knew. Toss helmet, toss keys on the counter, grab an iced tea. He finally felt content in the quiet fall evening.

Rifling thru his bag for a protein bar, he found it. She knew exactly where to put it. A note, a letter. He smiled recognizing her handwriting and one of the many nicknames she had given him.

Dear Cowboy,

I had such an amazing time with you, as always.

I care so much for you that I find the rest of this very hard to say. I love your vulnerability and your toughness. You are such a good, good man. I have no doubts that I want you in my life. I know you probably have doubts about being in mine. And that is okay for you, but not okay for me. I want the June Carter & Johnny Cash fairy tale. And if this isn't it, then I need to try to find it.

I walked into this with my eyes wide open. I fully realized what I was getting myself into. It is not your fault and it is not mine. It is what it is.

I hope you find what you are looking for. As do I. I do hope that search brings your feet, mind, and heart back to my door...and to me. What's next, Cowboy? What's next?

Always,
Your Seraphine

He stared at it for a long time, unblinking, and crumpled it into one tight fist. So much fear and angst it was hard to breathe. His hand ached as if attempting to compress the paper into dust.

She is right. I need to figure this out. She deserves more.

Sam looked down at the new scar on his wrist. It looked like the letter P but sharper, more dangerous somehow. It unnerved him to think he wasn't in control, that someone or something had done this to him.

Not sure when the scar appeared exactly, his thoughts were fuzzy as he tried to remember Salzburg and the bridge, the odd encounter with Nick and the creepy town, the train ride. Sam shook his head to clear it; it felt like cobwebs were being spun by evil spiders in his mind.

Thankful he was able to cover his auspicious mark with a thick gold watch band, so none of his family could pester him with questions he did not have the answers to. Only she had the answers, most likely, but he knew if he saw her again, it would be because he had made a choice. THE choice.

He turned and, in one motion, swiped the keys off the counter, heading back out to the motorcycle again, to ride until he figured it out, or he died. Sam didn't care which.

Sam cursed, *Another one wants to quit. Goddammit, things are falling apart. I was only gone three weeks!* He had rushed back to their main store front after Thanksgiving with the family up north, solving problems and fighting business fires for the past week, trying to set things right. His brother Matt, still on vacation, in Sam's opinion, dreaming about ways to grow the company as he wandered through the beautiful Pine Forest planting, trimming and logging.

Looking around his office with expensive new furniture, wood floors, a cowhide rug on the floor, Sam knew it was him, but yet it wasn't. *Only gone three weeks, yet things are the ever-loving same.* Bored out of his mind, he looked into the future: five, ten, twenty years, running the business, day by day, selling trees. He went numb. It is all he can do to handle the bleakness.

A thought of her, and he softened. Not a lot, but a little. Another reason to be numb. Numb is better. Better to be numb against the questions, numb against the doubts and fears. Still no answer came to him as he hoped, as he has continually hoped for days now. He knew she was out there, waiting. Patient as always, or maybe not, he supposed.

Anger returned swiftly and caught him by surprise. It almost took his breath away, but then he settled in with it; it was an old friend. Comfortable.

He remembered again:

Sitting at dinner, he watches her laugh and say something. She sometimes talks with her hands and sometimes she just sits and listens with a hand on her chin. So intent, so thoughtful. His thoughts burn as he wonders, always wonders, what she is thinking. She throws her head back and laughs. Silent laughter replayed like a silent movie in his mind. That throat. His thoughts move on to things he likes to do to that throat. How he likes to watch it in other ways.

Graphic images tumble by, Sam blinks and clears his throat. He hasn't moved from the spot he was standing, his heart beats fast. He didn't keep any pictures of her, thank God. He can feel he is getting hardened again. Hardened from where she split him open. It was good.

Obviously, she is not the one. Obviously. His chest hurt as he said that to himself. He laughed a cynical laugh that echoed in his office. If he closed his eyes, he could still feel her hands on his face. His eyelids flutter then snap open.

No. Not anymore.

Sam grabbed his sunglasses and headed out into the yard. The fall sun was bright and he stood there for a moment surveying his empire, his little world.

There's so much more out there in the world, he thought with a longing as deep and as dark as the sea. Sam noticed an employee helping a family.

They look happy. His chest burned with jealousy.

"No one is happy," he scoffed, under his breath. Discussing trees, the young couple were intent. The man seemed stressed and Sam watched the woman smile, a smile of love that made her beautiful. She reached out her hand and touched the back of the man's neck. It was a familiar caress, Sam could tell. The man looked over and a peacefulness fell across his face, looking down at her. Their heads were close, almost touching.

Sam's heart sped up and he remembered. He couldn't shut it off. Goddammit, he longed for her hand on the back of his neck. He starts to sweat and sat down on the retaining wall nearby. He rubbed his neck looking down at the gravelly ground, his shoes, anything.

Damn, damn, damn. His eyes filled, *how can I still miss her this much?*

He wanted to run away so bad; he bit his lip and tasted blood. His eyes closed, his hands fell next to him on the retaining wall and gripped hard. He wanted to tear it down. Burn the world down. Intent on his thoughts, Sam didn't hear little feet wander up, until a tiny hand steadied herself on his leg. His eyes opened to look into big hazel ones staring up at his face. Brown curly hair. He smiled. She threw back her head and laughed.

"Seraphina!" The man yells.

"Dada?" she answered and looked up at Sam. He was stunned. The man jogged up to them.

"Phina! I'm sorry, sir, she moves quick. She's an independent little thing. I didn't see…," he trailed off at his daughter not acting shy.

Sam looked down, "Hi, Seraphina," he said soft to her.

She looked up and stared, "Superman," another laugh peals out of her, a ribbon of delicious noise.

Sam chuckled, "It's no problem, sir. She is beautiful. Whatever you want today is on the house. Here's your daughter." He hands Serah back to a dumbfounded man. The little girl's face was one of joy.

Sam turned to walk out of the yard, walking past his employee, "Don't charge 'em. Not a cent." The employee nodded and watched Sam pass.

Sam swung into his truck, sat, and smiled. Turning on the radio he drove out. This time he knew exactly where he needed to go, and exactly why.

It's her. It's always been her. Onward, Gunnar.

Sam pulled up to a red light, the radio blared out AC/DC, and he couldn't help but smile at one of his favorite songs. His phone buzzed and he looked down: *Hi, can I see you? Missing you. Can't sleep without you next to me in bed.*

It was the past calling. A past that he couldn't resist. Sam tapped the steering wheel to the beat of the music and clenched his jaw. He loved to be needed. Like a drug, when he was needed by someone it filled the dark corners of his soul and made him think it was all going to be okay.

Good job, universe. Way to torture me.

"Is this the longest red light or what? Jesus," Sam asked the silent interior of his truck.

His phone buzzed again: *Seriously, Sam, we need to talk. You know I wouldn't text you if it wasn't a big deal. My dad is in the hospital again, my boss at work is trying to get me fired and...I'm late.*

He rubbed his face with his hands and groaned. He couldn't be sure what was true and what was fiction, not with Carmen. But he felt a responsibility to her. She didn't deserve to be treated in his usual callous way, the way he treated most in his recent past; no one did and not when she was going through so much.

Sam sighed and gripped the steering wheel hard. A horn honked behind him and he looked up to see the light was green.

Just try it, buddy. You have no idea how I'd welcome a good fight right now. I think you need a punch in the face...whaddya think? Sam thought while holding up his middle finger, so the driver behind him could see, and super slow accelerated on his way. Sam felt his heart harden into a rock as he drove past his original intended turn. Rage perched gracefully on the passenger headrest, drinking it all in.

It was never going to be, buddy. You know that. You know you don't deserve someone like her. You made your choice a long time ago. Sam nodded to the voice in his head.

Be there in 10, he quickly texted back, then reached up and violently turned off the radio. The truck filled with silence, and Rage sat content, as he drove.

Chapter 27

The kitchen smelled of turkey. It was Thanksgiving Day. A tradition for a few years now, Serah joined Ben and the three musketeers law school friends on most holidays. All three had a delicate family history they preferred not to revisit if they could avoid it; all three found solace in the family they had made together.

Serah was grateful to be included with this fun group. She had been celebrating holidays with Ben for years, but she knew she was also jealous. Never jealous of what Ben had really, she was so happy for him, but a quiet jealous, of what she, Serah did not. Well-fortified today with friends, wine and good food, Serah knew it would keep her warm and lighthearted and also keep the demons at bay for the day. The only one that really enjoyed its victims drunk was Rage. Rage worked well with liquor, the emotion was all the more sweet—to Rage anyway. Serah knew she could avoid Rage today staying in the warm house full of family and love. Rage was occupied elsewhere.

Ben's head was stuck in the pantry searching for another item missing from the list and Serah could tell his blood pressure was starting to mount. She knew Ben was a perfectionist and felt responsible for making "the perfect meal"—or close to it. Levi looked at Serah and raised an eyebrow, echoing Serah's thoughts, "Chef Ben wants to make the perfect meal today, I've never seen him so worked up!"

Serah laughed. It was also a tradition to forget something from the massive list of ingredients, "I'll make a run to the store, no problem. Write me a quick list and I'll scram."

Pulling out of the driveway, Serah cruised along the fairly empty streets. Her eye caught on a large jackrabbit that had been hit a few hours before on the street. *Poor baby.* It always made Serah sad. She could feel the animal's terror and confusion. As she got closer to the site of death, she saw it. Demon Fear. It looked up and blinked its blue eyes a bit in the late afternoon sun. Face bloody, it was a mess. It moved slow from the chill and slower from the meal. Fear was a carrion eater. Often preferring to eat the recently or not-so-recently dead, if they died by appropriate means, of course. Fear lingered. The beautiful jackrabbit with the impossibly long ears met with Fear as its last thought, its body reacting to the accident, pumping out pheromones to no avail. It died cloaked in its own juices of fear, and the demon could smell it.

"God. Bastard has no decency. Disgusting demon." Serah's stomach lurched a bit and she gagged as she drove by, feeling the edges of emotion and the traces of ecstasy from the demon's meal. She was surprised there weren't more. Usually, they flocked to carrion such as this. There was a lot of emotion to feed on. *A demon thanksgiving,* Serah thought and choked back a laugh.

A quick drive from the house and Serah pulled into the grocery parking lot. She sat for a second and closed her eyes, shaking off the feeling. With a sigh, she got out of the car in one graceful move and headed into the store.

Turning into Ben's driveway, Serah grabbed the grocery bag and walked up the path to the house, *relaxed,* she realized with surprise that she felt relaxed for the first time in a while. Turning her face up to the sun, she closed her eyes breathing a contented sigh. Continuing up the path to the house, Serah stopped. A dead bee. Serah squinted and paused to peer down at her feet, scrutinizing the sidewalk. She saw three, then four, five, she stopped counting, all in the space of a few feet, all lifeless, dead on the sidewalk.

"Huh, that's weird," Serah remembered a recent conversation with Ben and it made her worry.

Demons passing through could have an effect on an area, usually subtle and hard to notice. Honeybees are extremely sensitive to the environment. Scientists are now talking about how there is a noticeable decline in the honeybee population. All these bees are dying and scientists can't explain it.

Serah nodded, "I thought they figured it was global warming or pollution or something like that causing it."

"Sure, that's one reason and I'm sure its accurate as well. But because these guys are so sensitive, they are a warning beacon. If you see a group of them dead then you know something had to cross their path. Just use it as information. Be on the lookout and then you can be better prepared," Ben said. Strict on always wanting her to be ready, to use all her information, and "observe the world around you!" one of Ben's favorite lines, often shouted at her when she failed to recognize some clue he had tested her with.

Serah looked up quickly and around the front yard, the neighborhood beyond. It was an idyllic setting—the sun was going down behind the purple mountains. Dusk.

"Shit," Serah whispered. Why didn't she realize the time and delay, even for half an hour? That would have helped. But now she was out in it, a powerful time of day. And with dead honeybees. Serah sniffed the air. Salty air. It smelled like the ocean. Almost, but not quite. Dammit. Her head snapped around quickly taking in her surroundings, *what did I miss?*

Not seeing anything around, *maybe it was just lingering from a past encounter*, she reasoned. Then something told her to look up. She saw it then, as the thought to look up passed through the edges of her brain—the big blue eyes, like full moons blinking in and out, off and on, from its perch high on the power pole. Three crows, one on the ground and two sitting nearby on the high-tension power line, watching. Or waiting. She read once that crows, ravens, were very smart. Part of the corvid family of birds that could use tools, reason solutions to problems, rather quickly too. She wondered what this new sign meant. No time to think about that now, she prepared for what was to come. It was Demon Fear. Fear focused on her and she focused on Fear.

Serah recognized it as the same from the jackrabbit meal earlier in the day, it had to be; the eyes the shape of the symbol inside was exactly the same, she was sure of it. Serah paused, attempting to stamp the exact picture in her brain so she and Ben could log it later.

She wondered why this one was still out searching. It should be hibernating after the full meal. These demons seemed to be growing in appetite. Terrifying thought, she could barely keep up with them now. Serah's anxiety grew as she focused on Fear above.

Serah looked up and slowly backed up toward the house. The demon followed. It gracefully tiptoed from pole to wire, creeping along, Fear keeping her within sight.

Quiet as she could, Serah placed the groceries on the front porch then leaned her palm up against the door, closed her eyes, and whispered: "You shall not pass. My words are powerful, as is my will. My words are powerful, as is my will. You shall not pass. My words are powerful, as is my will You. Shall. Not. Pass."

Serah turned and stepped forward into the street with a smile. Her eyes narrowed on it as it crept closer. Her thoughts jumbled, hoping this would go down quick and clean. The street was empty, dark enough, and cold enough so most were inside. Any curious onlookers would just see a girl in the street, bouncing to stay warm.

Fear hissed.

Serah held out her hand and crooked her finger, teasing and shrill, "Here kitty, kitty, kitty." Fear stopped. Serah watched the form of fear waft closer, seemingly intrigued by the one who was not afraid. She looked to the left and grabbed a handful of rosemary from the bush off the front steps and quickly lit it with a lighter she carried in her pocket.

Herbs have power, Seraphine. They have been respected for centuries for their magic. Let's learn what you can use to protect yourself out there. Ben's words resonated through her mind.

"Rosemary for healing, protection, and strength," she whispered, as the flame grew and the moist herb smoked. Waving it like a smudge stick in a pattern of protection over the doorway, she turned and advanced on the demon.

She lit it again, and again, "Rosemary for healing, protection, and strength," she whispered like a lover to the flame. With each repetition she stepped forward, with each step Fear hissed.

Serah inhaled deeply as if taking a drag from the purest of magics, "I am not afraid of you." She held out her hand, warding it away and taking some of its power with the sign of the witch and all the runes that now adorned her arm. She blew the smoke and anger and incantation of her power of faith as hard as she could, like a wall of energy to dissolve even the worst Fear. She was only two feet away and the taste of the salt filled her mouth. She spat it out on the ground.

Fear danced and Serah smiled. She turned lightly on her feet and twisted the smoke in a ring around the hissing demon. Back and forth and back and forth, her feet light and her breathing soft, her mind focused.

"I am not afraid of you. Rosemary for healing, protection, and strength." The Demon slowly grew smaller, as if dissolving before her eyes. She stepped too close and tiptoed quickly back, gasping at the images that attempted to invade, to disrupt, to overpower. Eyes closed she quickly turned and called the quarters with the remaining smoke, North, South, East, and West, facing each direction with a prayer.

The rosemary was almost gone.

Seraphine grabbed the now palm-sized, wafting, wavering demon with her scarred hand and shoved the last of her talisman into its core. On a hiss and a screech, it disappeared, but not before it left its mark.

Serah dropped to one knee in the street, gasping at the torment only she could see and feel. Her scarred hand clenched and unclenched rapidly, as she fought out of the demon haze. She put her palms to her face where the odor of rosemary was still strong and it was just enough to help her heal. Serah opened her eyes to see a fine layer of salt misting a circle on the street. She knew better than to touch it, sure of its power even now. *Another one bites the dust.* Taking a deep breath, Serah stood and surveyed the now dark and still-quiet street. Three crows sat on a neighbor's fence watching.

"Hi guys, enjoy the show?" She softly called to them, as five more landed. The fence was crowded. Eight Crows. *Eight crows, eight rules. Fitting.* With a word of thanks to the rosemary and the universe that supplied it, she turned and walked back in the door.

Greeted with a chorus of tipsy hellos from the three musketeers, Ben grabbed the bag and dove in with frantic preparations to finalize the delicious dinner and dessert. Ben beamed as the rest of dinner prep went off without a hitch.

"I don't remember having a home cooked meal as good as this EVER," Serah pushed her plate and leaned back from the table with a bit of a groan as she rubbed her full belly. Everyone laughed and agreed.

"Ben should invite you over more, Serah. I don't like you living alone and working so hard. You need some meat on your bones. Look at you!" Lily said after the chuckles subsided.

"Ah, leave her alone. She looks tough. I wish I had her arms!" Levi added, "All I got was a slow metabolism and terrible knees. Thanks, Dad, by the way."

"But you got your beautiful skin and eyes from your mama!" Serah broke in laughing, "Ben, your derby pie is way too good." She patted her stomach for emphasis. She looked around and raised her glass, "To family" she said.

"To family!" the voices coursed.

Glasses clinked and conversation turned to the bar-exam-test prep, law school finals, and future law firm plans, slightly more somber than in years past. They had a lot to do, a lot of goals to meet, a lot of pressure to handle.

"To friends, together forever," Levi said with confidence. Lily and Ben nodded feeling safe in knowledge that there was nothing the three of them couldn't handle together. Serah sat back sipping her wine, quiet and happy, her heart full. These times with her adopted family felt like vacations for her soul.

Chapter 28

"Seraphine Macguire?" The nurse called at the office door. Serah looked up, grabbed her small bag, and followed the women in the white coat.

"Step on the scale, please," she motioned for Serah to put her things on the chair. Serah grimaced stepping on the scale.

"108 pounds," the nurse looked at the chart to mark it down and paused, "Your last visit you were 140, that was almost three years ago. Looks like you have been working hard, dear!"

Serah nodded and smiled a thanks, *yeah, it's the 'get chased by demons every night" diet Try it! It's fun!* Serah almost laughed at the sarcastic voice in her head. She knew it was also her intense training in the gym that was showing results as well. *All those miles, all those hours,* she saw a brief reflection of herself as she passed a mirror on the bathroom wall, her arm muscles clearly visible even under her T-shirt.

The nurse ushered her into a nearby room, took her through the usual BP and temperature check, "The doctor will be in shortly."

"Thanks," Serah plopped down in the chair with a sigh. She hated sitting on those benches with the awful paper, *does that really do anything for germs?*

Her phone pinged, a text from Ben: *How'd doc go?*

Ben had been concerned for a while about demon effects. Thomas in Salzburg had emailed the information he had, mostly rumors and chatter about other demon hunters and what they experienced. Rigorous records were hard to come by; something they all hoped would change as Thomas and Ben started a systematic search to reach out to as many demon hunters worldwide as they could. It was a long and slow process. Demon hunters were notoriously loners filled with the emotions of the preternatural beasts they hunted—that made them become volatile at worst and inconsistent at best.

Ben decided to mention his worry to Thomas, and they agreed it was a worthy topic to discuss.

Serah had protested, "Guys, I feel totally healthy and fine, I promise!"

"Yeah, and what about those headaches? Hmmm?"

"Headaches? What headaches?" Thomas questioned, from the FaceTime video on the phone which was propped up between them.

Serah threw a dark look at Ben. "Traitor."

Ben laughed, "Yes I am, but it's for your own good."

Serah texted back: *still waiting.*

A quiet knock and the door opened quickly.

"Hello, young lady. I'm Doctor Stern," he stuck his hand out and Serah shook it firmly.

"So how long has your blood pressure been this high? You look like you are very fit, so tell me, in your opinion, what's going on?"

"Welllll, I've been having headaches pretty regular after, um, exercise," Serah tiptoed around the truth trying to give as much information as she could. *How the hell am I supposed to tell him enough to make this worth it?*

"Your blood pressure could definitely be the cause of the headaches. And from your bloodwork we got last week, it looks like everything is normal except your sodium level. It is...very abnormal. I'm actually not sure how you are still even sitting here in front of me..." Dr. Stern scooted around on his wheeled stool to show Serah the lab results.

"A normal level for you—someone fit—probably taking electrolytes and a few supplements is usually a little bit high, around 145. But yours is 1150. This has to be a mistake or fouled test tube from the lab. You should be in a coma with this level...," he trailed off a bit. "We should probably get this redone, but given your BP level today..."

"Are you experiencing any other symptoms? Insomnia? Dehydration? Diarrhea?" Serah shook her head no at each question, she felt fine. *Except for the headaches.* Admittedly she was sleeping less and less but, some nights, after the Rage demon encounters especially, she slept like the dead.

"Well, then, let's get some new blood work to compare, and start working on that blood pressure. I'm gonna prescribe two things. One very, very minor dose to help the blood pressure. Try that for two weeks first, then if that isn't knocking out the headaches, take the second prescription as soon as you feel one coming on. First two weeks try Excedrin or Excedrin pm. They both work pretty well for OTC." Serah nodded along, she knew it wasn't her blood pressure, it was the demon salt, their salt and the frustration. *And the sadness.*

"Okay! Let's get you outta here, make an appointment for that blood work, and have them send it to me. I'll take a look at it and my office will call you to get you back in and discuss it, if need be."

"Thanks, Doc," Serah smiled and reached out her hand to shake his.

"My pleasure, Seraphine. Stay safe out there."

Serah tried not to grimace, "Always."

Chapter 29

Serah was pulling into the employee parking lot at Flyer's Club when she saw them. Him first and then: *her.* She sucked in a hot breath that felt like poison fire in her gut. It had been more than a month since she had heard from Sam.

Ben's voice roared into her head.

"I'm tired of waiting, Serah! I'm tired of being patient, tired of seeing you slowly torn apart inside by the demons and your sadness over Sam!" Stomping out of a recent training session with a plan of his own to find out the truth. He told Serah later that he traded cars with Lily on the pretext of needing to take his to the shop and then stealthily drove by Sam's work.

"You bastard," Ben whispered under his breath as he took in the scene. Sam was laughing, holding hands with a tall blonde as they talked with Sam's brother.

"Tall and blonde...so typical," Ben sneered to the empty car. He drove home slowly, debating how and when to break the news. He decided to tell her while drinking a beer one night at her house.

Serah closed her eyes and took a breath, "It didn't work. I tried so hard, and it didn't work."

"Thanks for telling me, Ben. I kinda figured it would be something like that...I'm just glad he's home safe." She gratefully turned back to Diego's insistent nose vying for her full attention.

"Serah," Ben stared at the coldness that was his friend, "Serah, it's not your fault. We didn't know what we were doing. We STILL don't sometimes. We tried...

YOU tried. Sometimes it's just not meant to be."

"I hate that saying, Ben. "It's just not meant to be,' sounds like a cop out to me."

"Serah—"

"Ben, stop. It's okay. Okay? This is my life and I want to spend the time I have left figuring out how to beat these bastards, so I can finally rest. And maybe be normal...someday..."

"He's too pretty anyway. Like devil pretty, ya know? I didn't trust those blue eyes either! I mean, really blue freaking eyes like the damn demons? Come. On. I'm glad, honestly. You deserve better! She can have him...and he walked funny too," Ben added and glowered at the talk of Sam hurting his dearest friend.

Serah laughed at her loyal friend, "He did, didn't he!" The two clinked their beers and went back to chatting on the back patio, relaxing on an unusually warm winter day, strategizing for the next step, the next encounter.

Serah shook herself out of the memory and pulled her car over at the loading zone curb. Serah seethed. A car door slammed and she smiled, slow. It crept across her face, showing one tooth and then the next. One tug to straighten her jacket, she turned, fierce yet casual, in her saunter toward the black SUV.

"Hiya," the Serah-dragon called out as she neared the two.

Sam's head poked out where he was leaning into the car grabbing something from the passenger seat. The blonde stood on the curb. His eyes cut a path from Serah, to the blonde, then back to Serah.

"Hey, Serah. How're you?" he continued quick, "Thought this was your day off..."

"Really?" her voice narrowed with her eyes. "Nice try, Sam."

Before he could say another word, Serah crossed the remaining few feet between them. She grabbed his arm and though he was way too muscled for her to move him. He let her yank him closer, her anger like a wall of heat.

"This is *My* place, Sam. *Mine*," Serah seethed. "After *Salzburg*, after all this time, after trying to *save you*, and I don't hear *anything*! Not one damn thing. And now you come *here*? With *HER*? I was *sick* over the thought that you were lost and alone, thinking I had *left* you!"

Serah's voice broke, she clenched her teeth bracing herself to continue, "Why are you so quiet? Why don't I get an explanation? What happened to you?" Her voice softened on each question until it became a whisper of pain.

Sam shook his arm, pulling it out of Serah's grasp, "Get a grip, Serah. I never asked to be *saved*. Salzburg was fun, but it's time to get real. I have a job, I have responsibilities. I can't go galivanting off around the world with you. Grow *up*." He turned and motioned to the stunned blonde. They started walking toward the hanger, leaving Serah clenching and unclenching her fists in the road.

"Oh, and fight your own imaginary demons, will ya, Serah? It's too draining for me to fight your battles for you," Sam tossed back over his shoulder as the automatic doors whooshed open and then shut behind them—mocking Serah with the last word.

Like a robot, Serah turned back to her car, she reached out to grab the door handle with an unsteady hand.

"Such a pretty day. A pretty day to fly," Serah whispered. She shook her head and wrenched the door open, as if wounded. She drove home in a daze after texting her boss Al she was going to stay home. *Take the day off, Serah. You deserve it*. Al's response to his best instructor gave her the strength to hold back the tears, climbing in bed with her two trusted companions—the only place she felt safe, loved. Sleep, a valiant try to heal the heartache that she knew nothing could cure.

It was dark when she woke. "I like to run at night, you know that," Serah smiled at the concerned faces of Diego and Rubi as they watched her lace up her sneakers.

A quick pat on Diego's head, "You hate running with me, pal," and she was out the door 8.6 miles round trip to the airfield and back. Time to run Sam out of her mind and out of her heart.

Chapter 30

Present Day

Serah sat in her sunny yellow kitchen sipping her third cup of coffee and remembering. The memories of her first demon encounter swirled, coffee and her warm kitchen were of little help.

"It does no good to dwell on the past," she heard Benjamin's voice again, his teaching embedded in her mind from their many training sessions. "We all wish, but no one gets a mulligan. There are no do-overs, Seraphine. Not in this world."

Ohh, Ben, you have to be wrong. With a sigh and a final sip, Serah turned and smiled as she took in Diego's expectant face. Setting down her coffee cup, she went for the leash. It was time to go enjoy this pretty day.

Once back home from their walk, the residue of the Rage bubbled up and Serah paced. The long run last night had worked well until she had run smack into Rage. And a pretty day filled with memories just made it worse. Sweat trickling down her back, she slowly turned as if on autopilot and walked to her pantry. The whiskey beckoned. *Just one small glass to take the edge off.* A smile that was not hers spread across her face and with rock steady hands she poured. The first sip was liquid gold tracing a warm path down to her gut where it curled up and burned away the pain, the anxiety, the abundance of emotion that felt like it was rotting away who she thought she was.

Fucking demons, fucking Sam, fucking mom, fucking life, Serah closed her eyes and sat down hard on the stool next to her small kitchen table, as the dark rage boiled. She gripped and relaxed, and gripped and relaxed her hands around the small glass; it felt as if she was on fire. Trying to fight fire with fire, she took another hefty swallow.

Diego padded up quietly and shoved his favorite toy into her lap, "No, Diego, not now," she said as she pushed his head away. "Stop it, buddy. I'm not in the mood," she said as he tried again with a short whine.

"No. NO, NO, NO! I said NO!" Serah screamed at her most treasured possession. She screamed and gripped Diego's coat so hard he squealed, twisting and turning trying to get away. Looking down, eyes burning and mouth set, her voice already hoarse from strain, "You need to LISTEN to me! STOP being weak, I HATE YOU." Rubi jumped on the table and swiped at Serah's arm, hard enough to draw blood. That swipe and Diego's yip yip yip of pain broke through.

"Oh my God. Oh my God, buddy, bubbs. Oh my God, oh my God." Leaning down she buried her face in his fur as he stood there shaking. She sat up and watched him slink away, tail tucked, the shame was overwhelming.

Looking at the whiskey glass, she turned and threw it as hard as she could against the wall where it shattered and dripped. Rubi jumped and scattered full speed at the noise. Serah blinked, grabbed her jacket that was tossed over the chair, and walked out the door; she knew exactly where to go.

A short drive later, Serah walked into Banderas. A local bar and restaurant favored by the after work, slightly ritzy crowd. Making a beeline for the bar, she looked strong; she felt strong. Strong *and crazy*—her presence causing a few to turn and watch her path.

"Jack, double, neat," she said to the bartender's look and settled on the leather stool. Slightly hunched over, she sipped her drink like a dragon in her lair. The tap on her shoulder made her smile again, *well that didn't take long,* she thought as she lazily turned to look into the blue eyes of a handsome stranger.

"Mind if I sit down?"

Serah nodded, "Sure, handsome, but I'm really not in the mood." She played hard to get with a flirty smile. *Always the fucking same,* she thought. It felt like coming home, this pain, to where she was meant to be, filled with rage in a bar ready to fight.

"Well, you sure are too pretty to have a bad day," handsome flirted back with a sweet southern accent.

Serah glanced down, "Are you a cowboy?" Gesturing at his boots, she almost felt bad for a second, then it all came rushing back. *Fucking cowboys.*

"Nah, I just play one on TV, little lady," he winked at her. "Why don't you put a smile on that sweet face of yours?" Handsome reached over and put a hand on her shoulder.

Serah shrugged it off, "Because I. Don't. Want. To." Her voice was hard.

"Well now, I was just trying to be nice, Miss…uhh." He extended his hand. "I'm Sam." Serah laughed and let his hand hang in the air; she laughed harder and turned back to sip her whiskey.

Handsome Cowboy's hand hung in the air for a second, then his eyes narrowed, "You don't have to be such a bitch." Those words melted into the air for only a second before his head came crashing down on the bar as Serah's hand, holding her glass, smashed into the side of his head.

"What the…?"

She swiveled and blocked his grab for her arm, *ahhh he has friends,* the gleeful thought passed through her head as she rose to meet the first who didn't really know what to do to when fighting a woman. Serah solved that by punching him directly in his face. It glanced off his nose, which gushed blood instantly. She smiled as she shook her numbed hand; the pain felt good. It didn't knock him down, she tsked a sound—she was still working on her technique. Cowboy number three ran up, grabbed her around the waist, and slammed her down on the ground. Serah impacted with a grunt, swept his feet out from under him with her leg, and leapt on top of him as he crashed to the floor.

Much easier to punch a face in this way, she thought as she haymakered his face once, twice, three times. The bartender vaulted the bar and grabbed her under the arms, as handsome cowboy, pissed and ready to regain some pride, sucker punched her in the gut. Serah kicked up, using the balance of the bartender to hold her back, she kicked with all her might at his chest, a double barrel shot with both feet square into his chest. Both men staggered back and the bartender's grip loosened. Serah shimmied out of his grasp and stood breathing hard, half hunched over with a small demonic smile on her face surveying her damage. She didn't see the fist until it was too late; she went down, lights out, with a right hook to her temple.

Serah woke up in the kitchen with an icepack on her face and the bartender kneeling next to her; he was half turned with his back to her talking to someone behind him.

"She's a regular, I dunno. I understand, but we can't call the cops. I know, I know, but they've been here three times this month and threatened our liquor license if they had to come here again." There was a mumbled answer and then the kitchen door swung shut. Serah could tell one eye was already swelling. She tried to sit up, "Hey, hey!" she croaked, and put a hand to her lips—one was bloody and swollen. The bartender swung his attention back to her and lifted her up a little, so she could sit against the wall. Serah put her hand on the sticky floor to brace herself.

"Okay, kiddo, I managed to hold off the guys and kick them out. I figured they were rude or did *something* to deserve what they got, but you are thiiis close," he held his thumb and forefinger apart by barely an inch, "to getting thrown out or taken to jail or worse. Jesus, what were you thinking?"

Serah couldn't stop the giggle that escaped her lips. She took over holding the frozen bag on her face and looked up with her one good eye at his horrified expression.

"Rage made me do it. I…Rage," she nodded, as if verifying the statement and closed her eyes with a sigh. "Could I have another drink?"

"No way, what you need to do is sit here, sober up, and call a friend to come get you." The bartender stared at her confused at how such a pretty girl could wind up on the disgusting kitchen floor bloody from a bar fight.

"Did you hear me, kiddo? No arguments. You can sit here until they pull up. Tell them to come around the back, service entrance…okay?" He shook her a little to get her attention.

"Yeshhh. Yeah, yeah, I will." Serah giggled a little again. The bartender shook his head and walked out of the kitchen calling over his shoulder, bluffing, "I'll give you thirty minutes, then I'm calling the cops, capiche?"

"Thirdy minutes. Yeah, yeah, thirdy," Serah slurred and waved her hand at him. Patting her pocket, she grabbed her phone and scrolled through the numbers.

"Sam, Sam, Sam, Sam, Sam," she whispered and clicked on Ben, "Ben, Ben. Yes, Ben. No more Sam," Serah started to cry as the phone rang.

"Ben, I need help." He didn't even question, only asked her where she was and told her to sit tight. He drove up ten minutes later and tucked her into the passenger seat of his car.

"Tell me what happened," he asked in a gentle soft way, as if coaxing a wild animal near.

"The others look worse," was all Serah would say. Ben didn't press. He knew what it was like to battle demons; he battled his own in his life. So, the silent car drove down the dark freeway into the quiet night.

Chapter 31

Ben's backyard patio erupted with angry voices. The neighbors, upon hearing words like "demons, tired of fighting, I'm DONE," would only shake their heads at the nonsense and continue on with their lives.

"Serah, you need to stay the course. We are making progress, slow but steady," Ben's calm response did nothing to ease the tension rolling off of Serah. He held his hands out in a gesture of peace. "Come on, sit down, sit down on your mat and take a breath. We will get through this together."

"Together? Look at my bruises, Ben! This is ridiculous. Bar fights? Really? I've been in five...no, six bar fights now! What's next? I thought I was supposed to be helping people not hurting them. This situation is worse than awful," Serah said as she paced.

"You've helped a lot of people, Serah..." Ben's soft comment caused Serah to stop and turn her thousand-yard stare toward him. Ben winced at the force of Serah's gaze of anger.

"Yeah, and spend the next two days barely holding it together. And for what? Who knows what actually happened? We have NO idea if any of this is really working to shift the balance."

"Serah, we need to see this through. You are chosen for this."

"We need! I need! I'm sick of what I *need* to do! You know what I need? A LIFE! A freaking normal life," Serah interrupted emphasizing her point with a chop of her hand. "Enough! I've had *enough*. How many more fights until we get the edge on these bastards?! I want to see real progress and feel like I'm actually *doing* something," Serah's shoulders slumped as she paused—her whole body out of steam.

"I want to feel the sunshine and the moonlight and not wonder where the next fight is coming from. I want to fall in *love*. I know what I'm doing is important. I really do. But I want…I want so much." Her words ended on a whisper, and she plopped down on her mat. Diego padded over to sit next to her—a quiet guardian of her pain.

"You can't give up Serah," Ben pleaded. "You have to keep going or the world is going to fall to evil. I truly believe that. I have felt their presence. You inspire me to fight it—fight the apathy, fight the despair, fight the rage," Ben sighed, and it was his turn to slump down on the mat next to Serah and Diego. "I know it's hard, I wish I could do more, I really do. But you can't give up." Serah put her arm around Ben's shoulders and their heads fell together in silent friendship.

"You know if Sam had chosen differently, I might have it in me to keep going. But he didn't. I lost big that day and I feel so responsible, so *broken*."

"He still might, Serah," Ben stopped, not one for empty promises.

Serah shook her head, "No, it would take a miracle. I need a miracle, that's what I need. A freaking miracle."

"Okay, let's take a break for the night. Go home, relax with Diego, write everything out and sleep on it, make a decision in a few days. I will respect what you want to do."

"Okay thanks, Ben," Serah pushed herself to her feet.

"Relax, write, think, okay?" He repeated.

"Yup, I will. Love you, friend," Serah turned like an exhausted warrior and patted her hip for Diego to follow.

"Love you back," Ben's voice followed Serah out the door, leaving him standing in his patio, silent, with only the trees to listen. Turning away from the cold evening, Ben grabbed his phone. He needed to let Thomas know; they needed to figure out more to do to help his friend. Texting Thomas: *She needs us, she's ready to quit, I don't know what she's going to do. Help.*

Thomas: *it happens with all of them, if she needs to quit, let her quit. For now. Unfortunately, this will follow her, the demons won't quit, soon she will realize she has no choice. I'm sorry to say.*

Ben tossed his phone down on the couch, sat next to it with his head in his hands. He was going to lose her and he couldn't stop it.

Easing herself behind the wheel with a tired grunt, Serah slowly started the drive home. Her mind raced.

"I know he cares, buddy, I know. But him and Thomas aren't living this. I have to DO something, gonna see what happens, gonna make a plan, gonna go big," putting one hand on Diego's scruff she nodded at her own words. She thought she needed a rest, but she decided she needed to end the fight. Once and for all.

"Go big or go home. I'm coming for ya, demon fuckers...I'm coming," Serah smiled as she drove down the dark empty street formulating her plan. *It was time.*

Chapter 32

The university campus was quiet as the armed civilian approached. It was early in the day, the sun peeked bashfully over the horizon. He looked around at the foliage turning on the beautiful trees that lined the entrance. He always wanted to be invited to a place like this—this lofty, beautiful, quiet place.

He snorted a laugh when he realized the snobs were waiting. He himself had been waiting for this day for a long, long time. The snobs deserved everything they got today.

His birth name was Ryan, given by parents who didn't care and didn't understand. It would matter greatly, who he was and what his name was, in the end. He had christened himself Nicholas. St. Nick, it had a nice ring to it. He would think of his new name and chuckle to himself. Destroyer of dreams, wolf in sheep's clothing, evil and decidedly not jolly. He liked being unexpected.

Ryan/Nick carried an AR-15 modified automatic rifle with five extended magazines placed in his vest pockets and more in his bag. He remembered his late-night trip out to Arizona to purchase this beauty, driving all afternoon then into the night. He felt like a desperado, and he loved the adventure. This place: Where such rifles were legal and it was easy to find someone to upgrade it for him, no questions asked. Maybe he would get his friend to write a book about him someday. She always wanted to write; this would inspire her! He knew it would without a doubt.

He liked the weight of the rifle in his hands. He felt powerful. He felt like a king. He knew they would all bow to HIM.

Four emotions—rage, horror, fear, and apathy—coursed through his veins. They also followed at a minimum safe distance in order to remain undetected and undisturbed for as long as possible. Rage, Horror, Fear, and Apathy drank the emotion with almost unrestrained glee. They knew they would not have to feed again for a long, long time.

Ryan/Nick beelined for a massive oak near the center of campus on the western edge of the courtyard. He sat and leaned up against the tree, his tools of the day close beside him, and breathed deep the crisp cool air. *Almost salty,* he thought and closed his eyes for a moment, the air smelled like his grandma's house near the water in Pacific Beach. He loved smelling that salty air from her porch. He loved his grandmother the best and was grateful she was not here to see what he had become.

His demon tribe hopped up onto thick oak branches staying hidden by leaves and mistletoe and birds' nests that adorned the tree. Not that anyone could see them, however, occasionally they ran into a few who could, once in a great while, one who could see and fight, and they would take no chances of being thwarted on this special day.

His watch beeped the hour. He could hear distant church bells ringing *oh that's sweet,* he thought, sarcasm and rage coursing through his veins. It was time. Standing up and brushing off a few leaves that stuck to his perfectly frayed jeans, he picked up his companion. He was ready.

The bell tolled and the people came. Students coming onto university grounds for the first class of the day. Some bleary, stumbling out of the library after studying all night, others leaving professors' offices from early morning office hours, the administration offices unlocked and opened one by one and computers slowly fired up by the staff. He had his pick. It felt like Christmas. He realized it actually almost was.

Giddy with anticipation of what was to come, Nick-Ryan picked his first targets and strode like the king of death himself toward a group of three laughing loudly as they walked on the path from the library. *Laughing? We will see about that. Fucking snobs always so happy all the time. Laughing!* The torrent of thought became vitriol—poison in his head. He strode forward, no one yet noticing the armed man, face contorted with rage and followed by his vaporous companions that few could see. The stage was set for a massacre. Saint Nick and his demons were the only ones who were ready.

Seraphine clutched her phone to her chest with a moan of fear. Her citizen app alert startled her out of her morning coffee quiet time. It was the only quiet she got these days and she treasured it.

shooting, mass casualty, university campus, situation in progress, police alerted, campus in lockdown.

She knew Ben was there. He had texted late last night saying he was going to catch up on his studies with Lily and Levi in the library, most likely all night. She wished him good luck and good coffee for fortitude, with a thumbs up reply at 10:55 p.m. That was the last she had heard from him.

Please, pleeeeaaase, be safe in the library. PLEASE. Serah prayed. She prayed over and over to a God she did not believe in, but hoped against hope something out there would hear. Serah now believed deeply that the universe was all energy; thoughts had power, depending on the strength of the thinker, and she knew she was very strong. *Please, pleeeaaaaase, stay in the library, hide, BE SAFE. PLEASE. I cannot do this without you. PLEASE, PLEASE, PLEASE, PLEASE, BE OKAY.* Serah tried again, and again, and again. She sat in her sunny little kitchen, dog at her feet, cat under her palm and tried with every fiber of her being to bend the universe to her will.

The "ping!" from her phone, a text message, made her gasp and open her eyes. She looked at the time, she had been at this for over an hour. It was Lily.

At the hospital, I can't find Ben. I thought I followed the right ambulance but I don't know anymore.

Are you hurt? Serah asked.

No, only scrapes. Ben pushed me down behind a rock wall in the courtyard. I don't know what happened. Omg, Serah.

I'm coming. I will be right there.

Flinging on a denim jacket and her fanny pack purse, Serah grabbed her keys and ran for her car.

Shot four times, induced coma to let his body heal. Talk to him, he can hear you. Young and strong, there's a good chance he will be fine. One bullet hit his lung, the other his liver, but we repaired the damage. There's no reason he shouldn't live a full, happy life…

The doctors, so many doctors and nurses. Their words reverberated in Serah's mind over and over. *Full, happy life. Full, happy life. Full, happy life.* Serah repeated those three words, like a mantra in her mind. She grabbed for Lily's hand and held on tight; both of them standing and staring at Ben in the hospital bed, hooked up to so many machines. Beeping, noisy, scary machines, breathing for him, draining fluid from him, keeping him free from pain as best they could tell. So many machines, so many noises. The one noise they never want to hear again, when his heart stopped briefly after surgery. *Never again, please.*

Serah squeezed Lily's hand and went to stand closer to the foot of Ben's bed. Leaning against the foot rails with her hands, she closed her eyes. Taking a deep breath, she pulled all the energy she could muster. *The energy of the heart can be detected many feet from the body, Seraphine. Use your energy, send it out to help guide the choice of those in need,* Ben's voice echoed. Serah almost sobbed, but tucked her chin instead and threw her energy out like a lasso of light toward her best friend.

Heal, my friend. Heal and come back to us. Use this light, use this energy. We are here for you. We are waiting. We love you. Feeling heat rush through her body, almost as if she had a powerplant warming up to nuclear level, never before had she felt such a rush of energy from this technique. It felt powerful. *She* felt powerful. Directing all of her love toward the sleeping man as best she could, she felt the power drain from her body—streams of golden light leaving her hands in her mind's eye. Taking a deep breath, Serah opened her eyes, surprised she saw her hands outstretched toward him, no idea she had moved.

A nurse cleared her throat and Serah dropped her hands to her sides, stepping back to make room.

Lily grabbed her hand again glanced over and whispered, "Serah, your hands. You are burning up."

"Hot coffee all around," Levi interrupted what Serah might have said to answer, as he walked into the hospital room, one arm in a sling from a ricocheted bullet on the courtyard wall. The two turned toward him gratefully and each grabbed a cup.

Serah half-sat and half-crumpled to the floor with her coffee in the corner of the room. Trying to stay out of the way, not caring it was a dirty hospital floor, *I would lay on a bed of nails for you, my friend.* She knew it was going to be a long night. Serah and the inward girl on the lake settled in.

Chapter 33

A Whisper of Demons

Serah laid her trap and waited. She picked the field behind the cemetery, an appropriate choice she thought, no visitors late at night and few to complain. She knew those under the ground were way past caring about anything they felt. There're no such things as zombies or vampires; the dead don't rise and the dead don't talk. They are dead, lost to us, but what they leave behind is powerful magic—good *and* bad.

She didn't really have a plan. *Ben would be so pissed*, she thought and almost laughed. At the thought of him, Serah closed her eyes and choked back tears; her chest hurt so bad with the effort. He still wasn't awake. It'd been almost a week. A week in a coma, *in the in between,* Serah nodded to the mental voice. *Yes, he has a choice to make.* She visited him daily for long stretches of time, trying to work her magic from deep within, Thomas giving her numerous tweaks and suggestions via text. She hoped it worked; she *needed* it to work.

Taking a deep breath, she lifted her head up to the sky feeling the night air on her skin and went deep, deep down inside to the girl on the lake. The place where demons couldn't go, the place that held all of her power. The girl in the lake was trailing her hand in the water looking serene and calm. She looked back at Serah and smiled. She was ready. Serah opened her eyes.

She wondered which demon she would get.

As the sun set, Serah saw a demon edge the field of graves, and she watched blue eyes blink from its perch on a tombstone. Her hands flexed on the rose weapon of thorns, hoping it would help tonight. Wrapped around the base was her grandmother's rosary beads. She was wearing her mother's dragon stamped necklace for extra power and armed with an unshakable faith that she would win. It was time to make a difference in this fight.

Patience, Serah waited. It sat. It rubbed its face and yawned. It sniffed again and caught the whiff of rat poison she had placed at the base of the cemetery sign. It smelled like emotion to them and tasted like heaven.

"Come on," Serah whispered. "Come on!"

It blinked and turned to the tombstone to its right. Another pair of blue eyes popped up and slinked over the top, then a third pair of eyes came into view. They sat, at the edge of the field of graves, smelling their dessert.

Three? Oh, man. Serah gulped and steeled herself, *a whisper, Jesus, Mary, and Joseph,* absurdly hoping for more, pragmatically hoping for less.

She had told no one where she was going to be; no one knew what she was going to do. Diego was locked inside safe. Her friends were safe. That was the way she liked it, *alone, gut it out alone.* She didn't want to hear arguments; she didn't want to wait and plan. She was ready. Breathing deep, she pushed herself into the calm space as she was taught and stepped out from behind the tree to face them.

"Hi, fuckers," she said and smiled sweetly, a strong figure in the ever-approaching night with a hand on her belt and a hand on her weapon. They hissed in unison. It was a chilling sound. She watched the three floating up and hover about six feet in the air. All eyes locked. The demons descended and the fight was on.

Striking first with the weapon of thorns, a demon screamed, and she was pleased. One hand held out with her talisman kept another at bay, she pivoted on one foot, turned, and struck the second. The third swung out of reach. She danced.

"My words are my weapons. I am lucky, I am strong. You cannot defeat me. You will not succeed. I am lucky, I am strong. I am not afraid. These are my words and I will it so." Not quite what she had practiced but close enough. She started to pant as they came faster. The third was quick, *it has to be Rage,* she thought. Her defenses were strong tonight, and she was just as fast, not allowing any of them close enough to fully know what brand of demons she was dealing with. Not yet.

Slash, pivot, turn, arm up, arm up. Slash, pivot, turn, arm up. Speak the words. It was a dance that grew tiring, fast. Her scars burned like salt in a wound. Serah knew she had to think of something. They seemed undaunted but a bit slower than before, staying at a respectful distance at times. She stepped backwards toward the trap of poison, grabbed some with her hand, and flung it. They scattered and descended upon it. Eyes turning white, all color was drained out of them.

What now?! Think, think, think. Serah could feel her arm burn, bleeding from a nick from one of their talons. The demon poison made it ache. Her thoughts turned to suicide. She imagined the rope, thick around her neck, she tried to swallow, it was thick. Her hand grabbed at nothing. Her breath came fast. Despair.

Goddammit. "I am strong. I am not afraid. I am strong. I am not afraid. This, too, shall pass. This, too, shall pass. My witness is my words. They are powerful and So. Am. I."

She stumbled forward and slashed at the scrum, a poison feeding frenzy broken up only by her interruption. They did not like it and white eyes turned on her. Rage was quick; it's now solid arm and claw reached out to slash her face. Pain seared down her neck as she turned to evade the blow. The three were strong together. Steeling herself, Serah felt the rush of adrenaline that always accompanied Rage. It pushed everything else out and she welcomed it.

Use it. Use it. The movie of visions started in her brain and it was useless to stop. She couldn't close her eyes against it; it was already inside.

"I am strong. I am lucky. I am not afraid. My words are my witness. They have power and so do I. This stops," she said as she noticed all three demons now lined up in a formation near one of the tombstones. Their path was large as they moved in to attack, grab, snap at the poison, or sit back and stare. She ran over to the headstone and they rose up to watch her with glee.

Turning, she spit out the rage on her words, "I am lucky. I am strong. I am not afraid. This shall pass. You are nothing and will become nothing again. My words are my witness. They are powerful, as is my will."

Almost screaming, she charged and slipped. Fear caught her first. Never had she been filled with more than one demon poison at a time, let alone three.

Fear, oh, sweet fear. Serah turned her head up to the night sky and howled her incapacity to feel any more. She couldn't.

Oh, God.

"Mom, help me. Please. Someone."

The Whisper of Demons moved back to watch and savor. They could smell it, the victory. The emotions pouring through the sweat in her shirt, the tears forming at her helpless fate. Serah shook the hair out of her eyes and tried to stand on legs that quaked. She stared at her demons arrayed before her, her weapon limp at her side and panting, eyes closing at the thoughts that consumed.

A brief smile crossed her face and she turned and ran. *Faster!* She ran toward the gardener's shed she saw at the corner of the lot. If she could get inside, she had an idea. She wanted to hide, she wanted to close her eyes and fall and give in.

If she closed her eyes, would they still see her? If she couldn't see them, did they exist? Silent, salty gusts of wind told her what she did not want to know. They were still there.

Racing up to the shed, she flung open the door to run inside. Skidding on one leg, she turned to bolt the door, no lock. *Doesn't matter anyway.*

Leaning her palms up against the wood-paneled door, eyes closed, her forehead pressed into the rough wood, "You cannot enter. You cannot enter. Unwelcome and unwanted, I do not allow you to enter here. My words are powerful, as is my will." She leaned and pushed all her power into the words. The door bounced once and then was still.

Serah turned to look around her. Shovels, picks, axes. Lawn mower, gasoline. Gasoline. She stared and visions of burning down houses tiptoed past her mind; peacefully sleeping people choking on smoke and their own death. She giggled and swallowed back the bile. *Stop it. Focus.*

Gasoline, fertilizer, garden tools—she saw them one by one and knew what to do. Grabbing the rest of the rat poison, she cleared a space at the back of the shed and placed a pyramid of poison under the small window. Fear gripped her and she swallowed it down. She trailed a bit of the poison over to the door. It was just enough.

Next, Serah took the sod knife with its curved wicked blade and slashed open the bags of fertilizer she had piled on top of each other. Only two bags, she hoped it was enough, then doused the stack with gasoline. Saving some fuel, she rummaged around for a few glass bottles and found an old milk jug, one glass coke bottle from what looked like the '70s, and a small vase.

They slammed against the door again, shaking the shed; she almost dropped the can. *Shit!* Running over, she leaned against the door. "You cannot enter, you will not. You are unwelcome and unwanted. My words are powerful, as is my will," she quickly whispered and then ran back to her plan. Filling each glass bottle with the gasoline, she soaked some rags in the same.

"Hellooo, Molotov cocktail," chuckling madly, Serah could hardly tell where the demon poison stopped and where she began.

Propping open the window, she knew the odor would reach them quickly. Blue eyes appeared two, four, six staring. Blinking. Purring. But They didn't enter. They couldn't, so They waited. Salty air, salty poison—it dripped from them as if they were salivating for more.

Serah crooked her finger at them, "Come here, little demons. Come heeere." On her invitation, they watched intent as she backed away toward the door. Without turning, used one hand behind her to open it, blink blink of their eyes, and they flew. Serah leapt for the other side of the mantra-protected door and crouched. They slinked in, carefully it seemed. But the scent got the better of them. Like a shark feeding frenzy, they curled and rubbed and purred and hissed and drooled on the pile of poison; eyes leaking blue, turning white again. Serah took a step back inside and then another, balancing on the balls of her feet.

Silent. Silent. She prayed, "I am lucky. I am strong. I am lucky. I am strong." A few more steps, she was close enough, *hurry, hurry*. Grabbing the lighter, she lit the first rag and hurtled the cocktail down next to the bags of fertilizer. She backed away quickly as it caught. The flames raced.

Backing out the door, her eyes glanced at the demons still feeding. At the doorway, she lit the second glass jar and tossed. It exploded outward, shooting flames and sparks toward the frenzy. Serah turned, grabbed the heavy wood door, and pulled it shut.

Quickly, quickly, she leaned against it with all her will, all her force, "You cannot leave, you cannot leave, you cannot leave. My words are powerful, as is my will. You shall not pass." The door was hot.

How long does it take for fertilizer to explode? She tripped backwards and scrambled further away, staring as the smoke curled out from the eves, from under the door. Serah ran around to the single shed window and saw their eyes, as if smashed up against glass that was not there, they could not escape. Hissing and howling, the stench was real. Fire cleanses.

The explosion knocked her off her feet, she landed on her back with a grunt and an alarming lack of air. Rolling over, she crawled to her knees, wiping the dirt and hair off her face. With an equally dirty hand, she stumbled over to the large oak that she hid behind earlier in the night. She crouched down and rummaged through the bag she had left there, pulling out her cell phone; she dialed.

"Sam. It's me," Serah whispered.

"Serah?" Sam yelled over music in the background.

"Yeah."

"Where are you? It's late!"

"I know. Can you come get me?" Serah continued to whisper.

"What? Where are you? What happened?" She could tell he was already walking, moving toward his car outside away from the loud music.

"There's a fire. I'm in the field behind the cemetery. You'll see. Please. Hurry."

"Okay. Okay, got it. I'm on my way." It was quieter now. She could hear his locks disengage and his car door open, "What the hell happened, Serah?"

"You'll see," she whispered. "You'll see." Serah hung up. Leaning back against the tree, she let the phone fall. She turned to see the shed burning against the night sky, her eye caught the glint of the sod knife still clutched in her left hand. Despair and fear and rage, she could feel the emotions boiling through her; she was weak. They bubbled up and she couldn't stop it. She felt black inside. Filled with a black emptiness, a black evilness she couldn't describe and wouldn't know how to if asked. She didn't know this feeling could exist until this moment.

The thought crept by, *If I cut me, I would bleed black.* Her very veins felt filled with a sludge of poison. She took the sod knife and pressed it into her fair skin, into the soft, sweet skin on the underside of her right forearm—skin meant to be kissed. The knife pressed deeper, its kiss was sharp, *but at least it felt real,* she thought on her gasp of the pain. She pressed and pulled it a quarter inch down that soft flesh. The despair bubbled; her blood welled. It was red, she stared. It was red. Serah started to cry.

That was how Sam found her. As soon as he saw the flames, he didn't care anymore if he drove over a grave. He pulled his truck up as close as he could get; leaving the keys in the ignition, he jumped out.

"Serah!" he called as he ran toward the shed and turned to see her bent over her arm, almost as if she had no strength to keep herself upright.

"Serah," he trotted over to her and grabbed her arms. He saw the blood and the knife. He shook her until her head bobbled a bit. She looked up with her tear-stained face close to his. His heart lunged in his chest, like being stabbed.

"It's red, Sam. It's still red," She whispered.

"Your blood? Jesus, of course it's red, Serah…" She smiled at him, he glanced over at the shed thinking a million things, but knowing they didn't have much time to get out of there before the fire department arrived.

"Come on," he heaved her to her unsteady feet. "Let's go." Reaching down, he opened her bag and threw her cell phone in. He grabbed the hand with the sod knife and twisted it out of her fingers, putting it in his back pocket, *no evidence,* he thought. His large hand encircled her upper arm as he led her down the short hill to his truck. The grass was dewy and wet, not much had caught fire yet. Only a few sparks here and there near the shed, Sam looked around taking stock as they went.

"Serah. Serah, get in!" He shook her gently, until she lifted her leg and tried to climb up into his truck, he boosted her the rest of the way. Trotting around the front, he smoothly stepped into the driver's seat. They drove out, Sam watching the glow of fire, the shed now fully engulfed, in his rearview mirror. Pulling out of the circle drive of the cemetery, he made a quick right heading out into the night.

"Where do you want to go, Serah? Where do you need to go?"

Serah thought of Diego licking her face, calmly surrounding her with love and his quiet presence. She thought of Rubi snuggled up for a long rest-filled nap. Sleep, yes, sweet sleep. She just might be able to sleep now. The tide had turned. She knew it, deep down, the tide had turned, just a little, just for now, and it was enough. Serah knew she was a warrior, she had vanquished three at once. She was a warrior now. She was ready.

"Home. Sam, take me home, please."

The End

Epilogue

"I am a witch, I'm a warrior, I'm a demon destroyer," Seraphine softly sang and surveyed her tools of the trade. She picked up the gilded handled "rose bush" type weapon custom made of Koa wood—the strongest wood on the planet. The metal-plated handle had one side open to the wood where she burnt inscriptions of her power symbols into it. Her grandmother's rosary beads were the final touch—inlaid and twisted throughout the thorny branches. This weapon connected her to the earth, fire, and her power; she *felt* connected and strong. Serah tossed the work of art in her hands gently, feeling the weight and the balance and her confidence grew even more. She saw her wrist and forearm where the fourth scar was now visible—stark white and slightly raised liked the rest of them.

The last scar appeared on the night she faced the Whisper of Demons—three demons at the same time—and was victorious. She smiled as she remembered climbing into Ben's hospital bed to show him after she cleaned up from the fight. The new scar-rune was The Helm of Awe, one of the most powerful Norse symbols, at least according to historians. Ben and Serah looked at each other, shouted "Demon Warrior Princess!" in unison and dissolved into laughter.

"Oh, God, Seraphine don't make me laugh. It hurts!" Ben groaned, still chuckling and grunting with the effort. He had only woken from his coma twelve hours prior. They determined almost the exact time the shed exploded and Serah won her victory. Heads together, they whispered ideas of what all this might mean, chatting and brainstorming until shift change when the night nurse came to tell Serah visiting hours were over and shooed her away, so her patient could get some rest.

Raising her arm up to eye level, she whispered the symbols of power under her breath and saw a tracer of light follow her words on each scar. Diego padded into the room with a soft click click of nails on the hardwood floor. Smiling, she dropped down to love on her loyal companion. She could feel his light, she could feel his energy. They were entangled forever in this universe and the next. Diego pushed his head into her chest and chuffed; it was a potent potion of love.

The Viking man smiled as he read the last gilded page of Seraphine Macguire. The sunlit lettering ended on the page, but he knew it was not truly the end of her story. Her story had only just begun.

As much as he wanted to follow this one, it was time to find the next chosen one. The balance had to be restored, the scales had to even out. It was why he existed in this place, this library of souls. He patted Garm on the head and eased himself out of the chair toward the endless shelves. Garm pushed himself off the floor to join him. They paced back and forth for a while. It was always this way. One would speak to him, he was patient.

Finally, the whispers of intuition increased and he walked over, the soul book was quite gilded and fancy—unlike the one he just finished. He scowled a bit at the gold and silver *pompous and spoiled,* he thought with a grimace. Garm laughed, panting slightly, looking up at his partner in this realm, *this one is going to be fun.*

Samuel Gunnar read the name in delicate letters on the spine. With a sigh, the man settled back in his chair and started to read.

Afterword

God speaks to each of us as he makes us,
then walks with us silently out of the night.
These are the words we dimly hear:
You, sent out beyond your recall,
go to the limits of your longing.
Embody me.
Flare up like a flame
and make big shadows I can move in.
Let everything happen to you: beauty and terror.
Just keep going. No feeling is final.
Don't let yourself lose me.
Nearby is the country they call life.
You will know it by its seriousness.
Give me your hand.

~ Rainer Maria Rilke

Dear Reader, this story is not intended to make light of or to trivialize mental health. The idea for this story was actually born during a time of deep personal grief and loss. If only fighting our personal demons was as easy as in this book.

I believe mental health is an important topic—one that humanity needs to shed a massive light on, dispel judgements and stereotypes about, and create hope for all who struggle with it.

If you are struggling with a particularly difficult time in your life, please know you deserve to feel better—you *can* feel better. May you all find a "Ben" in your life to help you on your journey.

Here are some resources that might be a place to start:

Better Help
https://www.betterhelp.com/

Mental Health First Aid
https://www.mentalhealthfirstaid.org/mental-health-resources/

National Alliance on Mental Illness (NAMI)
https://www.nami.org/

The Trevor Project
https://www.thetrevorproject.org/

Active Minds
https://www.activeminds.org/

The work of Charlie Mackesy, online and in print, including his award-winning book *The Boy, the Mole, the Fox, and the Horse.*

Acknowledgements

I'd like to thank my family and friends for cheering me on and always believing in me that I could actually write a book even when my own belief failed me.

Thank you to the muse for coming back, over and over again even when I was sure she had grown tired of my procrastination.

Thank you to my uncle who shared with me, among other first-rate advice, "There are three rules for writing a novel. Unfortunately, no one knows what they are," a quote by Somerset Maugham, freeing me to be the writer I really wanted to be.

Thank you to myself for never giving up, for continuously pulling this novel out of the deep dark drawer it hung out in for over a decade and bringing it into the light of day.

About the Author

Kate Chambers is a first-time novelist with a book that only took her twelve years to finish. She's hoping the next one will be a tad quicker. Kate is a wannabe witch and beach girl at heart, who now finds herself under the hot desert sun where she lives with her supportive husband, two retired K-9's, three spoiled horses, and an affectionate donkey named Frank. Her favorite form of yoga to take and to teach is Yoga Nidra because it mostly involves lying down and relaxing. In her spare time Kate enjoys deep dives into wellness, wine tasting in beautiful locations (or at least by a window), and wandering through animal sanctuaries all over the United States.

Relax with Kate at: www.theoutlawcowgirl.com

www.ingramcontent.com/pod-product-compliance
Lightning Source LLC
Chambersburg PA
CBHW032211030726
47494CB00020B/952